Time Is Irreverent

Marty Essen

ENCANTE
PRE

D0880471

Copyright © 2018 by Marty Essen

This is a work of fiction. Names, characters, organizations, places, events, and incidents are either products of the author's imagination or are used fictitiously. Any resemblance to actual persons, living or dead, or actual events is purely coincidental.

All rights reserved. No part of this publication may be reproduced or transmitted in any form or by any means, electronic or mechanical, including photocopying, recording, or any information storage and retrieval system, without written permission from the author, except for inclusion of brief quotations in a review. Additionally, e-book versions of this publication are licensed for the purchasing reader only and may not be resold or given away to other people (unless additional copies are purchased for each recipient). Thank you for respecting the hard work the author put into creating this book.

Published by:

Encante Press, LLC
www.EncantePress.com
SAN: 850-4326

Interior layout and cover design by Tugboat Design

Publisher's Cataloging-in-Publication data

Names: Essen, Marty, author.
Title: Time Is irreverent / Marty Essen.
Description: Encante Press, LLC, 2018.
Identifiers: ISBN 978-0-9778599-4-8 | eBook ISBN 978-0-9778599-5-5
LCCN 2018900252
Subjects: LCSH Alternative histories (fiction) | Nuclear weapons--Fiction. | Aliens--Fiction. | Presidents--United States--Fiction. | Science fiction. | Satire. | Political fiction. | Humorous stories. | BISAC FICTION / Science Fiction / Humorous | FICTION / Science Fiction / Time Travel | FICTION / Satire.
Classification: LCC PS3605 .S6756 T56 2018 | DDC 813.6--dc23
10 9 8 7 6 5 4 3 2 1

By the same author:

Cool Creatures, Hot Planet: Exploring the Seven Continents

*Endangered Edens: Exploring the Arctic National Wildlife Refuge,
Costa Rica, the Everglades, and Puerto Rico*

Special thanks to:

Mary Tracy, editing
Deb Essen, proof reading
Autumn Conley, additional editing suggestions
and
All my readers, and friends on social media, for their
encouragement and support.

CONTENTS

For

Sean & Heather Essen

Tom Duffin

and

Diana (Essen) Duffin
January 29, 1955 – May 21, 1989

PROLOGUE

I've been abducted by aliens. Hmm. Is *abducted* the proper word for it? Sure, the aliens began our relationship in the traditional way by placing me on a brightly lit laboratory table where they checked all my fluids and examined me quite extensively. On the other hand, they never even hinted at firing up the dreaded alien abduction drill or bringing out the intimidating tray of assorted scalpels. Instead, these masters of the stress-free abduction kept me higher than a kite and respected my privacy. In fact, only two, dressed in festive pink lab coats, actually saw me naked, and they were always careful not to embarrass me or inflict any pain.

Honestly, who could blame them for wanting to check a few of us humans out? They didn't even know we existed until 2020 when America's sanity-challenged President Handley dropped some huge ones, claiming he was smart enough to launch nuclear missiles here and there without negative consequences. Less benevolent otherworldly beings would have just invaded and enslaved us, eaten out our brains, or done something similarly undesirable.

These aliens? They simply distracted the president by giving him a debilitating case of Koro syndrome—or at least worsening the one he already had—then gassed the rest of us with the alien equivalent of vaporized cannabis. Soon peace broke out, at least until the gas dissipated, allowing them to easily gather a few human specimens to study before plotting their course of action.

As for me, I had blissfully walked over to what appeared to be a giant rainbow-striped hose, and they sucked me into their ship. Once on board, they greeted me by name, Marty Mann, led me to a touch-screen, and invited me to "build my own euphoria." I selected several choices at random, placed a mask over my mouth, and inhaled. Before I knew it, every pore on my body oozed with a pleasure I'd never known before.

After my examination, I spilled my guts and told them everything I knew about the human race. In the end, the aliens didn't even suggest destroying Earth or letting us foolish earthlings destroy it ourselves. Instead, they concluded that a simple correction to our past was all we needed to right the wrongs of our world. With any luck, I'll be sent home soon. Right after a slight detour to Galilee in AD 31. . . .

CHAPTER 1

Meet the Keithrichardslys

"Wait! Wait!" I shouted. "This is all happening too fast. Only five or six hours ago, you sucked me into your ship. *Now* you're telling me to prepare for a trip back to the time of Christ?"

I was sitting in a delightfully comfortable chair on the bridge of the coolest spaceship I'd ever been on. Okay, technically, it was the first time I'd ever been on a spaceship, so it was the coolest by default, but I was sure it could give all other vessels a run for their money.

Everywhere around me, aliens busied themselves with various tasks. They all had tall, graceful bodies with a bit of a hump across the tops of their buttocks to accommodate their hind brains. Truly, they were a beautiful humanoid species, or perhaps *exotic* would be a better word to describe them. Although their skin generally resembled human skin, including variations according to races, colorful blotches—mostly oranges, pinks, and purples—on their necks, cheeks, and arms enhanced their looks. Most striking were their expressive eyes with fiber optic-like eyelashes that terminated in dots of light. Sure, those attributes would have prevented anyone from mistaking them for humans, but certainly we weren't the only standard on which to base attractiveness.

As for the bridge, it was just as colorful as the aliens that inhabited it. All surfaces were rounded and smooth, and most were some shade of purple, blue, or pink. Adding to the effect were lights that illuminated all the controls and gadgets and even chairs with a slight pinkish glow.

Even more striking than the colors was the bridge's vertical layout. On Earth, ships typically have horizontal layouts, but human limitations didn't apply to these aliens. The gravity here felt far lighter than that on Earth and even lighter than it was in other areas of their ship. The pull was just strong enough to keep beings grounded if they so desired, yet weak enough to allow anyone working in one of the lower sections to reach one of the upper ones in only a few graceful bounds. The layout made sense because the ship featured a giant rectangular window that allowed a natural view from the front, beside an equally large screen that simultaneously showed a checkerboard of views from external cameras aimed front, back, left, right, up, and down. Consequently, everyone had an unobstructed view, and those in back never had to shout, "Hey! Down in front!"

The aliens could obviously apply gravity with precision since various small items at workstations stayed put, while chairs could either float, attached to simple tethers, or lock into place on narrow platforms that protruded from the rear wall.

One of them, quite apparently the captain, sat in the centermost chair and swiveled around to face me. "You've been here for nearly a week."

"A week! How is that possible? I only remember arriving on your ship, the nice doctors who examined me, and bits and pieces of an interview with two of your associates. It seems like I was on Earth just this morning . . . and I don't recall ever meeting you before."

"I'm sorry you feel that way. You've actually seen me many times." He looked me in the eyes and half smiled. "Let's just say that we miscalculated how sensitive your species is to our *chemistry*. Our self-serve euphoria dispensers work well for most, and since you appeared to act normal, it took us a while to discover that there was a problem. As of today, all the dispensers have been reprogrammed to automatically recognize humans and offer customized human euphoria options at the proper dosage. Your memories of the past week should return soon."

"Thank you."

"What you remember of your stay has been pleasurable though. Hasn't it?"

I stood on the platform, still a bit woozy, and looked out toward my tortured home planet. "Certainly. Of course, anything is better than melting in the midst of President Handley's game of Dodge the Mushroom Cloud."

"Your president will not be dropping any bombs for a while." He covered his mouth to repress a chuckle. "We slipped him some medication that . . . altered his mindset a bit. Right now, the so-called commander-in-chief is staring into a full-length mirror, convinced that his genitals are receding into his body."

"Ah! I remember the Koro syndrome thing! No drugs could make me forget that. Still, I seem to be at a disadvantage here."

"How so?"

"For starters, you know much more about me than I know—or at least remember—about you."

"Feel free to ask me anything you want."

"Okay. What should I call your species?"

"We're the Pzzants."

I bit my lip to repress a laugh. "Um, I don't think it's wise to refer to yourselves that way, at least not in this solar system. Especially if you ever want to change tactics later and make people think you're badass. Just out of curiosity, did you mention to anyone on Earth what you're called?"

"No. We communicate directly with other planets only as a last resort. What do you suggest as an alternative?"

"Well, you've obviously been studying Earth and downloading our history into whatever you call the equivalent of a computer."

"A computer."

"Then why don't you just take the name of who you think is the most amazing person ever to walk on our planet and create some variant of that?"

The captain cast a glance toward one of his crew members.

She tapped a handheld device, paused for a second, then nodded toward the captain's chairside monitor.

"Keith Richards? Very well. From now on, we'll be known as the 'Keithrichardslys.'"

I repressed a snort. "How about just the Krichards?"

"If you think that's best," he said with a nonchalant shrug.

"And what should I call you?" I asked.

"As I'm sure you've figured out, I run this ship. Our titles are somewhat different from what you use on Earth, but you may call me Captain Weezeearffputput."

"Pffft! How about we stick with the theme and call you Captain Jagger?"

"If you think that's best."

* * *

Two days after Captain Jagger—Ha! I was going to be laughing about that one for a while—caught me up on everything I'd been too high to remember, I felt like myself again. Since a euphoria dispenser was just down the hall from my cabin, nothing stopped me from taking full advantage of the hospitality it provided.

Most recently, I chose "Margaritas in Maui" because I was feeling a bit nostalgic for a vacation I enjoyed there once. The great thing about Krichard euphoria meds is that they're realistic enough to give you the feeling you want, but without negative side effects, such as addiction and hangovers. And, of course, the recently discovered memory loss problem was no longer an issue.

I can't say whether it was physical or psychological, but just like a real pitcher of margaritas would eventually make me have to pee, so did the virtual pitcher from the euphoria dispenser. Back on Earth, no space-oriented sci-fi book or movie I'd seen ever mentioned public facilities for ship occupants to take a leak. As I stepped into one of the restrooms on my way to the observation lounge, it occurred to me what a missed opportunity that was. I could just imagine such a scene in *Star Trek: The Next Generation*, with Captain Picard standing at a high-tech urinal, only to have an inquisitive Data pull up next to him.

Here on the Krichard ship, I could use the private restroom in my cabin or any of the public restrooms along the hallways. The public ones were unisex, with privacy screens around each urinal. I guess freezing-up is a problem for males of their species as well. The urinals were similar to what we have on Earth, but without the stink or the puddle. To accomplish such an amazing feat of male cleanliness, an auto-sensor instantly adjusted the height to optimum for each user. If someone still managed to drip or splash, another sensor waited for the messy humanoid to step back before engaging a mechanical arm that reached out from the wall to squeegee and blow-dry the floor. At least that was what I was told, since it never had to do that for me.

As for the toilets, they were just as automated. No more cling-ons or inconveniently ripped toilet tissue. If the Krichards ever shared their restroom technology with humans, germaphobes would be in heaven.

I gazed into the restroom mirror, and a stranger stared back at me. The Krichards were preparing to whisk me away to the ancient Middle East to "correct an error in history," as they put it, so they temporarily altered my Scandinavian blond hair and features. "That's gonna take some getting used to," I muttered, as I took in my darkened skin, hair, and beard.

Fortunately, most of the other preparations were simple, at least on my end, albeit a bit invasive. My new Krichard friends had installed a communications device in my head that would allow me to instantly understand and speak any language they programmed into it. Additionally, it would allow them to communicate with me over time and space. I was a little concerned about the potential lack of privacy, but I understood the necessity and was relieved I wouldn't have to learn Aramaic.

A familiar face greeted me as I left the restroom. "Follow me to the conference room," she said.

Chrissie, the science and hospitality director, was my main contact on the ship, though that wasn't her real name. Like her colleagues, her given name was far too difficult for me to pronounce, or even to spell out. Luckily, she and the others saw the wisdom of taking temporary, pronounceable Earth names, and they were happy to adopt whatever I suggested.

Since rock and roll was an important part of my life, I decided to dub all nineteen crew members with the names of the rock stars they most closely resembled. Because some Krichard features didn't translate well to human features, I had to be imaginative. Chrissie was easy, however, since she had straight, luxuriously thick, dark brown hair with bangs and a sassy look reminiscent of the Pretenders lead singer during her early thirties.

Chrissie had what seemed to be the toughest job of our history-making mission. In addition to readying me, she had to learn biblical history and program my implant. Fortunately, her hind brain was ideal for the task. Early in the Krichards' evolution, the extra brain provided primitive memory functions. Later, as the Krichards advanced into a time-traveling species, they artificially enhanced the organ and even added a wireless computer interface. Now their hind brain functions as a virtual solid-state memory chip, allowing them to quickly assimilate the massive amount of information needed to intelligently interact with new species via all forms of communication.

Once we reached the colorful, brightly lit conference room, I sat in a puffy chair while Chrissie perched precariously on the edge of a tall stool. We waited a moment for the first officer to join us. He was a muscular man with wavy black hair, so I named him Bruce in honor of Mr. Springsteen.

"Here's the problem," Chrissie said. "We'd like to send you to the Sermon on the Mount, but the Bible is just about the least accurate historical book we've encountered on any planet. There are countless translations, and it's full of contradictions and errors. Even your own religious scholars disagree with each other about a wide range of details. In fact, we can't even verify with certainty that Jesus, the main character of the New Testament, actually existed. What if the Bible is just an early, poorly written novel that got a lucky publicity break?"

Bruce looked at me without a hint of emotion. "We could accidentally send you into the midst of some violent conflict, and the locals of the time might very well confuse you with an enemy or proclaim your sudden appearance demonic."

"Yeah," I said with a snort, "I suppose they wouldn't have any 'Sympathy for the Devil.'"

His eyelashes flashed deep purple. "You must take this seriously, Marty. All of our top personnel will be able to communicate with you through your implant, but the burst of energy necessary for time travel will deplete the ship of most of its power. Wherever you land, you'll be stuck there for at least twenty-three Earth hours, while our systems recharge. And if some piece of equipment malfunctions, well—"

"I know," I interrupted with another snort. "'You Can't Always Get What You Want.'"

He moved closer and stared directly into my eyes. "Chrissie, is Mr. Mann on any medication?"

"Nothing medically necessary. He's been so agreeable and low maintenance. We let him go self-serve at the dispenser right after installing his internal communicator."

"Effective immediately, we're restricting Marty's access to the euphoria dispenser."

"You mean 'I Can't Get No Satisfaction'?" I asked with a grin, before swiveling in my chair to face Chrissie. "Help me out here."

"It's a 'Bitch,' Marty, but until Bruce or the captain says otherwise, I'll have to keep you 'Under My Thumb,'" she said, joining in the fun.

"Ooh! You catch on fast."

Her eyelashes flashed bright green. "Our species was traveling faster than light-speed before yours even resembled a 'Monkey Man.' I memorized the entire Rolling Stones catalog faster than you can *Get Yer Ya-Ya's Out.*"

Bruce scowled. "Can we stop this nonsense and concentrate on our mission?" Then his left eyelash twinkled medium green. "Marty, if we can pull this off, we will save your planet, but we must do it before your president's Koro syndrome goes into remission and he figures out how to get . . . *A Bigger Bang.*"

Considering what was happening to my planet, thinking seriously should have been easy. But for me, silliness and laughter have always been defense mechanisms. Without them, I might very well have curled up into a little ball in a corner of the ship, unwilling to move. Perhaps that was also why I had been overdoing it at the euphoria dispenser. My country, which had always prided itself in being the good guys, had really screwed up. A weakness for charismatic TV stars, coupled with a resurgence of our long-repressed dark side, allowed a man more qualified to be a cult leader than a president to win a surprising election. Now the entire world was paying the price.

My selection as the human to save humanity certainly wasn't because of any superpower. Sure, I'm reasonably fit, but I'm no gym rat or martial arts fighter. If I was successful, it wouldn't be because of any heroic physical feat. Instead, both the Krichards and I hoped my experience as a travel writer would help me as a time traveler, and my belief in science would assist me in places and times where others fell prey to superstition. If all else fails, at least I'll go down laughing, I told myself more than once.

Chrissie entered something in her handheld computer, and a few moments later, two additional Krichards joined our meeting: Tina, the rough-edged, dancer-legged time-travel specialist, and Clarence, the big man in charge of security.

After a bit of small talk, Tina said in a smoky voice, "We're accomplished time travelers, but that doesn't mean this mission will be easy. This ship is an older model, only capable of sending one person on each time jump. Also, I've heard how sensitive you humans are to our euphoria dispenser. I will have to compensate for your inferior physiology."

"Hey!"

Even though he was seated in a chair similar to mine, Clarence towered over me. "Now is not the time to be offended, Marty. We're here to help, and she is stating facts. That's all."

"I understand. Sorry."

"When you arrive in the first century," Clarence continued, "you'll be on your own. I can give you a few pointers to help you in a fight. Other than that, I can't do much." He stood and motioned for me to do the same. Then he took a fighting stance and said, "Let's see what I have to work with. Suppose someone comes at you like this. . . ." He made a fist and cocked his arm. "What would you do?"

"Uh . . . run?" I said with a smirk.

"That isn't what I had in mind, but . . . Well, how fast are you?" he asked, looking me up and down as if he thought retreat might be my best option.

"I'm reasonably quick on my feet. Then again, if I'm going back to AD 31, I should be downright speedy. Think about it. I'm six feet tall. Making me anywhere from five to ten inches taller than the majority of men I will encounter in Galilee. Plus, I have the benefit of a lifetime of superior health care and nutrition."

Clarence placed a giant hand on my shoulder and looked toward Chrissie. "What do you think?"

"Marty has a point. Also, he'd likely be outnumbered in any encounter. I say he should run."

I broke into song. "Tramps like us, baby—"

"Marty!" Bruce shrieked.

"Sorry."

Chrissie added, "We will dress you as authentically as possible, in a long tunic, cloak, and sandals. I suggest you practice running in them before you leave the ship."

I smiled at the mental image of hightailing it away from an angry mob in ancient footwear and said, "I most definitely will. 'Man's Valiant Attempt to Save Planet Earth Foiled by Face-Plant,' would make an unfortunate headline for some intergalactic news service."

"Does anyone have anything else to add?" Chrissie asked.

We looked at each other in silence.

"Very well," Bruce said. "Let's make our initial attempt in two days."

Initial? Attempt? My nervousness ratcheted up several levels.

Tina stood and waved me toward her. "Come with me, Marty. We must take measurements so we can fabricate a wardrobe for you."

"Huh? You're in charge of time travel *and* clothing fabrication?"

"Yes. Do you doubt my ability to perform multiple jobs?"

"No. It's just—"

"Marty, this ship is staffed with only nineteen crew members. Nobody does just one thing. For me, it's mostly data input anyway. The main computer runs both the auto-weaver and the time-travel attachments."

Attachments? Oh, boy.

CHAPTER 2

Panic in the Hose!

By the time the big day arrived, I was such a nervous wreck that Chrissie permitted me a half-dose from the euphoria dispenser. Because I needed to believe anything was possible, I chose "Cubs World Series 2016," and the meds did ease my stress a bit. The only downside was that "Go, Cubs, Go!" kept looping through my brain, and I was unable to resist bouncing around the bridge in my first-century getup.

"Look at him," Bruce said, shaking his head. "The fate of his planet is in his hands, and he's dancing."

Captain Jagger shrugged. "I wouldn't worry about it. Chrissie let him visit the euphoria dispenser. The effects will dissipate the moment he time travels."

I expected that we'd have to slingshot around the sun or something similar, but the Krichard time-travel process was all about energy displacement inside a rainbow-striped cylindrical force field they affectionately called "the hose." In the simplest terms, they explained that the ship would hover over the North Pole, and they'd shoot me out through the same hose they had used to suck me up in the first place. This time, however, the hose would pass through their special time-travel attachment.

All along, the Krichards were friendly and forthcoming with me about just about everything, except their technology. Their reasoning, I suppose, was the same as advanced militaries on

Earth have for not readily sharing information with others about the manufacturing and launching of long-range nuclear missiles. Earth was far behind the Krichards in most areas, but with access to their technology, an egomaniacal leader like President Handley could make us dangerous to other worlds in a hurry.

Still, I had to know more about what I was getting myself into. Before leaving for the hose room, I launched across the bridge and landed neatly in an open seat next to Captain Jagger. "Won't the primitive people of Galilee freak out if they see a big hose falling out of the sky?"

"What is primitive depends on your perspective." He paused to thoughtfully consider his next words. "To my people, your species is rather primitive. You haven't even advanced beyond nuclear weapons or traveled faster than the speed of light. Essentially, the difference between twenty-first-century humans and first-century humans is the same as the difference between our two species today."

"So are you going to disperse some happy gas first?"

"That won't be necessary. To put complicated science into understandable words, all the energy going through the time-travel attachment will move the hose into another dimension. No one will see it. You'll seem to appear out of nowhere. But even that the local people won't witness since we'll drop you off at night."

"If they can't see the hose, I won't be able to see it either. How will I get back?"

"We'll have to power down the hose while we recharge, but our time and location sensors will make sure it drops in exactly the same spot twenty-three hours later."

"What if I can't make it to the same spot?"

"You must. Our version of time travel requires precision. As you already know, we'll be able to communicate with you through your implant. But you can't expect us to just drop the hose a mile away. If you force us to do so, we'll lose the time trail and have to reconfigure all time and location settings. That could cause a substantial delay."

Even with the euphoria drugs coursing through my body, the muscles in my neck knotted up with tension. So much could go wrong, and I was just a normal guy. Surely, Earth had someone with a nerd brain and a football player's body who was more suited for this task. Besides, even if all the time-travel logistics went exactly as planned, how was I supposed to correct the past? The captain claimed the key to success was convincing people to abandon supernatural thinking in favor of logical thinking. Whether that would require discrediting Jesus Christ, kidnapping his disciples, or something else, no one knew for sure. He and his crew wanted to wait until I was in position and had a chance to assess the situation before recommending a course of action.

Chrissie entered the bridge from a side door, pushed off the wall, and landed on the captain's platform with a barely audible *thump.* "It's time to go, Marty."

Amazing technology and countless hours of preparation had all led up to this moment. I'd be winging it until further notice.

* * *

Tina was standing next to the control panel when Chrissie and I entered the hose room. As soon as I was within arm's reach, she handed me a small, orange plastic box. "If you feel along the right side of your tunic, you'll find several hidden pockets. Place this in one of them. It contains a butane lighter you can use to wow the locals if necessary. In addition, here's a pocket watch, so you won't be late for your pickup time, and food and water packs to strap around your waist under your clothing."

I followed her instructions and asked, "What's next?"

"From your point of view, it will seem like an airlock on a submarine, only you'll be able to breathe naturally the entire time. We'll seal you in, pressurize the hose, open the outer hatch, and send you on your way."

My eyes widened.

Chrissie added, "From our point of view, it will be much more complicated than that. We have to prevent you from freezing and then from burning up, get you to the proper time and place, and, as if those things weren't enough, keep you from splattering on the Earth's surface."

"You two sure know how to make a guy feel *safe.*"

Chrissie flashed an eyelash. "Don't worry, Marty. We're good at what we do."

Tina motioned for me to climb into the airlock. After she sealed me in, I was fine for a few seconds. Then claustrophobia seized me. I had forgotten to tell her I was terrified of tight spaces. I banged on the wall and yelled, "Let me out! Let me out!"

Tina's voice filled my head. "The process has already begun. We can't abort."

"Slow your breathing, or you'll throw off our calculations!" Chrissie added.

Two women in my head at once? It was like trying to concentrate on a final exam in high school while having crushes on the girls in the desks on either side. Wait! Could I have a thing for Tina and Chrissie? I barely know them. They're not even human. My breathing grew faster. I need to slow down and—

Whoosh!

Everything went white.

Everything went black.

I landed with a thud—"Ow!"—stood up, and looked around. "Oh, shit. Something went terribly wrong. I'm blind!"

"Marty, this is Chrissie. You're not blind. It's nighttime in the first century. It should be very dark. Just give your eyes a moment to adjust."

"Okay. . . . Damn, it's hot and humid here, and it smells like wet forest. And I don't know if it's just the aftereffects of my ride, but the ground seems to be vibrating, ever so slightly."

"Actually, that's quite odd," Tina said. "Hold on while I scan to verify your time and location."

My head went silent, leaving me sweating alone in the dark.

As the silence continued, the panicky feeling of being trapped in the airlock crept back into my brain. What was taking her so long? "Tina, are you there?"

"Just a moment."

Oh, this can't be good.

"Um . . . Marty. All the hyperventilating you did in the hose. Well . . . it kind of threw everything off. You're actually in the late Cretaceous period—some sixty-seven million years in the past."

"*What!*"

"Didn't we originally suck you into our ship from a state called Montana?"

"Yes, I've lived there many years."

"Welcome home!"

Chrissie reentered my head. "This is very important, Marty. If possible, don't move from where you are. The hose will return to fetch you as soon as our systems recharge. If you're not in the correct location, you could be stuck there for a long time."

"That shouldn't be a problem. I can barely see six feet in front of me and seem to be surrounded by trees. I'll just stand here and—"

Scrunch!

"Whoa! Did you two hear that?"

"Yes," Tina said. "Hold on again. I'm doing a search of scientific documents on Montana during the Cretaceous period. . . . Here it is. Big dinosaurs, from *Triceratops* to *Tyrannosaurus rex,* could all be nearby."

I'd never been more thrilled and more terrified at the same time. When I was a kid, all I ever talked about was dinosaurs. Later, as a travel writer, I commonly sought locations that were home to large, exotic reptiles. Even so, I knew a *T. rex* could use a young boa constrictor as dental floss, and I had no weapons and no hope of rescue for nearly twenty-three hours. So all I could utter in response to Tina's announcement was an anemic, "Cool."

She continued. "In addition to the dinosaurs, some of the plants may be poisonous. Don't touch anything you don't have to."

I jerked my hand away from a tree trunk. "The next time you send me anywhere, please pack a flashlight."

"Remember the butane lighter I gave you? Take it out. See if you can find something flammable to burn."

"Wait!" Chrissie warned. "Before you move an inch, you *must* mark your location."

I pulled off my cloak and ripped it in two. Then I flicked on the lighter, spotted a slender tree within my reach, and tied one of the halves around it. Once my location was flagged, I took a chance and reached up and broke a branch off the tree I had touched earlier. Next, I wrapped the other half of my cloak around the skinny end of the branch and lit it. Now, at least for a few minutes, I had a torch.

Working fast, I gathered leaf litter, pinecones—anything that looked flammable—and tried to ignite it with my torch. When my torch began to burn out, I ripped the sleeves off my tunic and added them to the tip. If necessary, I'd burn everything I was wearing. No other humans existed to be modest around, and, fortunately, Tina hadn't made my clothing flame retardant.

Eventually, I gathered enough burnable materials to keep a small fire going. As I stared into the flames, it occurred to me that I was already changing history. Not only was I the first human on Earth, but I had also built the world's first campfire. The elements would certainly erase all traces of my presence, but if something were to happen to preserve this site, archeologists would be forever perplexed.

Scrunch! Scrunch!

Whatever was out there was getting closer. I resolved not to run. After all, where would I go? Besides, I was pretty sure all top-of-the-food-chain predators throughout Earth's history had the same instinct to chase the running meal.

Scrunch! Scrunch! Scrunch!

I frantically searched for anything to enlarge my fire, but everything in close proximity was too wet or too green. As I waved my dying torch around, something shiny caught my eye at the base of a nearby tree. I crept closer for a better look. *"Wowww!"*

"What is it?" Chrissie asked.

"I'll tell you in a second." I reached down, and as I grabbed the object, it crinkled in my hand. "I think I've just confirmed that scientists are correct. Dinosaurs *are* reptiles."

"How do you know that?"

"Skin! They shed it just like modern reptiles, and—oh, my God!—it's huge."

"Any theories on what kind of dinosaur it is?"

"Are you asking if it'll make a snack out of me or not?"

"Yes, basically."

"I can't tell. The skin isn't complete. I'd love to examine it more carefully, but—"

"Burn it!"

"That's exactly what I had in mind, Chrissie."

Scrunch! Scrunch! Scrunch! Scrunch!

"This better work! The *Scrunchasaurus* is almost on top of me." I ripped off a piece of the shed skin and tossed it into my campfire. It burned but not nearly as well as I hoped it would.

Scrunch! Scrunch! Scrunch! Scrunch! Scrunch!

"God, does that stink!" I covered my nose. "It smells like burning hair. . . . No, make that burning sasquatch." I paused to listen.

Scrunch . . . Scrunch . . . Scrunch.

"Chrissie, I think we've just invented dinosaur repellant."

"So it's moving away?"

"Yes."

"Good job, Marty!"

Now, feeling less stressed, I replenished my torch with another swatch of clothing and took advantage of the extra light to make two piles: one of anything dry enough to burn and one of torn strips of dinosaur shed. "How soon until sunrise?" I asked anyone who was willing to answer.

"About six hours," Tina offered.

"I'm going to try to get some sleep."

"Good idea," Chrissie said. "One of us will be here the entire time if you need anything."

"Okay. Good night," I said, trying to make myself comfortable on some leaves. "Hey, you won't be able to hear my dreams. Will you?"

"Only if you dream about me," Tina said.

"Or me!" Chrissie added, with a smile I could hear.

Oh, great. Now my thoughts could spend the night alternating between one dangerous *Scrunchasaurus* and two flirtatious eyelash-flashers. I'd never fall asleep.

* * *

After mostly dozing, and then getting an hour or two of sleep, I awoke shortly past sunrise. "Breaker! Breaker! Come in, alien spaceship."

A moment passed before Tina asked, "Breaker? What's broken?"

"And must you call us *aliens?*" Chrissie added.

"Sorry, my good friends. Nothing is broken. 'Breaker! Breaker!' is just an old Earth phrase. I thought you two knew everything about my planet."

"We know a lot and are learning more each day," Tina said. "But even we double-brained aliens have our limits."

"Well, anyway, I just wanted to let you know that I'm awake. After I have a snack from my food pack, I'm going to go on a little hike."

"Marty, this is Clarence."

"Hey! It's the man with the deepest voice in space. What are you doing in my head?"

"I've been monitoring your mission from my workstation. Stay where you are until we pick you up. It's too dangerous down there. Humans and dinosaurs don't mix."

"That's not what the Young Earth Creationists say."

"You don't believe that bullshit, do you?"

"Of course not. I'm a man of science. And science is the very reason I'm going hiking. No human has ever had the opportunity to see what I could see today."

"Marty—"

"Think of it this way. I'm a curious traveler just like your people are. Look at the risk you took to make contact with Earth. For all you knew, we had the technology to blow you out of the sky."

"Humans wouldn't have to literally blow us out of the sky to destroy us."

"How else? You can travel faster than the speed of light."

"Not during a recharge cycle after a time jump. Then, to use an Earth term, we're *sitting ducks*. At this moment, we have only sub-light-speed propulsion and minimal shielding. If President Handley or anyone else were to attack us with a nuclear missile, the electromagnetic pulse would fry our circuitry, and the radiation would kill everyone on the ship."

"See, we're both taking risks. Besides, if a dinosaur eats me, you have several other humans on your ship who are capable of finishing the job. I need to do this, Clarence, and I promise to be really, really careful."

"I can't make you stay. But if anything happens to you, I'm going to kick your ass the next time I see you."

"Understood," I said with a smile, secretly thankful for his concern.

* * *

Thick forest surrounded me, but when I looked east, toward the sun, I saw a welcoming break in the trees. I headed that way, glancing behind me occasionally, both to memorize my return route and to make sure no dinosaur was following me. Never before had my senses been so attuned to my surroundings. I listened for twig snaps, watched for movement, and smelled the air for whatever dinosaurs smelled like.

With all the precautions I was taking, travel was slow, but the hike was worth it. The break in the trees marked where the land dropped into a deep, wide valley. Looking down, I saw a lush, green meadow, bisected by a clear stream. I followed the stream with my eyes to a small lake, and at the edge of that lake—

"Dinosaurs! I see dinosaurs!"

"Tyrannosaurus rexes?" Tina asked.

"No. Nothing that big. If I describe them to you, can you look them up on your computer?"

"Perhaps. Let's give it a shot."

"Okay, near the lake but not in the water, I see seven small— and by small, I mean roughly eight feet long from tail to head— bipedal creatures. They appear to be herbivores because they are leaning down to graze. Hold on, I'm going to move closer." I descended fifty or so feet down the valley wall before continuing. "Now I can see that they also have high-domed skulls with nasty-looking spikes on their muzzles. The spikes continue in a ring around their heads. Basically they're overgrown badass kangaroos with what I presume are scales."

"Based on your description, I can narrow the species down to *Dracorex, Stygimoloch,* or *Pachycephalosaurus.* Then again, it could be all three."

"How could it be all three?"

"Paleontologists disagree on the fossil evidence. Some think the fossils indicate three separate species while others insist they are just differing stages of juvenile, near adult, and adult. To complicate matters more, the males and females could be more physically dissimilar in these species than in others. That alone could account for the confusion."

"From where I'm standing, they all look pretty much the same. You didn't happen to hide a portable bionic eye at the bottom of my food pack, did you?"

"No. Your mission was to correct history, not to go on a scientific field trip."

"But this is one hell of a field trip, isn't it? And maybe we could correct history from this point in time. Instead of taking me back, you could send down a team of young, progressive thinkers. We could start the human race from here and avoid all the pitfalls of superstition-based societies. Imagine how many fewer wars we'd—"

"Marty, this is Captain Jagger. We cannot give humans an almost sixty-seven million-year head start! You might enjoy the romantic concept of being an Adam surrounded by numerous Eves, b—"

"Especially if they're redheads," I chimed in.

He ignored my comment and continued, "But even with an educated beginning, who knows what could happen? Look at the abrupt turn your people took in a single election cycle. Who would've guessed that *post-truth* would ever be a thing?"

"You're right, of course. Although why would making a correction from AD 31 be any more effective than doing the same thing from where I am now?"

"Aside from the fact that your band of humans would never survive, it might not be. What I do know is that by the first century, your species had time to evolve naturally, and we can see more clearly which events had long-term negative effects on human development."

"Do you ever worry about the ethics of playing God?"

"*Playing* God? Who says we aren't gods? And if we are, wouldn't we have the right to return to correct a mistake *we* made in your history?"

"Okay, you're freaking me out a little now. I'm alone, sixty-seven million years in the past, watching dinosaurs, with multiple people speaking in my head—who may or may not be gods."

The captain chuckled. "Sorry about that. This really is our first time here. And the definition of a god depends on one's perspective. Perhaps we can continue this philosophical discussion when you return to the ship. In the meantime, I'm going to try to be one fewer voice in your head and leave you in the capable hands of my crew."

During my conversation with the captain, I had continued

my descent. Now I could see more animals—not just dinosaurs, but birds and insects as well. On modern Earth, I knew the bullet ant to be the insect with the most painful sting. Here I had no way of knowing how painful the sting of an ant, or any other insect, would be. Quite possibly, somewhere in prehistoric Montana, were insects that could make bullet ant stings feel mild in comparison.

I looked around and spied numerous insects marching up and down tree trunks. Without getting close enough to examine any individuals, I had to assume they all had the potential to sting. I made a mental note not to grab a tree for any reason, including breaking a fall. And slipping and falling was a distinct possibility here since the valley wall was both steep and wet.

Eventually, I reached a wide, rocky outcrop that jutted sixty or more feet from the wall and provided a good vantage point for both animal-watching and safety. I crept out to the tip of it and swept my eyes up and down the valley. If the sights hadn't made me feel so puny, I would have felt like I was the king of the world.

"Tina, are you still there?"

"Yes."

"I have another dinosaur for you to look up. It's an herbivore. This one is about twenty-five feet long, with a stout body, spiky armor, and a wicked-looking club at the end of its tail. It's kind of like a cross between a wolverine and a pangolin."

"Okay."

"Wait! I'm having flashbacks to my childhood toy dinosaur collection. I think it's an *A . . . Ankosaur* or something like that."

"I think you mean *Ankylosaurus.*"

"That's it! I'm watching an *Ankylosaurus.* How cool is that?"

"As cool as an ice cube down your back?"

"That was a rhetorical question. But sure. As cool as an ice cube down my back . . . and front as well."

"Ooh!"

As I continued scanning the valley floor, the wondrousness of it all practically overloaded the connection between my eyes and my brain, but as I relaxed, more animals came into focus. Most were small, though some were large. Many of all sizes sported rudimentary feathers. The closest I'd ever come to a sight like this was when I was working on a story in Zimbabwe and saw baboons, warthogs, impalas, greater kudus, and elephants all in the same scene.

I was just about to describe another species to Tina when a rodent-like animal below me squealed and darted into a hole. Some things never change. My mind drifted back to present-day Montana where I'd seen countless ground squirrels do the same thing to avoid hunting eagles and—*Oh, shit!*

I dashed away from the edge and dove behind a boulder as an airplane crashed onto the outcrop! Okay, it wasn't exactly an airplane.

"Tina," I whispered. "Can you look up another dinosaur for me?"

"Sure. What have you got?"

"Some sort of *Pterosaur,* only bigger than I ever imagined they could get. It landed on the same outcrop as I am on. Its wings are folded, and it's slowly walking on all fours—kind of like a bat. It's as tall as a giraffe, with a beak long enough that my entire body could fit inside. And I wouldn't want to be on the receiving end of a head-butt because it has a huge crest."

"First of all, that's not a dinosaur. It's a flying reptile, most likely a *Quetzalcoatlus.* If my identification is correct, paleontologists speculate that it's a terrestrial stalker, scavenger, or both. It may not have landed specifically to attack you, but if you get too close, it will swallow you like a french fry."

"Well, if I have anything to say about it, keeping some distance between us won't be a prob—Oh, God! It's coming toward me."

Whether the *Quetzalcoatlus* heard me, smelled me, or saw me, it really didn't matter. It was shuffling my way with its head cocked slightly to the side. Maybe it just wants to be friends, I told myself.

Snap! Snap!

Or maybe not. A well-aimed snap of its beak would rip me in

half. I couldn't stay where I was since the boulder was too small to protect me. But how does one escape a powerful reptile with the wingspan of a four-seat, single-engine airplane?

Snap!

The only two things in my favor were mobility in tight spaces and, presumably, greater intelligence. I scanned the hillside for a cave or a tight stand of tall trees. No luck with the cave. However, I did see some promising trees, level with my position, some forty yards away. I'd never make it in a run, so I needed to use my superior brainpower to come up with a distraction to give me a head start. I picked up a tennis ball-sized rock, yelled, "Here, boy. Fetch!" and threw it as far as I could.

The *Quetzalcoatlus* just glared at me.

Well, it was worth a try.

Snap!

I resorted to backing up and beaning the reptile with whatever I could get my hands on: fistfuls of pebbles, rocks, and sticks. It ignored the pebbles, the rocks pissed it off, and it either ignored the sticks or caught them in its beak and pulverized them. My arm tired quickly, but I couldn't stop. I twisted a rough branch off a small tree and screamed as my hand began to burn. I dropped the branch and picked it right back up. If the branch burned my hand, what would it do to the inside of a predator's mouth? I lobbed it at the *Quetzalcoatlus's* beak.

Snap!

I sprinted for the tall trees, hoping they were close enough together to protect me. As I neared, I realized they were spaced too far apart. I chanced a glance over my shoulder. The *Quetzalcoatlus* wasn't pursuing me. Instead, it had taken to the air and was headed toward the lake.

"Marty! Marty!"

"Ow! You don't need to yell."

"You weren't answering any of us!" Chrissie barked. Then, in a much softer voice, she added, "We thought something horrible had happened to you."

"Me? No. I was just feeding a fire stick to the local *Quetzal-coatlus*. But now my hand is swelling up, and it's burning like hell."

"I told you not to touch any of the plant life," Tina said in the sing-songy voice shared by moms across the galaxy.

"I really didn't have a choice."

"You need to get as much of the poison off your hand as you can," Chrissie said. "Unfortunately, we don't have enough information on the indigenous plants to suggest an antidote. Water is your best bet."

"I'm heading for some right now. There's an animal trail that leads from my current position to a stream below."

"Need I say, *be careful?*" Tina said, still using her mom voice.

"And try not to linger," Chrissie added. "Sunset is in six hours. You absolutely must be back to the pickup location by then. You'll never find it in the dark."

I regressed to my child voice. "Don't worry. I will be careful and on time."

As soon as I reached the stream, I searched for anything potentially unfriendly before plunging my hand into the water. Ah, sweet relief!

Once the burning began to fade, I could better concentrate on my surroundings and committed as much of it to memory as possible. I was the first and only human being to see living dinosaurs. What I would give for a camera! In addition to photographing dinosaurs, a selfie would be awesome. Later, after returning to my own time, I could show people the photo and announce without the slightest bit of exaggeration, "This was me when I was the strongest, smartest, and sexiest man on Earth." Come to think of it, the photo would also show me when I was the weakest, dumbest, and ugliest man on Earth, but that little fact could be left unmentioned.

Time passed quickly as I hung out by the stream. I hardly noticed the increasing temperature, courtesy of the rising sun, and the valley grew quiet. Grazing animals moved to the far side where they could rest under clusters of shade trees, burrowing animals moved underground where they could cool off in their tunnels, and Cessnas with beaks abandoned the sky where they could . . . do whatever they did in the heat of the day. I had just enough time to check out the lake and make it back to the pickup spot before sunset.

I waded across the stream and started hiking toward the lake. Once I was moving, the heat felt uncomfortable. Sweat trickled down my face, and the little clothing I had left was soaking wet. A quick, cooling swim would feel great. But could I risk it? What if the lake was home to the Cretaceous equivalent of the Loch Ness Monster? When I had looked down from above, I hadn't seen any creatures swimming in it, but bushes and trees shielded much of the shore from my view.

I picked up my pace until I was within a few hundred feet of the water. Then I methodically approached the shoreline in a deep crouch.

Splash!

Several animals disappeared into the water, but two remained on shore.

"Crocodiles? *In Montana?*"

"Did you say something?" Chrissie's voice startled me.

"Oh. Sorry. I was actually talking to myself. But as long as you're here, I was just commenting on what an unusual sight crocodiles are in Montana. I'm sure they aren't the same species that lives in present-day Florida, but to my untrained eye, they're damn close."

"I'm looking them up now. . . . Crocodiles have been on Earth for about eighty-five million years, and their ancestors date back over two hundred million years. How big are the ones you're looking at?"

"Not huge. One is roughly six feet long, and the other is three feet longer than that."

"Hmm. They're most likely a long-extinct species of crocodilian called *Borealosuchus*. You should be okay if you keep your distance."

"Yeah, well, they've kinda ruined my swimming plans, but—"

"Swimming!" Clarence, the universe's only living subwoofer, vibrated my skull. "I've been patient with you, Marty, but you've done enough exploring. Get back to the pickup spot, now!"

"I'm on my way, boss." Oh, wait! That's Bruce. "But first, I want to skip just one rock across the lake. No matter how many times it skips, I'll set a world record that will stand for sixty-seven million years."

"I said *now!*"

"*Okaaay!* I'm going," I fibbed. He couldn't see me, so what the hell? I took a few steps closer, found the perfect rock, and let it rip. I turned and started back toward the animal trail with a smile on my face.

A few minutes later, Chrissie whispered in my head, "How many?"

"Nine," I whispered back.

"Congratulations!" she said with a laugh.

Once I made it to the spot where the animal trail met the stream, I looked up the valley wall. The climb back to where the land flattened out again was steep, and the height of the wall looked much greater from the bottom than it did from the top. I estimated my climb would take forty minutes, which would get me to the pickup spot with plenty of time to spare.

Before taking on the wall, I stopped at the stream to soak my hand again. Much of the swelling had gone down, but the burning had come back some. I was lucky that I'd been able to skip a rock at all. Had my hand been uninjured, I certainly would have added more skips to my world record.

While I was sitting, I took some time to relax and finish my food pack. Hey, I had just invented the picnic! Then I stood and turned in a complete circle, slowly taking in the verdant beauty of the meadow one final time. Three small dinosaurs—and by small, I mean bigger than a black bear—were working their way down the opposite valley wall. Rather than waiting until they were close enough to identify, and risking Clarence's wrath once again, I crossed the stream and started my ascent.

Initially my climb was easy because I had the animal trail to follow. But on my way down, I hadn't taken the trail the entire way. Now clusters of trees and bushes kept me from simply looking up to see where it went. Considering the consequences of getting lost, I had to return exactly the way I came. Once I reached the stand of tall trees, I cut directly across to the rocky outcrop. There, I took a short rest before locating the first in the series of landmarks I had memorized during my descent. Confident I would be to the top in no time, I picked up my pace in anticipation.

Scrunch! Scrunch!

Oh, boy. Here we go again. I looked up and immediately spotted the source of the heavy footfalls. "Chrissie! Tina! We have a problem."

"What's wrong?" Tina asked.

"There's a dinosaur at the top of the valley wall effectively blocking my route to the pickup spot."

"Describe it to me. I'll get you an identification."

"There's no need for that. He's a *Tyrannosaurus rex!*"

The *T. rex* glared down at me as if daring me to climb higher. Instead, I retreated a few steps and traversed the wall, heading toward my destination. The dinosaur stayed on top and mirrored my sideways move. If I moved faster, he kept up. If I moved the opposite direction, he did the same. If I moved down, he just . . . leaned over farther.

"Hey guys. I have good news and bad news."

"Marty, this is Bruce. What's the bad news?"

"Bruuuce! Where have you been? You haven't said a word to me since I landed in this *jungleland* that will someday be called Montana."

"Your mission is the primary responsibility of Tina and Chrissie, not me. However, no one can work nonstop. Chrissie was optimistic your climb up the wall would be uneventful, so she ran down the hall to grab a quick bite to eat. I'm filling in until she gets back."

"Okay, the bad news is that the *T. rex* isn't going to let me up on the flat land unless I join him for dinner . . . as his main course."

"What's the good news?"

"*Tyrannosauruses* are top-heavy. I don't think they do well on steep inclines."

"How does that help your situation?"

"Somehow I've got to get him over the edge."

"You can't possibly—"

"I agree. Even if I had a long rope and, by some miracle, managed to lasso him, I don't weigh enough to pull him over. I'd be little more than a charm on a necklace."

"Let me confer with Tina. Maybe we can come up with an idea."

I continued my parallel line dance with the *T. rex*. As terrifying as the experience was, it was also fascinating. Every kid who grew up playing with toy dinosaurs imagined what it would be like to come face to face with a real one, and the big boy above me did not disappoint. He was fast, nasty, and absolutely stunning. Yes, unlike the solid gray, black, or brown *Tyrannosauruses* in movies and in books, this one was colorful. His chest was whitish green, and his sides were a deeper green with bright orange speckles that shimmered in the sunlight. His forelimbs, while short, didn't appear to be as weak and useless as those of the *T. rexes* I'd seen in movies or in books either. They had some heft to them. As for his overall size, he was as enormous as I had expected. He balanced on his hind legs, like a teeter-totter, with his massive head far out front and his tail providing a counterweight. His hips were the fulcrum, and they appeared to be several feet higher than a basketball hoop.

Crack!

I glanced below. The three dinosaurs that I had seen coming down the opposite valley wall were now working their way up the wall I was on. They climbed with determination and didn't seem to care if any bushes happened to be in their way.

"Bruce, are you there?"

A few seconds ticked by before his voice filled my head. "Yes."

"There are three Komodo dragonlike dinosaurs coming up from the valley floor—beelining for me. I don't know what species they are, but that's not important right now. What *is* important is that they're definitely predators, a little bigger than me but significantly smaller than the *T. rex.*"

"Lunch."

"That's exactly what I was thinking."

"I don't follow you," Tina said. "How will one of the smaller dinosaurs be a *T. rex* lunch with you in the middle?"

"I'm not sure." I looked around. "I've got it! Give me a few minutes of silence. This isn't gonna be easy." A twisted old tree clung to the valley wall, one hundred feet to my right. It was just out of the *T. rex's* reach. I traversed partway to the tree and called, "Here, boys!"

Okay, I could have timed that better. The dinosaurs scrambled up the hill much faster than seemed possible. I raced the rest of the way, leapt for the lowest branch, and pulled myself up. When I realized I wasn't high enough, I yanked myself two branches higher—"Ouch!"—and scraped my already aching hand in the process. The dinosaur trio arrived seconds later.

I assumed the creatures were aware of the danger above. So to make it possible for *Mr. Tyrannosaurus* to do his job, I needed one of them to become so focused on me that it would carelessly move higher up the wall. I was currently on the side of the tree opposite the *T. rex.* I had to take a chance and switch sides. That would be a feat easier said than done, with the Cretaceous period equivalent of three full-grown hyenas glaring at me from below and a giant African lion glaring at me from above.

I hugged the tree as tight as I could and eased my way around. "Ow! Ouch! Ouch! Ouch! Ow!"

"What's wrong?" Tina shouted.

"I'm up a tree. It's crawling with stinging ants."

"Get down!"

"I can't. The three smaller dinosaurs are below me, and they look as hungry as the monster above me."

I frantically brushed off the ants and pulled myself up to the next big branch. "Ouch!"

Aside from the welts bubbling up on my arms and chest, my plan seemed to be working. But the *T. rex* snacks were still out of reach. I had to move out from the tree trunk. I stood on the branch and stretched for the one above me, hoping to steady myself. Then, on tiptoes, I shimmied out. God, I hate heights!

To the *T. rex*, I must have looked like I was offering myself up on a two-pronged fork. To the dinosaurs below, I was a piece of meat hanging precariously from that fork.

I pretended to slip. Or was it a real slip? I'm not sure. A frenzy erupted below. It still wasn't enough. I inched farther out, my legs involuntarily shaking.

Crunch!

The *T. rex* grabbed the smallest of the dinosaurs. The other two fled down the hill, if only for a moment. This was my chance! I swung down like an Olympic gymnast on the uneven bars—and landed on my ass. I got up and ran like an Olympic sprinter—and fell on my face. A sharp rock had given me the worst charley horse ever. I got back up, gritted my teeth, limped a bit further along the hill, and climbed the short distance to the top.

As I reached level ground, the pain in my ass began to fade, and I chanced a look back at the *T. rex*. I wish I could say he stopped what he was doing to acknowledge my ingenuity with the dinosaur version of a tip-of-the-hat, but instead, he threw back his head and swallowed a large, bloody piece of flesh.

I sprinted to the pickup spot and found my marker sooner than expected. "Hey, everyone, I'm here. Suck me up!"

"You're early," Chrissie said.

"Six and a half hours early, to be precise," Tina added.

"What? You said six hours—" I began.

"Until sunset," Tina finished. "Do the math. We dropped you off a little after one, you built a fire, you slept until seven in the morning, and now it's a little past five thirty in the evening. We'll be ready to pick you up just after midnight."

"Okay, I'll just sit here and try not to look like a *T. rex* after dinner mint. . . . Even though I *am* cool and refreshing!"

"Gather up some sticks and build a fire before it gets too dark," Chrissie said.

"Don't forget to add some dinosaur shed," Tina added.

"I just need a few minutes to catch my breath. Then I'm on it."

* * *

When I was a kid, time never passed slower than when my parents made me go to church. Later, as an adult, time never passed slower than when my sense of obligation made me sit in a dentist's chair. Gathering sticks in the darkening forest, surrounded by who knows how many ravenous dinosaurs, made those experiences whiz by in comparison. Now time wasn't even crawling. I needed a distraction.

"Chrissie, are you there?"

"Yes."

"Why did you and your crew choose to get involved in Earth's affairs? You could've just passed us by and let us blow ourselves to pieces."

"Yes, we could have, but not everyone on your planet has reached the same stage of mental evolution. Why should those of you who are peaceful, open-minded, and willing to care for your people and your planet die because others are warlike, bigoted, and too selfish to worry about how their actions affect others?"

"I agree. But I still don't understand your generosity."

"Long ago, we had much in common with the primitive thinkers on your world today. We had to learn the hard way what holds societies back, and what makes them hate. We barely survived. Later, as our ships grew faster, we learned that countless other inhabited planets suffered similar fates. We couldn't just stand by and do nothing, so our top scientists worked around the clock to perfect time travel. Then we made it our mission to help as many worlds as we can. At this moment, numerous ships from our planet are in other solar systems helping other worlds."

"Are you always successful?"

"Of course not. Some global societies are beyond help, and sometimes the planet's representative—in Earth's case that is you—fails. Earlier today, you mentioned to Clarence that other humans could serve as a replacement should something happen to you. That wouldn't work. In selecting you, we ran billions of computer simulations to make sure that if you changed Earth's timeline you wouldn't eliminate yourself. After all, how can you go back in time to correct an error if that correction causes you never to exist in the first place? It's a confusing paradox."

"Mind blowing is more like it."

"And only a small number of people on each planet come from stable enough family lines for corrective missions."

"So I wasn't selected because of my travel experience and my belief in science?"

"Yes and no. To put it in Earth terms, your stable family line made you a finalist just like all the other humans on the ship. Computer simulations don't take long with the experience and technology we have. You never would have made it onto our ship without a time-travel-proof line."

"But I willingly walked—"

"Perhaps not as willingly as you believe. Then, once you were on our ship and we got to know you, your travel experience and belief in science quickly moved you ahead of the others. Sure, technically, we could replace you with someone else, but what if that person failed, and the person after that? We could be here a long time. With so many planets in need of our services, each captain is under orders to conduct just one try per planet. Some-times fate has to be fatal."

"Wait! I just failed. Does that mean Earth is doomed?"

"No, *you* didn't fail. *We* failed. It's our obligation to get you to the correct time and place. We'll stick with you until that happens.

Then you'll have one overall opportunity, which can include up to two follow-up time jumps, to succeed or fail."

"No pressure there!"

"Hey, you asked."

"How much time is left until the pickup?"

"Did you lose your pocket watch?"

"No. It just seems to be running a little slow."

"Four hours, fifty-three minutes."

I glanced at my watch. "Hmm. I guess it is accurate. It's been such a tense and exhilarating day. . . . I'm so tired."

"Would you like to take a nap?"

"How can I safely do that? Mr. *T. rex* or any of his toothy colleagues could show up. Next thing you know, I'd wake up dead."

Chrissie giggled softly before replying in a serious voice, "Not necessarily. Once you get your fire going and fall asleep, I will listen through your ears for any danger. Just like last night."

"Huh? I knew you were with me last night, but it never occurred to me that you were listening through my ears."

"I didn't want to make you feel self-conscious—especially if you talked about any women in your sleep. . . . Okay, that wasn't what I meant to say."

"Oh?"

I could almost feel her changing to a darker shade of . . . her colors. She cleared her throat and continued. "Remember, when we get you to Galilee, we will need to eavesdrop on everything. It's not as if your ears turn off when you go to sleep."

"Okay, fine. A nap it is. But if I start mumbling names, wake me up."

"I will, Marty."

Although I doubted she'd actually wake me if I started talking about anyone in my sleep, my thoughts quickly changed to discouraging a dinosaur visit. I now had a large pile of sticks and other burnable materials. I flicked on my lighter, and with a little strategic blowing, coaxed my campfire to a roar. Then I added some dinosaur shed and made myself as comfortable as possible. I fell asleep within minutes.

* * *

Scrunch! Scrunch!

"Marty, wake up!"

"Chrissie. . . . Oh, fuck! It's the *T. rex!*"

"No, no, don't worry about the dinosaur. I've been monitoring the sound for about twenty minutes. It's not getting closer to you, and it sounds as if it's walking on four legs, not two. More than likely, it's a *Triceratops* or some other large herbivore."

"That would be so cool! When I was a kid, my dream was to see a *Triceratops.*"

Tina spoke up. "Sorry, but this isn't a dinosaurologist expedition. It's time to go."

"I don't see the hose, Tina. What do I do?"

"Stand beside your marker. That will be close enough for the hose to find you."

I followed her instructions.

Whoosh!

Everything went white.

Everything went tight.

CHAPTER 3

Circling Uranus

"Let me out! Let me out!" I screamed. Yes, my claustrophobia kicked in both going and coming.

Tina opened the hatch and greeted me with a smile. She offered her hand and pulled me out with surprising strength. I was still breathing hard, so she waited a second before giving me a quick, polite hug. "Welcome back, Marty Mann!"

Chrissie grabbed me as soon as Tina released me. She looked me in the eyes, her eyelashes glowing steady pink, and pulled me into a long, warm hug.

My knowledge of Krichard customs and emotions was rudimentary at best, so I tried not to read too much into her warmth. Still, I couldn't help thinking—

"You are filthy and disgusting!" Chrissie said, interrupting my fantasy before it even had time to heat up. "I can't believe I touched you. Look at all those big, red welts on your body! We need to get you to the medical lab and then into a shower." She paused to sniff the air. "On second thought, perhaps a shower first, *then* to medical. *Yech!*"

Oh, yes. She was definitely falling for me.

* * *

I'd take you through the play by play of my medical examination and shower, but the exam was just as boring as exams on Earth, albeit with fancier equipment, and the shower was sans Chrissie and, therefore, equally boring. Had Chrissie joined me for hot, wet interspecies sex, I would have been a gentleman and withheld the intimate details anyway. So remember, this isn't a sleazy romance novel. No matter what happens in these pages between me and anyone else—even if it's super, super hot—there will never be any "glistening," "writhing," "moist petals," "throbbing manhood," "heaving breasts," or "raging with passion." Well, maybe heaving breasts, but that's it. Shall we move on?

Once the ship's doctors, Ann and Nancy—I swear they were sisters—certified me healthy, clean, and thoroughly disinfected, I retired to my cabin for a wonderful night's sleep. The cabin itself was awesome and far more comfortable than sleeping on the ground in a wet forest, worrying about being devoured by an ancient carnivore. Since the Krichards are tall, and any aliens they meet during their travels could be even taller, it was quite spacious. It was also well appointed. My favorite feature was the dial-a-gravity bed. Forget all the fancy adjustable beds on Earth. You haven't slept until you've plopped down on a Krichard mattress with your effective weight less than that of a humming-bird. In fact, I set mine even lighter. I would have floated away if the blankets hadn't been tucked in so tightly that they held me in place. Need I say that none of the cabins had ceiling fans?

* * *

When I woke up, I was thrilled to see that my hand and skin were pretty much back to normal. Whatever the doctors had given me did wonders.

I padded over to the cafeteria for some breakfast. As a travel writer, I always made it a point to eat local, no matter where I was. So even though the Krichards are capable of replicating any Earth food I desire, other than when I first got on the ship and was too high to ask for anything else, I have insisted on eating Krichard fare.

And what a wonderful adventure for my taste buds! Krichards didn't eat anything with a heartbeat, but they did synthesize a meat-like substance that absolutely did *not* taste like chicken. They also used a wide variety of spices, but just like their faux meat, those spices didn't taste the way I expected them to. Also, as you might expect of a good-looking humanoid species with flashy eyelashes, much of what they eat is sweet—minus the pesky long-term side effects of weight gain or diabetes.

I could name some of their foods for you, but without something for comparison, they would just be meaningless combinations of letters. Just as the Krichards came from roughly forty light-years from Earth, so did all their ingredients and cooking techniques. Imagine the most exotic dish on our world made from ingredients you didn't even know existed, and you'd be somewhat close to the concept of Krichard food. Consequently, it took me a while to learn what I could eat that wouldn't make my stomach turn cartwheels. And like most kinds of food—whether belonging to a specific ethnic group or a specific alien group—some of it was unappetizing, and some of it was heavenly.

As for this morning's breakfast? It was nummy!

Once my stomach was full, I decided to look for Chrissie. First, I checked at her workstation. When I didn't find her there, I walked to her cabin and caught her just as she was heading out the door.

"Hi, Marty! How are you feeling today?" Her eyelashes began glowing pink again. The Krichards may be more advanced than humans are, but they'd make terrible poker players. As near as I could tell, their eyelashes were virtual mood rings.

"Considering that just yesterday, prehistoric plants, insects, and reptiles were all out to get me, I'm feeling wonderful. And I'm still pinching myself. I actually got to see dinosaurs. Can you believe it? *Dinosaurs!*"

She subtly pointed with her head to indicate we should start walking. "I'm glad you're taking things so well. If you had died down there, I never would have forgiven myself."

"It wasn't your fault. I was the one who hyperventilated and threw everything off."

"Yeah, but we should have been prepared for that."

I turned my head toward her and smiled sympathetically. "No worries. I had an unforgettable adventure. When do we try again?"

"In three days. Tina is rechecking and recalibrating everything to make sure the same problem doesn't happen again." She let her hand brush against mine. "In the meantime, you should just relax, or perhaps we could . . ."

I couldn't breathe as I anticipated her next words.

"take a spin around *your anus.*"

I stopped dead in my tracks, unsure if I'd heard her right. I looked into her eyes. She showed no emotion. Even her eyelashes failed to glow. I continued staring until her left one twinkled ever so faintly, and the corners of her lips eased toward her squinting eyes. A giggle escaped and grew into a laugh. "I've been watching you," she said, "and I'm picking up on Earth's sense of humor. I really had you there, didn't I?"

I laughed as well, but more at how cute Chrissie was at making her first Earth joke than at the joke itself. "You did. And I'm flattered. But you should know that my sense of humor is not typical of what you'd find on Earth. Still, pronouncing *Uranus* to sound like *your anus* is a classic . . . for teenage boys worldwide. And, of course, coming from you, someone who—if you were serious—could actually circle Uranus, adds an extra element of realism to the joke."

Chrissie's eyelashes flashed again. "Good, because I was serious about that part. Even at the speed we travel, our missions are long. Sometimes we just need to get off the ship and have some fun. We have a couple of Chromosphere Cruisers on board. We should take one out for a ride."

"Can they really fly into the chromosphere of a star?"

"Oh, no. That's one thing my species has in common with yours. We like to give our vehicles exaggerated names. Chromosphere Cruisers not only melt in extreme heat, but they also barely exceed light-speed. Still, they're loads of fun, feel faster than they really are, and can circle Uranus with ease."

"Okay. It's a date!" I flushed when I realized what I had said.

Chrissie didn't let me squirm for long. She reached up with a long finger and ran it down my cheek. "It's a date."

Oh, yes. I was most definitely falling for her.

* * *

Two hours later, we were in the cruiser bay looking at a spacecraft that was beyond dazzling. Obviously, the Krichards exaggerated much more than just its name. The Chromosphere Cruiser was dark pink with high fins, triple-indented sides, and a rounded, clear top that covered the cockpit and small studio cabin.

"This looks like more than something you'd just take out for a quick spin," I said.

"That depends on your definition of quick. It has a range of four light-years, but only enough food and liquid to sustain two humanoids for the equivalent of six Earth months. The longest I've known anyone to take one out was for a little more than a month." She stepped inside the plush, violet interior and motioned for me to follow.

"Can I drive?"

"I've read about how you human males always like to be in control. But in my society, pilots are chosen based on skill, not sex."

Reminiscent of the big ship, the cruiser had a vertical cockpit. As soon as we strapped ourselves in standing side by side, the gravity eased, eliminating all fatigue.

Chrissie pushed a series of buttons, grabbed the floor-mounted control stick, turned to me, and flashed an eyelash. "Hold on!"

"But the door isn't op—"

We shot toward the bay door. It opened just in time.

"Woo-hoo!" she yelled before looking at me and calmly adding, "I've been studying Earth interjections."

I had been in space long enough that much of the novelty had worn off, but when the big Krichard ship moved, it was barely noticeable. This was a completely different feeling. We whipped past the moon, then circled back around it—coming in low, just over a mountain range. From there, we shot toward Mars, circled it, and did the same with the dwarf planet Ceres. Incidentally, I didn't know all of those celestial objects by sight. A screen beside me educated me as we went, conveniently displaying a map of the solar system translated into English.

If humans were to travel to Mars via a NASA rocket, the trip would take six to eight months. Our trip, via the Chromosphere Cruiser, took less than fifteen minutes, and we weren't even going full speed.

Next, we hit a long stretch of nothing but the blackness of space. As the cruiser hummed, my thoughts bounced between the euphoria of where I was at that moment and the sorrow I felt for what was happening back on my home planet. Less than a year ago, I was living a fulfilling life in Montana, hoping that our president wouldn't turn out to be as unstable and dangerous as I feared. Now I was alone with a beautiful alien, and the sun was behind us, getting smaller by the second. Should I be depressed or thrilled?

My parents and my sister died young, and I wasn't currently romantically involved with someone, so at least the disaster on Earth wasn't quite as personal for me as it could have been. Even so, I was painfully aware that while I was gallivanting around the solar system, close friends of mine were living through hell. On the bright side, my Krichard friends were giving me the opportunity to make things right again. But what will a timeline change do to Earth? Will I even recognize it when I return? Will that change make it so people I care about never existed? And what if I want to stay with Chrissie and the rest of the Krichards? Will they allow me to do that?

Chrissie reached over and nudged my shoulder with a finger. "Hey. You've left me for a bit. What are you thinking?"

I shrugged. "Oh, nothing earth-shattering."

Chrissie tilted her head as if she didn't believe me. Then after a pause, she smiled, pointed, and giggled. "Look how big Uranus is!"

We had now purposely pronounced the planet's name with the accent on the second syllable so often that neither of us could say it the unfunny way even if we tried. Laughing, I replied, "It's beautiful! And to think I was a little worried it might be butt ugly."

"Seriously, don't you love its bluish-gray color?"

"I do, and I didn't expect it to have all those dark rings. Can we land on it?"

"No. It's a gas giant. And even if we could, we wouldn't see a thing. We can land on one of the moons if you want."

Minutes later, we buzzed Uranus and began searching for a moon to land on. The planet has at least twenty-seven moons, so we had the luxury of being choosy. We selected one between the sun and the planet and landed on the dark side. We couldn't leave the cruiser without putting on spacesuits, and neither of us felt like going outside anyway. Instead, Chrissie pushed a button that reclined the entire cockpit just enough to give us a perfect view of Uranus.

I felt like I was back in high school, sitting in a car with my date on Skyline Parkway. I was just about as nervous as I was back then too. If Chrissie were human, I'd have no doubt about her intentions, but she was a humanoid from forty light-years away. Maybe they're just overly friendly. Maybe only females make the first move. Maybe they restrict romantic relations to their own sex. Maybe . . . who knows?

Perhaps the same thoughts about my species were going through her head, and neither of us wanted to risk making a wrong move. Finally, I turned, looked deep into her eyes, and said, "May I kiss you near Uranus?"

Slap!

Chrissie glared at me, her eyelashes glowing fiery yellow. Then she tightened her lips to restrain a snort, and her eyelashes flashed pink. Her attempt to recompose to a scowl failed miserably. Soon she was laughing, and so was I.

We kissed.

"That was out of this—" I began.

We kissed again.

"—world," I finished.

"So you liked that?"

"Very much."

"When you first caught my attention, I did some research. I was so pleased to learn that your species uses mating positions similar to mine."

"Mating?"

"Am I going too fast?"

I hesitated. "Well, we don't even know if our parts are compatible. We could both be in for a big disappointment."

"Oh, we're compatible. I looked that up too."

I tried to slow my heartbeat and appear more relaxed than I felt. She looked so delectable at that moment—her face lit by both the reflection off Uranus and her twinkling eyelashes.

Before I could utter another word, she continued, "There's just one thing. From where I come from, the girls are the aggressors, not the boys. So undo your cockpit belt, and no more Uranus jokes. Follow me into the back. The view will be just as good from there—no matter which way you look."

* * *

One hour later, we were basking in the afterglow, just talking.

I felt more compatible with Chrissie than I ever had with anyone on Earth. She was sexy, sassy, and smart enough for two brains. Still, I didn't know her nearly as well as she knew me.

"Tell me about your life. Hell, I don't even know the correct name of your planet."

"Well, as you know, our species name sounds very much like the Earth word *pissant,* so we call our planet Pzzantia. However, we're not as attached to names as you are, so Krichardia is just fine."

"Do you have family or a spouse on Krichardia?"

"Yes and no." She tapped a button to reset the gravity, allowing us to hover above the bed, parallel with the clear ceiling of the cruiser. "My parents and older brother still live in the same city where I was born. And if I had a spouse, I most definitely wouldn't be here with you now."

"I hope this isn't too forward, but how old are you, and how long does your species live?"

"Those are fair questions. Because my years are different from yours, the answer takes some calculating." She closed her eyes, presumably to access information via the wireless interface in her hind brain. After a few seconds, she opened them and continued, "I am thirty-seven in Earth years, which would make me two years younger than you. And if nothing happens to me sooner, I will die when I reach seventy-five."

My eyes widened. "That seems rather precise."

"We're a beneficial suicidal species."

"How is suicide beneficial?"

"We believe in the greater good. Look at your planet. It has far more people than it can support without incurring long-term, catastrophic environmental damage. In the twentieth century alone, your population grew from 1.65 billion to 6 billion. It would have soon reached 8 billion if your president hadn't started dropping nuclear bombs. Even without the bombs, your population was doomed to crash in a very painful way because of pollution, famine, disease, and wars over resources. To prevent such a thing from happening on Krichardia, we work to keep our population down on both ends of life. At the beginning, we encourage small families and generously provide birth control. At the end, we appreciate the certainty of an exact exit date. What could be more loving for your children and grandchildren than to leave them with a healthy planet and memories of you before your mental and physical health deteriorate?"

I stroked Chrissie's cheek with the back of my hand and wondered what it would be like to know for sure that your life was almost halfway over. Still, I couldn't argue with the logic of her species. "Can I ask one more question?"

"Only one. Then I want to curl up next to you, enjoy the view, and taste something from Earth."

I raised an eyebrow.

She smirked, realizing that my mind had gone straight to the gutter. "No, silly! When we first reached Earth, we sucked up part of a grocery store. Just as you are curious about our food, we are curious about yours. I stashed several bottles of wine in the cargo hold along with an assortment of sweets, cheeses, and crackers. I thought we'd start with a white wine and maybe try a red later on."

"That sounds perfect, but now I forgot my question." I paused and stared at her for a moment. "Oh, yeah," I said, tapping the side of my head as it came back to me. "How long have you been in space?"

"I've been working on ships for roughly fifteen of your years. For a while, I was promoted to faster ships and better positions every six months or so. It's difficult to form and maintain close relationships with others when that happens, but my ultimate goal was to get on a time-correction ship. I've now had my dream job for a little over two years and hope to stay where I am for many more."

"Let's break out the wine!"

"Yes, sir!" she growled.

* * *

We spent another hour on the moon. The bottle of wine Chrissie brought was a large one, and since she had never drunk real alcohol before, I probably should have cut her off at two glasses. Instead, she downed more than half the bottle.

47

"We s-s-should . . . go," she slurred.

"You're pretty drunk. Are you sure you can get us back okay?"

"Wa . . . We're in space. Wh-What'sss the worst thing I can do? Fly into Uranus?" We both snorted at that one.

We moved to the cockpit and strapped ourselves in. Chrissie pushed on the control stick to lift us awkwardly off the moon. Then she yanked it back to narrowly avoid a mountain.

"Does this cruiser have autopilot?" I asked nervously.

"S-S-Sure, but that would take all the fun out of it. Hold on!" She slapped the control stick to the left, then shoved it the opposite way. For a moment, I feared we actually were going to pierce Uranus, but she managed a last-second course correction, and we banked away. "Neptune, here we come!"

"Neptune? I thought we were heading back to the ship."

"We're . . . jussst taking the looong way."

"You're the boss."

"Yes, and don't youuu ever forget it. Look at the map on your side screen. If we head directly back, we just go through empty space. But if we go around, like thisss. . . ." She reached over and pointed. "We can check out Neptune and Saturn and even take a spin around Jupiter."

"Won't the captain expect us back before we can do all that?"

"I'm sending him a message now. I haven't had a day off in months, and Tina is making all the preparations for your next time jump. Who wants to sit around on a big ship when we can go s-s-space camping?"

"Space camping? I love it!"

As I studied the solar system map, Chrissie inputted our estimated travel times at light-speed: Uranus to Neptune was 185 minutes, Neptune to Saturn was 206 minutes, Saturn to Jupiter was 41 minutes, and Jupiter to Earth was 34 minutes. She then flashed an eyelash in my direction. "You're a travel writer. This should be right up your alley. We'll just explore until we find a suitable spot to stop. Then we'll have a bite to eat and some red wine."

I couldn't help smiling. Was I the luckiest guy in the solar system, or what?

"Watch out!" I shouted. "Meteor!"

"I see it!"

She swerved just in time.

"That was close. We could have been space dust."

"Nope. Chromosphere Cruisers have numerous built-in s-s-safety features. If I hadn't swerved first, the autopilot would have eventually taken control and s-s-swerved for me."

"Eventually?"

We exchanged glances as an eyelash lit up the cockpit.

We raced toward Neptune. After a bit, Chrissie wisely changed her mind about drunk flying and put the cruiser on autopilot. "I need to take a nap. Would you like to join me? The cruiser will wake us when we reach Neptune."

Even though I wasn't tired, nothing in the entire solar system could have been more irresistible to me than the opportunity to lie next to this captivating woman. We crawled into the back, and she rested her head on my shoulder and fell asleep in seconds. I nodded off several minutes later.

* * *

"Neptune! Neptune! Neptune!"

"Shut up!" Chrissie yelled. The proximity alarm complied.

We rolled out of bed and shuffled into the cockpit. There was Neptune. Of all the planets in our solar system, Uranus and Neptune may be the most alike. Uranus is slightly larger, with the two planets coming in third and fourth when compared to the others. Additionally, they are both gas giants, sometimes called ice giants, made up primarily of hydrogen and helium.

"It looks a lot like Uranus," I said.

"Neptune is a little bluer," she said.

"Hmm."

"Hmm. Would you like to go back to bed? We don't have to sleep."

"Sounds wonderful."

"I'll set the autopilot for Saturn, as well as that damn alarm."

* * *

"Saturn! Saturn! Saturn!"

"Shut up!" Chrissie yelled. The proximity alarm complied.

We rolled out of bed and shuffled into the cockpit.

"That's more like it!" I said.

"It's gorgeous," she added, "but it's another gas giant, so we can't camp on it. The computer says Saturn has at least sixty-two moons. Perhaps we could land on one of those."

"If I remember correctly, scientists speculate that one of those moons may support life."

She tapped her computer screen. "Here it is: Enceladus. It has a thin atmosphere and vents in the southern region that shoot out water vapor, methane, and other materials. Obviously, if life exists there, it would be microscopic and deep inside the moon. I think your scientists are a bit optimistic with their speculation."

"But it sounds like a fascinating place to camp."

"As long as we don't go hiking without spacesuits."

"Enceladus is inside one of Saturn's outer rings," I said, pointing to her screen. "Will the ring material hurt the cruiser?"

"No. While some of the rings contain large hunks of rock and ice that we should avoid, the one where Enceladus resides is made up mostly of what is emitted from the vents."

"This is going to be the best camping trip ever! Can we make s'mores?"

"What are s'mores?"

"It's a traditional Earth camping delicacy. You roast a marshmallow over a fire, and while it's still hot, you squeeze it, along with a slab of chocolate, between two pieces of graham cracker. It goes great with red wine."

"I'll have to check our supplies. We should be able to do that. But first, let's get to the moon. I have to concentrate in case the ring contains any unexpected debris. So let's hold off on any more conversation until we touch down."

Chrissie's eyelashes went dark as she focused simultaneously on her navigation screen and the view out the front window. Passing through the ring was like flying through a cloud. Next, we headed for the southern tip of the moon. The plumes spewing out the vents were visible from far in the distance, and with only a thin atmosphere to restrict them, they made Old Faithful in Yellowstone National Park seem scrawny in comparison.

We were just about to land when Chrissie's daredevil instincts took over. She sped up and slalomed through some plumes. Then when she spotted a level place to land, just far enough away from the plumes, she banked around, made three high-speed, low-ground passes, arced high above the moon, and looped backward before gently setting the cruiser down on the surface. She looked over at me—my fingers clutching the side support bars of my stand-up seat—and said, "Chromosphere Cruisers are built for fun!"

I glanced out the windows as Chrissie methodically shut down any systems we wouldn't need on the ground.

"Want to go for a hike?" she asked.

"What? It's cold out there!"

"Aw. Is minus 295 Fahrenheit too cold for you?"

"Well, I *did* grow up in Duluth, so maybe not. But I generally prefer to breathe oxygen on hikes."

"Your species is *so* sensitive." She flashed an eyelash. "We have spacesuits in the back. We should have one that will fit you. I recommend you take a pee first. Then you won't have to worry about a wet diaper later."

"You mean I can't just open my fly and let 'er rip?"

"Oh, that would be very bad—for a lot of reasons."

We took turns using the restroom, then Chrissie showed me a selection of spacesuits—all in dark pink, of course. Because Krichards are taller than humans are, I had to wear a women's medium, which was slightly embarrassing. But hey, I was going to walk on Enceladus!

After we squeezed into our suits, we passed through a relatively spacious airlock that didn't spark my claustrophobia and stepped onto the surface of the moon.

"Hold on, Chrissie," I said, tugging on the sleeve of her spacesuit. "Humans have a tradition each time we step onto a new moon. Let me see if I can do this correctly. . . . That's one small step for man, one giant leap for man—"

"Don't do that!" Chrissie yelled.

It was too late. Up I went . . . and went. Just when I was getting panicky that I'd continue right out into space, I felt my ascent slow and reverse. My anxiety dissipated. Knowing I was okay, I corkscrewed several times on the way down and stuck my landing. Then I continued my speech exactly where I left off. "—kind, two perfect pirouettes—one for women and one for drag queens—and a dozen eyelash flutters for the most beautiful Krichard in the solar system."

Chrissie applauded. I took a bow.

"How high did I jump?"

"It's hard to tell because there's not a tall geological feature nearby for comparison, but I'd guess between 100 and 125 feet."

"When we get back to the ship, I need to write that down and add it to the other records I've set lately."

"Sorry, Marty, but that's going to be the shortest record ever!" She leapt into the air, rose well past my achieved height, and punctuated her jump with a series of graceful flips on the way down. Then, smiling like a child who had just beaten an older sibling in a contest, she took an extra deep bow.

"Is that the best that you can do? I wasn't trying the last time. You're going down, babe! Of course, the only way we'll know for sure is if we both jump at the same time."

"You're on!"

"Okay, on three. One . . . two . . . three!"

We took to the air, giggling as we climbed. Eventually, I felt the pull of gravity and Chrissie continued past me—until I grabbed her leg. Then, slowly, we tumbled back to the surface, laughing hysterically.

At just 314 miles in diameter, Enceladus is small compared to Earth's moon, which is 2,159 miles in diameter. The difference is even greater for gravity since our moon has 17 percent of what we have on Earth, while Enceladus has only 1 percent of what we have on Earth. No wonder we could jump so high.

Enceladus is an ice moon with craters, valleys, and mountains. One of its many unusual features is fine, dry snow that blankets almost every surface. Even though most of what shoots out the vents escapes into space, some of it drifts back down to the surface as perpetual flurries. I tried to make a snowball, but the snow was just too powdery.

Consequently, I realized that Chrissie's daredevil landing routine had been more purposeful than it appeared. She had been scanning for a solid place to land while simultaneously using the cruiser as a high-tech snowblower. Had she not done that, we would have been in continual danger of falling into a deep, hidden crevasse. Now, instead, we had a long swath of crusty, light-blue ice to walk on.

That our walk would be limited to a swath took nothing away from our stunning view. Saturn, the second-largest planet in the solar system, dominated more than a third of the sky. It was truly a breathtaking sight—like a golden marble, with a hint of purple and green, encircled by rings in similar earth tones. Also, depending on where we stood, the remarkable geysers of Enceladus added a fireworks-like touch to the scene.

Even though a walk on a moon, with the most amazing view ever, should have been instantly romantic, it took a while for me to get into the spirit of things. We were bundled up in spacesuits, holding hands through gloves so well insulated we could have been grasping hot coals without feeling a thing. Additionally, the frolicsome things new couples often do when they walk in the snow just weren't going to happen. Even if the snow had been wet enough for a playful snowball fight, neither of us would have felt a thing through our spacesuits. And, of course, kissing was out of the question.

On the other hand, Chrissie had an implant similar to mine, which allowed us to talk directly into each other's head. Or in her case, since the implant was part of the artificial enhancements to her hind brain, perhaps I was talking into her buttocks. Physical locations aside, communications were incredibly intimate because our spacesuits deprived us of all senses other than sight. With Chrissie inside my head, I felt as if we were two—make that three—brains sharing the same body.

I turned and looked into her eyes. "What does it feel like to have two brains?"

"I don't know. I've never had just one, and most of the augmentations to my hind brain were installed shortly after birth. Who knows? Because we originated on separate worlds, we could perceive an infinite number of sensations differently, from the taste of food to the appeal of colors to the feel of sex. Obviously our perceptions aren't dramatically different, but some mysteries will always remain between us."

"I agree. There will always be mysteries, but I'm a naturally curious person who likes to find answers whenever possible. That's why Truth or Dare was my favorite game in middle school."

She looked at me inquisitively. "What is Truth or Dare?"

"Well, when you're in middle school, it's an excuse for boys to get a peek at a girl's boobs and for girls to confirm who has a crush on whom. Sometimes we called the game Spin the Bottle because several of us would sit in a circle, and we would take turns spinning the bottle. When the bottle stopped, whomever it pointed at would have to declare *truth* or *dare*. Then, if the victim chose *truth*, the person who spun the bottle would ask a question, or if the victim chose *dare*, the person who spun the bottle would propose something outrageous to do."

The inside of Chrissie's mask lit up. "That sounds fun! We should play it now."

"But we don't have a bottle, and I've already seen your boobs."

"Perhaps you'd like to see them again sometime. We can just take turns. Ladies first!"

"Um . . . truth?" I said, wondering what I'd gotten myself into.

"Who is better looking, Krichard women or human women?"

"That's complicated. The women of my species vary in appearance much more than yours do. And I have to admit, flashy eyelashes take a while to get used to. Emotions also have a lot to do with how attractive someone seems. For instance, when I first saw you, I thought you were cute. But now that I know you . . ." I paused to add a bit of drama. "I think you're the most beautiful woman I've ever seen in my life."

"Ohhh." Lights flashed inside her helmet and then went dark. "Are you okay?"

She smiled. "I'm great. Now it's your turn. I also choose truth. Give me your best shot!"

"Well, let's just reverse the question."

"I agree that your species varies in looks more than mine does, so the question doesn't have a definitive answer. Regarding humans, the most difficult thing for me was getting used to your *lack* of light-producing eyelashes. We can't read minds, but with our eyelashes, we don't need to. Although we have some control over them, they ultimately betray our feelings. Humans are more guarded, and sometimes that makes me uncomfortable. With you, I'm learning to read your face for less obvious clues to what you're thinking. And yeah," she flashed a mischievous smile, "I think you're kind of cute too."

"Okay, it's your turn to be the virtual bottle spinner. This time, I choose dare."

"Hmm. . . . That's tough when you're on a moon that has no oxygen and barely an atmosphere. Considering that it's minus 295 out, asking you to give me a peek at a certain body part would be inadvisable—especially with the plans I have for you later. Almost any dare would be too dangerous. . . . Okay, I dare you to jump into the air and do five flips before landing."

I pushed just high enough to complete five klutzy flips. Chrissie applauded weakly as I landed.

"Dares here are boring," I said.

"Then let's change the game and play Truth Without Dare."

We started walking. "Tell me something nefarious about you. You can't possibly be so perfect."

After an awkward pause, Chrissie answered in a soft voice, "I cheated. Both Tina and I are attracted to you. And since the females in our society are the aggressors, it's traditionally up to us to decide who gets an unclaimed male. Had we followed tradition, the two of us would have had to wrestle in the nude while you watched. If after an hour, there was no clear winner, only then would you get to choose."

Visual images flashed in my head, and I allowed myself to enjoy them for a few steps before asking, "How did you cheat?"

"Isn't it obvious? By snatching you away for this interplanetary camping trip, you've now been claimed."

"But what if I don't want to be claimed?"

She punched me in the arm, playfully but hard. "Oh, you love it! Besides, you wouldn't really want to watch Tina and me getting all hot and sweaty wrestling anyway. . . . *Would you?*" She stared me down.

"Well, no," I lied meekly. "Won't Tina be mad at both of us when we return?"

"Maybe, for a short time. Our species doesn't typically hold grudges. She knows I would lick her ass in a wrestling match anyway."

"Pffft! The correct Earth phrase is 'kick her ass.' But thanks. My mind will go straight to that the next time I see you and Tina together."

"I know the correct phrase, silly." She flashed an eyelash. "Are all Earth men so easy to get hot and bothered?"

"Actually, there's a big difference in the way men, *and women,* on Earth think. Some just get bothered. The possibility that the wrong type of person might have sex with, or fall in love with, the wrong type of person gets a certain segment of our population very uptight."

"Well, that's just rude. If all people involved are consenting adults, why is it anyone else's business?"

I shrugged. "Religion, I suppose."

"That's a common problem on other worlds as well. When societies are primitive, religion becomes a tool to control certain segments of their population."

"On my planet, it's women and people who are not heterosexual that most major religions try to control."

"That's not surprising. Planets that have advanced beyond religion generally don't need help from my people. It's the ones that cling to it that most often destroy themselves. The worst are the worlds that have just two or three dominant religions fighting for supremacy."

"Are we still playing Truth Without Dare?"

"Do we need a game to have a conversation?"

"No. In fact, I have to say that I've never met a woman as easy to talk with as you."

"I feel the same way about you. Our conversations are effortless."

We stopped walking and turned around.

"Look how far we've come! The cruiser is almost below the horizon."

"We are on a tiny moon," she said.

"I feel like s'mores now. How about you?"

"That sounds wonderful. Shall we head back?"

"Okay, but let's play one last game. How many jumps would it take you to make it back to the cruiser?"

"I can do it in six."

"I can do it in five."

"You're on!"

* * *

I won't say who won our little jumping contest since it's really not important in the grand scheme of things.

"I kicked your ass again, Marty! I thought men were physically dominant on your planet."

"We are . . . on Earth. Here, I have to be careful. If I used all my strength, I'd never come down. You'd have to use the cruiser to pick me up somewhere in Saturn's rings."

"Oh, is *that* it?" she teased.

For the first time, I was a bit perturbed by Chrissie. I consider myself a liberated guy, but even the most socially liberal human men have difficulty losing to the opposite sex *and* being razzed about it.

Then Chrissie tilted her head and smiled at me.

And, I might add, that even the most socially liberal human man melts when a beautiful woman—of any species—gives him *that* look.

"Would you like to go inside and play with melted chocolate?" she purred.

I was a puddle.

* * *

Back inside the cruiser, we wiggled out of our spacesuits and made ourselves comfortable in minimal clothing.

"Watch this," Chrissie said. "Bubble mode." She pushed a button, and the cruiser began to hum. Next came vibrations and the *clunk-clunk-clunk* of unlocking clamps. Then, slowly, all the outside opaque surfaces receded to the underside of the cruiser, leaving us in what was essentially a long, clear bubble. "Welcome to space camping—Krichard style!"

"How fun! It's like being inside a reverse snow globe. Too bad we can't have a fire and actually roast the marshmallows for our s'mores. We'll just have to light 'em on fire and blow them out."

"Who says we can't have a fire? You open the red wine, and I'll take care of the rest." She pointed to the dining table near the center of the studio cabin and added, "Just don't stand anywhere near that."

Two button-pushes later, and the floor under the dining table opened up. The table descended into the opening, and a panel from beneath slid over and up to fill the space. Atop that panel was a realistic campfire contained within a ring of artificial rock.

"Does this work like the gas fireplaces on Earth?"

"Very much so, only it's more sophisticated." She flashed an eyelash and added, "Of course, it's not sophisticated enough to understand its purpose is ambience, not heat. I'll turn down the cabin temperature, so we don't break into a sweat. Then we can cuddle by the fire, make some s'mores, and drink copious amounts of wine."

I didn't think anything could beat watching Uranus from the dark side of a moon, but sitting around a campfire with snow gently falling and Saturn dominating the sky just might have been the most exhilarating atmospheric experience someone could have in Earth's solar system. And the company wasn't bad either.

"Oh, damn!" cried Chrissie.

"What's wrong?"

"I got melted marshmallow in my eyelashes."

I looked at her seriously, leaned over, and began licking off specks of the sticky white confection. Soon we were giggling, and my licks became more about making her laugh than removing remnants of marshmallow. The texture of her eyelashes gave my tongue a sensation it had never felt before. They were thicker than human eyelashes but certainly not wiry. Even more unusual than the texture was how they made my tongue tingle, as if an effervescent tablet was dissolving in my mouth.

After our giggles died down, I took a deep breath to compose myself and said in an instructive voice, "The key to making s'mores is to work slowly and use minimal force. Don't worry. The marshmallow will still melt the chocolate. Just remember that they're called s'mores, not smashes. Here. I'll demonstrate." I laid out two graham crackers and a slab of chocolate. Then I put a marshmallow on a long fork and began expertly roasting it over the fire. I turned to Chrissie and—she was naked.

I don't remember what happened to the s'more.

* * *

I woke up several hours later and was surprised not to have a hangover. Chrissie was still sleeping, so I propped up my head and watched her gently breathe—her face bathed in the diffused Saturn glow. Eventually she opened her eyes, and I kissed her on the cheek. "Good morning, gorgeous. How are you feeling?"

"Not bad." She moaned softly. "How long have I been asleep?"

"A little over four hours."

"Is breakfast ready?"

"I would have prepared something, but I'm not very good at reading your language. I was a little worried that instead of hitting the *on* button that I might hit the *eject* button."

"Oh, that would have been a rude way to wake me up." She worked her way to her feet and padded toward the food station. "I'll have something delicious programmed for us in just a minute."

"Hey. Before I forget, did you like red or white wine better?"

"I think red goes best with Saturn and white goes best with Uranus."

"Do you have a bottle of rosé wine in your stash? I hear it goes great with Jupiter."

"As a matter of fact, I do!"

We enjoyed a leisurely breakfast, marveled at Saturn for a while longer, and decided to break camp. Unlike on Earth, where breaking camp can be a chore, here it was easy. Chrissie simply pressed the appropriate buttons, and within minutes, the Chromosphere Cruiser put itself back into flight mode. We moved to the cockpit, strapped ourselves in, and took off for Jupiter.

* * *

Each time we traveled between planets, I had to pinch myself to make sure that I wasn't imagining it. Without exceeding light-speed on this relatively short trip, we still made it from Saturn to Jupiter in less time than it would typically take to drive from Milwaukee to Chicago. Seeing Jupiter up close required another pinch since it's the largest planet in our solar system—equivalent to eleven Earths wide.

Because Jupiter is a gas giant, we couldn't land on it. Nor did we land on any of the planet's more than sixty moons. This time, the awe factor of observing from orbit was more than enough for us.

"It's so beautiful," Chrissie said with a smile. "Look at that eye, or as your people call it, the *Giant Red Spot.*"

"It hardly seems fair that something so gargantuan can be so gorgeous. Okay, in the last two days, we've seen Earth, Mars, Ceres, Uranus, Neptune, Saturn, Jupiter, and who knows how many moons from space. Which is your favorite?"

"As you've surely figured out, my people love colors—the deeper, the brighter, the more outrageous, the better. So Jupiter is my choice. I love all the different bands and the intense hues. How about you?"

I paused for a moment to consider all that we'd seen before saying, "Saturn was my favorite as a kid, and now that I have viewed it up close, my opinion hasn't changed. The rings and the earthy colors are so dramatic. It's too bad we don't have time to see the rest of the planets, so we can rate them all. When this is all over, can we check out Mercury, Venus, and Pluto?"

"Pluto? I didn't think your people considered it a planet."

"It was a planet until 2006 when the International Astronomical Union kicked it out. For many of us, however, Pluto will always be a planet."

"As for your question, we'll have to get Captain Jagger's permission, but I'm sure he'll have no problem with it. After timeline corrections, he traditionally keeps the ship nearby for a few days while he and other crew members confirm success. Unless something unexpected comes up, we could go while they're doing that."

"What are the planets like in your solar system? Are they just as beautiful?"

"Oh, yes!" Her eyelashes glowed steady orange. "We have thirteen. Two naturally support life, one was artificially transformed to support life, three are basically big space rocks, and the rest are gas giants. Our gas giants aren't as big as yours are, but they all have vast ring systems."

"Interesting."

"And Krichardia is the most colorful planet in the entire solar system."

"Now *that* doesn't surprise me at all. I'd love to know more about your home planet."

"Sure. Physically, it's a bit larger than Earth, with fewer oceans but more lakes and rivers. We also have spectacular, tall, red mountains and stunning, thick, blue forests. As for life on Krichardia, we used to have frequent wars, but after we embraced science, they became extremely rare and usually small. We once suffered mass animal extinctions, but again science—with the help of a planet-wide environmental movement—not only stopped the extinctions, but in some cases actually reversed them by using preserved DNA and frozen embryos."

"That's impressive. What else?"

"Let me think. Oh! We have fewer countries than Earth does because we've found that eliminating artificial borders leads to a greater understanding among ethnicities. We've tried just about every kind of government imaginable, and though each country is self-governing, they all strive to utilize the best parts of a wide range of political systems."

Chrissie paused when she noticed me staring out into space. She didn't need to see glowing eyelashes to know that I was wishing my planet had been able to overcome the obstacles hers had.

When I turned my head toward her, she smiled meekly and continued, "That isn't to say everything on Krichardia is better than what you have on Earth. For instance, we still have a few remaining religious sects that not only reject science, but also raise their children in near-colorless environments. It's torture for the young ones, and as a result, they almost always grow up to be maladjusted adults. Also, while I admit that my experience is limited, I think humans are better at lovemak—"

"Chrissie, come in!" Captain Jagger barked over the cockpit communication system.

"Yes, Captain."

"I need you to cut your planetary tour short and return to the ship immediately. We think President Handley is preparing to launch a nuclear missile at us!"

CHAPTER 4

At Least Tell Me You're Naked

In less than an hour, we reached the ship, parked in the cruiser bay, made ourselves presentable, and walked into the conference room. Tina, Bruce, Clarence, and Captain Jagger were already sitting at the long, oval table.

"There's been a change of plans," the captain announced. "We're here to help, not to die or make things worse. As we do on every mission, we continually monitor government communications on any planet we help. Normally we have no issues, but President Handley is no ordinary man. He's erratic and seems willing to do anything to boost his fragile ego—including hurting his own people." He paused for a second, before pointing to Clarence. "Tell everyone what you told me."

"Yes, Captain. I have been researching Earth's history. In 1962, the United States conducted a test called Starfish Prime, which detonated a 1.4 megaton nuclear bomb 250 miles above the Pacific Ocean. The electromagnetic pulse from that bomb was much larger than scientists had predicted. It ended up blowing out streetlights and damaging phone systems in Hawaii, 900 miles away."

Clarence nodded, and the captain continued in a grim voice, "We have to assume that Handley has been advised of what happened with that relatively small nuclear explosion. Consequently, we've moved our ship into orbit directly over

Washington, DC. If a nuclear missile explodes anywhere near us, it will paralyze the entire Northeast. We don't think he'd be insane enough to attack us now, but we don't want to risk more human lives than necessary. Therefore, we've transported all the humans on the ship, except Mr. Mann, to Australia for their safety."

The captain pointed to Tina, and she turned to me. "Marty, this next part concerns you. As you know, this ship is an older model. The time-travel attachment is just as old. Generally, neither the ship nor the attachment gives us any problems. However, since your dinosaur adventure, I've had reservations about sending you directly to AD 31 without first conducting a shorter test to confirm that everything is calibrated properly."

"What we'd like to do," the captain added, "is send you thirty days into the future. It's low risk, and with just a few exceptions, you can go anywhere you want in the United States. We prefer that you choose a place you've been before, so you'll know your way around. Once you arrive, we'd like you to get online somewhere and look for news reports about a nuclear attack on our ship. Even though we have the technology to search into the future from here, I'd feel better with information gathered on the ground, in real time. If we have accurate, advance notice that we need to take evasive action, we can save countless lives. After you've completed your task, you can enjoy the rest of your stay until we pick you up again."

"Can you send me home to Montana?"

"I'd rather not. If the government is looking for you, your dyed skin, beard, and hair will make you too easy to spot there. Can you pick somewhere that's not so . . . white? I'd hate for you to be captured and tortured."

"Yeah, the torture thing doesn't appeal to me either. How about Everglades City? The town's residents are predominantly white, but dark-skinned people are much more common in Florida. I've been to the town several times and can easily acquire internet access, lodging, and anything else I need there."

"Everglades City is fine. Tina, Chrissie, can you have Marty ready to go in two hours?"

"That shouldn't be a problem," Tina said.

Chrissie looked across the table at Bruce and asked, "Can you remove Marty's euphoria dispenser restriction? I want to give him access to whatever he needs to avoid another panic attack in the hose."

"You've got it."

The captain stood and swept a hand toward the door. "Okay, everyone. Let's get to work."

* * *

One hour later, Tina called me into her office, next to the hose room. Getting ready for a simple jump thirty days into the future was much easier than preparing for a jump to the first century, and being able to wear my own clothes felt like such a luxury. Even though arriving at my destination with luggage wouldn't look out of place in modern-day Florida, Tina still wouldn't let me carry much more than I did on the previous jump. Apparently, the attachment could only compensate for a small quantity of non-living substances. But hey, at least I wouldn't have to be like the Terminator and arrive naked.

Tina did permit me to carry two very important additional items: a counterfeit driver's license and a debit card. Since I obviously couldn't use my real name, she asked me to come up with a fake one. I, of course, suggested Marty McFly, but getting anything past a Krichard is next to impossible.

"Pick a name that doesn't belong to anyone famous—real or otherwise," she said.

"How about Martin Tall"?

"No."

"Martin Steve?"

"No! Clever variants of famous names won't fool anyone."

"Marty Montana?"

"No."

"C'mon! I've never heard of anyone famous named Marty Montana. Plus, you've gotta admit, it rolls nicely off the tongue."

She wagged a finger at me. "No."

I took a deep breath. *"Fine.* I'll be Marty Smith. There have to be hundreds of Marty Smiths in the United States."

"That works. Give me forty-five minutes to get your license and debit card fabricated and to open up a prepaid account for you. Then we'll be ready to go. Oh. How much money should I put into your account?"

"Where's the money coming from?"

"I'm pulling it directly out of one of President Handley's many bank accounts. He'll never know what happened."

"In that case, take a million dollars. I won't need a fraction of that, but maybe I can find some worthy cause to donate the leftover money to before you pick me up."

"You do realize that when you finally change the timeline, Handley's money won't ever have existed, don't you?"

I shook my head. "That's too confusing to think about. All I know is that the president would be horrified if he knew his money was going to an organization, such as Planned Parenthood or the ACLU. However fleeting that donation may be, I'll get much satisfaction out of making it."

"Okay. I'll do it."

With nothing left for me to do before the time jump, I toddled down the hall to the euphoria dispenser and looked at the screen. Needing to be relaxed, not high, I selected "Beach Massage in the Bahamas." I inhaled my dose and toddled back toward the hose room. I was halfway there when I turned around, retraced my tracks to the dispenser, and added, "In-head music: Sade. Drink: Tequila Sunrise." Now I was ready.

There was still plenty of time left before the jump, so instead of going directly to the hose room, I walked to the observation lounge, plopped down on one of the couches, closed my eyes, and let the euphoria take over: *Ahhhh . . . the strong hands of a beautiful masseuse. Mmmm . . . the smell of warm cocoa butter and cold tequila. Just a little to the left. That's perfect. Oh, it's 'Never as Good as the First Time,' and this most definitely is a first. Yeahhhh. . . . Right there. I don't suppose a happy en—*

"Yow!" I cried as Tina jolted me back to reality with a vigorous shake. "That was mean."

"We were looking all over for you. You need to get to the hose room. Now!"

"But . . ." I glanced at the clock beside the couch and discovered an hour had whooshed by. "Sorry! I must've fallen asleep. I'm on my way."

* * *

Five minutes later, Tina and Chrissie had everything ready for the jump.

"Here are your food and water packs, driver's license, and debit card," Tina said. "I attached a sticker to the back of the card with your PIN, so you can make cash withdrawals. Don't leave it there. Memorize the number and destroy the sticker."

Two minutes after that, Tina sealed me into the airlock. Right away, I could feel myself getting panicky in the close quarters. I closed my eyes and summoned my beach massage euphoria. Sade began singing "Paradise," and my muscles relaxed.

Whoosh!

Everything went white.

Splash!

Everything went wet.

I choked as salty water poured into my mouth. I've never been a good swimmer for this precise reason: I sink. Between coughs and wild splashing, I finally squeaked out, "Help! I'm drowning!"

"Stand up!" Tina yelled.

"I can't"—*Cough! Cough! Blaaa!*—"breathe!"

"Stand up!"

I stood up.

"Oh! That was"—*cough!*—"embarrassing. The water is only waist deep." I wiped my eyes and looked around before continuing. "You definitely got me to Everglades City. I recognize some of the buildings. But the town is flooded, and it looks abandoned. Did a hurricane come through recently?"

"No," Tina said.

"Then why is—"

"Welcome to the year 2056!"

"What? Don't you have to do a verification scan first? How do you—"

"Because I sent you there."

"You bitch!" Chrissie screamed.

"Maybe next time we have an unclaimed male, you'll follow the rules."

"Oh? You're going to pull *rules* on me? You just wanted a plaything."

"And you wanted something more? Do you really think the captain would have let you keep him?"

"Ladies, I can hear you."

"Shut up!" they screamed in unison.

"Bring him back!" Chrissie demanded.

"Sorry," Tina said matter-of-factly. "I wiped the time and location sensors. Without my help, it'll take weeks to find him. By then, we'll be long gone."

Crash!

"I thought your rules stated that fights over an unclaimed male had to take place in the nude with the said unclaimed male—that would be me—watching."

"Shut up!" they screamed again.

Crash!

I didn't know whether to be terrified or aroused. Well, I am a glass half-full kind of guy. "At least tell me you're naked."

"Will that shut you up?" Tina spat. "Then yes! We're stark-naked and sweaty, and I have Chrissie's face in a scissor hold!"

Crash!

"Thank you," I whispered.

I listened as the fight continued, but on my end, all I could hear was an unnerving chorus of grunts, crashes, and what sounded like some very creative swearing. Unfortunately, the communicator in my head didn't translate Krichard swearing into English. It also struck me as kind of odd that I wasn't more upset than I was, standing in waist-deep water, in 2056, with alligators all around. Perhaps the high from the euphoria dispenser hadn't quite dissipated. Wait . . . *alligators?*

"Alligators! Chrissie! Tina! . . . Alligators!

"You'll be fine," Tina said, breathing heavily. "You stupid humans ignored global warming, and the rising oceans turned the Everglades into a salty marsh of death. Alligators are most likely extinct. You probably don't need to worry about saltwater crocodiles or sharks anymore either. Starfish might still exist in the wild, however. If you stand there long enough, they may start to nibble on you. Just—"

Crash!

"What's going on in here!" Clarence boomed.

"Tina sent Marty to Everglades City—in 2056! Then she wiped the time and location sensors."

"Damn you, Tina! I never should have . . . Wait. Can Marty hear this?"

"Hi, Clarence."

"Turn off the communicator. *Now!*"

Chrissie shouted, "Marty, I won't leave y—"

Silence.

I screamed back, "Chrissie!" but I knew it was hopeless.

Were my prospects in Everglades City doomed as well? As I glanced around, I never would have guessed the year. I had last been in the town in 2018, and other than some obvious growth, aged buildings, and roughly three feet of water, not much had changed. Why hadn't technology overcome global warming? Where were the ultramodern buildings and the flying cars?

I was thankful that Tina had at least sent me to a familiar area.

Otherwise, I wouldn't have known which direction to walk in. I slogged north on Copeland Avenue, cut east on Datura Street, then headed north again on Collier Avenue. Picking the streets was tricky since some were in deeper water than others. Collier Avenue was the farthest inland, and the water was only knee deep there. That was fortunate since following it was the only way to leave.

Walking through an abandoned town where I'd previously vacationed was an eerie experience. I had visited ghost towns before, but they were never this real. It's one thing for people to choose to move on because a gold rush ends, and it's quite another for people to have to move on because Planet Earth couldn't take it anymore. And where were the birds? I should have been listening to a symphony of squawks, quacks, trills, tweets, and chirps. Instead, the only sound I heard was the lonely sloshing of my cautious footsteps.

One sliver of good news was that I could see the waterline on some of the dilapidated buildings. I had arrived at high tide, or shortly thereafter, and already the water had dropped at least an inch. I continued to the edge of town where Collier Avenue became County Road 29. As I looked out over a sheet of water, I knew that was where my real problems would begin. The road dipped until it disappeared from sight, and if I remembered correctly, it wouldn't rise again until it crossed the Tamiami Trail, some five miles to the north.

If given the opportunity to mentally prepare myself, as opposed to being dropped from the sky and starting in a panic, I was probably capable of swimming several hundred feet. Swimming five miles was well beyond my ability, however. I turned and headed back into town. It was time to do some breaking and entering.

Breaking into any building, whether it was a house, hotel, or shop, was easy. In fact, some of the doors were already wide open. Buildings that weren't open had broken windows to climb through or rotten doors that required only a simple kick to break them down. Finding materials to make a raft to float me to safety was another matter. In one house, I stumbled upon some wire. In another, I found a rusty hammer and some nails. In an old gas station, I located some plastic oil drums. Finally, from the deck of a condominium I'd rented during a previous visit, I acquired some sturdy boards.

Once I had all the materials together, I assembled a raft. It wasn't pretty, but it would work. Unfortunately, by the time I was ready to go, the sun was too low in the sky to risk a trip. I decided to wait until morning. Besides, with any luck, Chrissie's sweet voice would enter my head before I embarked, and I could return to the Krichard ship instead of paddling to what I hoped would be dry land.

My old condominium seemed as good a place as any to spend the night. The final owners had stripped the place clean, but at least the stilted building was above the high water level, and the old carpeting had not been removed. I made myself at home and enjoyed some of the food I had with me. In retrospect, the fact that Tina had given me food and water packs for a trip that shouldn't have needed one should have tipped me off that she was up to something. Nevertheless, given my present situation, I was glad to have them.

* * *

"Chrissie, are you there?" I asked as soon as I opened my eyes. I didn't expect a response but needed to try anyway. Other than an aching shoulder from sleeping on the hard floor, I had made it through the night without any drama. In fact, I was surprised that it took the sun peeking over the trees to wake me.

Now that I was up, it was time to push off or, in my case, pull on. The tide was now much lower than it was the previous day, and only a half foot of water covered Collier Avenue. I found a short length of rope, attached it to the front of the raft, and started pulling.

For a while, I thought I'd be able to walk right out without even having to use the raft. At the edge of town, deeper waters dashed those fragile hopes. I climbed onto the raft and used a two-by-four as a pole to push my way along. The going was tedious but not dangerous. My biggest concern was that my drinking water was already half-gone, and the hot sun was making me sweat profusely.

As I moved closer to higher ground, negativity dominated my thoughts. At that moment, I felt lonelier than when I was the only person on Earth in the Cretaceous period. Finding people would most likely reverse my loneliness. But would I be able to relate to them? Would I be some primitive novelty? And would society have changed in a positive or negative direction? The fact that I was on a raft, where I was once in a car, gave me little reason for optimism.

I finally reached dry land, a little past what used to be the intersection of County Road 29 and the Tamiami Trail. Remnants of the old Chamber of Commerce building, which sat near that intersection, confirmed my location. Once County Road 29 rose out of the water, it was unmaintained but easily walkable. My plan was to continue north until I found someone who would give me a ride to civilization.

The road looked pretty much like I remembered it, with forests of slash pine and cypress trees on both sides and a wide strip of swampy water on the east side. The main difference was that many of the trees were dying or dead, and their condition progressively worsened as the swamps narrowed and disappeared.

I walked fast, stopping only occasionally to wipe my brow or wring out my soggy shirt. Since the south end of the road dead-ended in water, I wasn't initially surprised that I didn't bump into anyone. As I put on the miles, though, the lack of people began to freak me out.

Eventually, in the distance, I saw a vehicle on the shoulder. It was most definitely not a flying car. I jogged ahead, not quite believing my eyes as they took in a mid-1950s Ford truck. What was a one-hundred-year-old truck doing on the side of the road? Had Tina sent me to 1956 instead of 2056? No, that wouldn't have been possible since Everglades City wasn't an underwater ghost town at that time.

When I reached the truck, I looked around and didn't see anyone. The driver's side window was open, so I peeked inside. No 1950s truck I'd ever seen had an interior like that! Everything had been modernized, but only so far. While the exterior was 1950s, the interior was 1980s—complete with red velour bench seats and what appeared to be factory-installed seat belts and a cassette player. Personal touches included a cross hanging from the rearview mirror and miniature photos of Presidents Handley and Reagan stuck to the dashboard.

I was still peering in the window when a man yelled from the edge of the trees, "Whatcha lookin' for, son?"

"Oh! Hi. I'm so glad to see you!" I shouted back. "My car broke down near the end of the road. Would you be so kind as to give me a ride to a service station? I'll buy you a ta—a couple of new cassettes for your trouble." I almost said *tank of gas,* but who knows what kind of fuel trucks used now. I also crossed my fingers that the debit card Tina gave me would work in whatever strange year this was.

The man, who had graying brown hair and appeared to be in his mid-sixties, walked toward me, carrying a dead bird in one hand and a shotgun in the other. He stopped six feet away and looked me up and down. "What's someone like you doing here in 'Merica?"

"What do you mean?"

"You look like one of them Muslims."

"So?"

"Muslims ain't allowed in 'Merica."

Oh, shit. I had to come up with something plausible. I blurted out the first thing that came to mind and hoped it made sense: "Me? I'm not a Muslim. I'm with the Army, just back from overseas. I was working undercover to intercept an important document from a terrorist organization. I had to dye my hair, beard, and skin for the mission. I usually revert to my natural appearance when I return to the United States, but sometimes the hair dye chemicals give me migraines. I decided to hold off for a few days in case the situation escalates and the Army sends me back. I drove here because it's one of the few places away from the military base where I can get outside and not be seen. My ancestors are originally from Scandinavia."

"You're a lyin' Muslim too!"

"Well, it was nice talking to you. I'll be going now." I turned and started up the road, hoping I wouldn't hear the cock of a gun.

"Hey, mister!"

I turned and looked back.

The man stuffed a pinch of tobacco in his cheek without taking his eyes off me. "I didn't say I wouldn't give ya a ride. I just don't want no cassettes. You can come with me for free, but if ya don't want me to turn you in to the authorities, it's gonna cost you five gallons of gas."

"You still use g—" I stopped myself just in time. "I mean great. You have a deal."

"Hop in then." He flicked his hand, motioning me toward the passenger side. "I can take ya as far as Immokalee. There's a service station there where you can gas up my truck and send a tow truck to fetch your car."

"Thank you." I slid onto the bench seat and buckled my seatbelt.

The man did the same. Then, after a pause, he wiped his dirty right hand on his pants and offered it to me. "Ray Dixon."

"Marty Mann." I wanted to pull my name back as soon as I said it. I was supposed to be Marty Smith, and already I was screwing up. Since Tina knew she was sending me to 2056, she must have had a good reason for insisting I use a false name. Was I just a blip in history, who was a mildly successful travel writer? Was I a traitor to Planet Earth, who conspired with the Krichards? Or was I something in between? I needed to get to a computer or a library as soon as possible to catch up on the past thirty-six years.

Fortunately, Ray didn't appear to recognize my name. Instead, he steered the truck onto the road, pulled a cassette off the seat, and asked, "Do you like Billy Bob Jennings?"

"Oh, I love him! Is that his latest album?"

"It sure is!" He pushed in the cassette, and soon Ray was singing along with Billy Bob, only slightly off key.

I had no idea who Billy Bob Jennings was, but country music was still country music. I listened for a short time—to get the gist of the song—and then joined in, slightly off key as well.

After a few songs, Ray turned to me and said, "I ain't never known no Muslim to sing country like that. Are you really *Scandanuvian?*"

"Yes, and I can prove it." I yanked out a strand of hair. "See? Look at this root. It's blond where it's grown since it was dyed."

Ray took the hair and examined it.

"Watch out!" I yelled as the truck drifted toward the shoulder.

Ray swerved the vehicle to the left, then, still holding the hair in front of his eyes said, "What d' ya know? It looks like I was wrong about you."

"I like your pictures of President Reagan and President Handley."

"Yup, the two greatest men in American history!" He paused for a moment before tilting his head to look at me. "Wait. Don't ya mean Supreme Leader Handley? Nobody's called him President Handley since he chased them aliens back to where they came from."

I mentally kicked myself again. "Of course. Sometimes I just get sentimental for the old title of President."

"That's understandable. Handley was also 'Merica's last president. But praise Jesus! Because of our late, great supreme leader, we no longer have to worry 'bout the four evils of the Liberal Apocalypse: elections, Muslims, feminists, and environmentalists."

"Yes, praise Jesus!" I said, cringing internally. I wasn't quite sure how far to play along. Sooner or later, I'd say something that would give me away. I decided to risk a question. "Being that the sea levels have risen so much, don't you think we should have listened to the environmentalists?"

"Are you crazy? Them's the reason for all this floodin' in the first place! If corporations hadn't been handcuffed by all those environmental regulations, we woulda had enough of those insulatin' gases in the sky to block the sun's rays and keep us cool."

"I'm so glad to have met you, Ray. Your reasoning is so . . . *logical.*" Was I piling it on too thick?

Ray smiled. "I've got a daughter about your age. She's a bit rebellious and in need of a good military man like you. Ya married, son?"

"No."

"Attached to anyone?"

"Hmm. That's a tough question."

"I tell ya what. How 'bout after we stop at the service station, you come over to my house for supper? My daughter lives next door. I'll have her join us."

My first instinct was to get as far away from Ray as possible. Then, just as quickly, I changed my mind and said, "Well that's mighty nice of you. I'd love to have a meal with you and your daughter. However, if you're going to feed me, I insist on filling your tank all the way to the top." I had no idea how long I would be stuck in 2056. The sooner I made some friends, the easier it would be to adjust if Chrissie and the others never returned.

"That won't be cheap."

"That's okay. You've really bailed me out."

Several more off-key country sing-alongs later, we reached Immokalee. I fingered my debit card as we pulled up to the service station. Ray turned off his truck, and I inserted the card into the pump. *Please, Tina. Let the debit card work. It was Chrissie you were mad at, not me.*

When the pump started, I repressed an audible whoop. It worked! I was a millionaire. When the pump stopped, it deducted

$272.32 from my card. Obviously, a million dollars wouldn't last as long as it used to.

As I climbed back into the truck, Ray shot me an inquisitive look. "Well? Aren't you gonna make arrangements for your car?"

"Oh, yeah. . . . Wait here. I'll be right back." I walked into the service station, grabbed some random items off the shelves, and stepped up to the counter. "Hi! How are you?"

A gaunt man with dirty fingernails looked at me from across the counter. "We don't serve Muslims," he said.

"Really? I just bought almost three hundred dollars of gas from you."

"Only 'cause I didn't see you first."

"How do you know I'm a Muslim? Lots of people have dark skin and hair."

"Not around here, they don't."

"Maybe I'm Hispanic."

"You could be. But if I'm wrong and I get caught, it's a twelve-hundred-dollar fine. You won't find many businesses around here that will take that chance."

I noticed Ray watching me from his truck, so I pointed as if giving instructions. Then with a big smile, I said, "Well, I'm sure I don't have to tell you what rejection feels like. You know what they say, small mind, small penis." I turned on my heels and walked back to the truck.

"All set?" Ray asked.

"Yes. They're going to send a tow truck. Depending on what they find, my car will be ready either tomorrow or the next day. I need to check in to a hotel and clean up before supper. Can you recommend a place for me?"

"One of my cousins runs a little motel in the old section of town. If we go in the back way and I introduce you, he won't care that ya look like a Muslim."

"Perfect! And if we can swing by a drugstore, I won't look like a Muslim for long."

"There's one on the way. Want me to go inside for ya?"

"That would be great. I just need some blond hair dye, shaving cream, a razor, and a couple bottles of natural beige foundation makeup. Also, if they have flowers, I'd like to buy some for your daughter."

"Will do," Ray said with a grin. "She loves flowers . . . and blonds."

As we pulled up to the store, I had a moment of panic. Even though Ray looked trustworthy, I couldn't just hand him my million-dollar debit card. While I doubted he'd steal it from me, if he remembered my last name, he might notice it didn't match the name on the card and turn me in to the authorities. "Hey, Ray. Is there a bank nearby where I can make a cash withdrawal?"

"Son, there ain't been a real bank in this town for fifteen years." He pointed out his open window. "If ya need cash, that machine across the street is your best bet."

I scanned the area to make sure no pedestrians were milling about. "Okay. I'll be right back." I jogged up to the ATM and inserted my card. When prompted, I entered my PIN and the dollar amount and hoped for the best. Soon I had one thousand dollars in crisp twenties and hundreds. As I counted the bills, I noticed they had been redesigned: President Reagan now graced the front of the twenties, and Supreme Leader Handley graced the front of the hundreds. On the reverse side, all the bills featured a portrait of a Caucasian Christ with the motto, "Jesus: Official God of the United States of America."

I rolled my eyes and jogged back to join Ray in the truck. Now I had a new problem. Had the prices for hair dye, makeup, and flowers skyrocketed at the same rate as gas prices? To be on the safe side, I handed him three hundred dollars and prayed it was a realistic amount.

Ray looked at the bills and whistled. "Ya must like expensive products."

"Sorry. Except for shaving supplies, the military covers everything for me. I'm kind of clueless as to what cosmetics cost, and I want to make sure there's enough money left over for a nice bouquet. I trust you to bring me back the change."

"Of course! Stealin' from a military man would be like . . . well, almost as bad as stealin' from Jesus!" He saluted me and stepped out of the truck.

I slouched in my seat and pulled out my water pack. So much had happened since I met Ray that I hadn't realized until that moment just how thirsty I was. I sucked down every last drop.

A few minutes later, Ray returned with my supplies and a vase containing a variety of red and white flowers. He also handed me a wad of assorted bills.

"Thank you so much. While you were in there, I was thinking. I want to look and feel my best when I meet your daughter." What I really meant was that I'd like to log on to the internet and get up to speed on the world I was now living in. "Since my car won't be ready for at least a day, and hair dye often gives me a migraine, can we move supper to tomorrow night instead? I'm sure your daughter will appreciate a little advance notice as well."

"That'd be just fine. I'll introduce ya to my cousin and draw ya a map to my house. It's only a ten-minute walk from where you'll be staying. You can come over 'round five."

Minutes later, we were at the motel. Ray's cousin, Duke, seemed like a nice enough guy. I kept the chitchat to a minimum, though, because every time I opened my mouth, the chances increased that I would say something to blow my cover. As soon as I could politely do so, I bid the two men farewell, stepped into my room, and collapsed on the bed.

CHAPTER 5

God Bless Our Supreme Leader

I allowed myself a short nap before I shaved, took a shower, and got to work on my hair and skin. Even though I had zero experience at dyeing hair, the instructions seemed straightforward enough. Or so I thought. Ultimately, my hair turned out blond with streaks of blue. I would have fit in perfectly at a 1980s punk club. Here, I wasn't so sure. Next, I applied way too much makeup to my face, neck, arms, and hands. Obviously, getting my makeup to look natural was going to take some practice. My slightly blue, somewhat crusty appearance made me feel self-conscious, but all that really mattered was that I looked a hell of a lot less Muslim than I did when I started.

It was time to go shopping.

While in the truck with Ray, I had kept my eyes peeled for a shopping center. If I remembered correctly, a promising collection of stores was located about four blocks to the south. Items I hoped to acquire included clothes—especially long-sleeved, high-collared shirts—basic toiletries, more hair dye and makeup, and whatever the current equivalent was to a laptop computer. Then, in the morning, I'd see what kind of automobile I could buy with a debit card.

I walked down the street, and sure enough, the shopping center was where I remembered it. There I was able to find almost everything on my list. Still, these were most definitely strange times. I naturally expected giant leaps in technology, fashions, and designs. Instead, just like Ray's truck, most products seemed to emulate the 1950s and the 1980s—at least in appearance. Thank God, they left the 1970s alone. Elephant bell pants and leisure suits should never come back.

Laptops were, perhaps, the most interesting. While they obviously couldn't emulate the 1950s, and the 1980s designs were just too primitive, they didn't appear to have advanced at all since 2020. In fact, they seemed to have regressed a bit because they were a little thicker and quite a bit heavier. The one I purchased came with the Leviticus 20:13 operating system, but it had the look and feel of Windows 98. I wondered if the geeks had replicated the older software's fondness for locking up and going to the blue screen of death.

About the only things that weren't retro were the price tags. My laptop, for instance, cost me a little over four thousand dollars.

I headed back to the motel with all my worldly possessions in a large shopping cart. I may have looked like a street person at that moment, but thanks to Tina, at least I wasn't destitute.

* * *

As soon as I reached my motel room, I booted up my computer, installed some software, and logged on to the internet via the motel's network. The internet worked basically as it had during my original time, except porn sites no longer existed—hey, I had to check—and most liberal web pages were either blocked or out of business. For instance, I couldn't set up *HuffPost* as my home page. Instead, the native internet browser required me to choose from a list of government-approved Christian home pages.

Once I figured out how to navigate past all the religious propaganda, I found some old news articles and pieced together why the United States had leapt backward instead of forward. As expected, the Krichards unwittingly played a part in that regression. When President Handley began dropping nuclear bombs to "protect American interests," his popularity plummeted. That all changed when the Krichard ship parked in orbit over Washington, DC. With great drama and showmanship, he addressed the nation while standing in front of a gigantic missile and holding what appeared to be a red game show buzzer. "Aliens want to destroy the world," he shouted, "but I will destroy them first!"

Before he could formally order the launch of multiple nuclear weapons—damn the consequences—the Krichards slowly backed away. Given the chance to avoid paralyzing the Northeast, the president then amended his order and launched unarmed missiles, just for show. The ship disappeared shortly thereafter, never to be seen again.

Although I suspected the Krichards departed mostly because of what Tina did, Handley manipulated the event to turn himself into a godlike hero. He became so popular that all the states, except California, Washington, Minnesota, and New York, ratified an amendment to the U.S. Constitution to anoint him as Supreme Leader for Life. While they were at it, they eliminated separation of church and state and proclaimed Jesus the Official God of the United States of America.

Armed with virtually unlimited powers and a compliant Supreme Court, Handley subsequently kicked out the four dissenting states. California then became an independent country, while the other three joined Canada where residents affectionately began calling them the Canadian Claw Provinces.

Even though Handley died long ago, conservative politicians and religious leaders kept his reign alive via two successive supreme leaders—both claiming to have been chosen by God. To this day, the United States remains the most powerful theocracy the world has ever known.

Here, if you are a heterosexual white male, life is full of privileges. If you are an unmarried white woman, your father determines your rights. If you are a married white woman, your husband determines your rights. If you are a nonwhite minority (not that there are many nonwhites left in the country), you have the same rights as a horse. If you are gay, lesbian, or bisexual, you will be imprisoned one year for a first offense and ten years for a second offense. And, of course, since Jesus is the Official God of the United States of America, if you are caught practicing any religion other than Christianity, you will be immediately deported.

I now understood why Ray was so confident his daughter would join us for dinner. She didn't have a choice.

I also better appreciated Tina's wisdom in insisting on changing my name before sending me back to Earth. One of the news stories I found reported that several people had witnessed me approaching the Krichard hose and being sucked up by it. When that happened, Handley declared me an enemy of America and ordered me shot on sight. While the chances were slim that anyone would believe I had managed to avoid aging over the years, the name change would help keep me out of trouble if anyone got too curious.

Finally, my crash course in American history confirmed why retro 1950s and 1980s products were so common. During my time, conservatives often pined for the 1950s—or at least their idyllic version of it—because in those days white men were in charge, women were submissive, and gays and lesbians were in the closet. Those same conservatives also loved the 1980s because it was the decade of Ronald Reagan, whose presidency they puffed up and sanitized to the point where he became a demigod. Now, in a country ruled by religion and conservatism, it was only natural that the past be an important part of their culture. After all, what is conservatism if not a political philosophy designed to slow or reverse progress?

Whew! With everything that had happened since I splashed back onto Earth, I had absorbed as much as I could. Tonight I would try to get a good night's sleep. Tomorrow I would buy an automobile, have dinner with Ray and his daughter, and attempt to come up with a plan for the rest of my life—or however long I was stuck in this reality. Would a road trip to either the country of California or the province of Minnesota be on my agenda? Such a drive was beginning to look like my best option.

* * *

In the morning, I set out in search of a car and found the first thing I admired about 2056: a replica 1959 Ford Thunderbird convertible in Brandywine Red. Other than the addition of a cassette deck, it was just like the original, complete with a 430 cubic-inch, 350-horsepower, V8 engine. Obviously, Americans had abandoned all pretense of conservation or innovation when it came to automobiles. Perhaps their reasoning was that if they were going to drive countless species to extinction and run the planet into the ground, they might as well do it in style. Or perhaps, using Ray's twisted reasoning, they actually thought putting more carbon dioxide in the air would slow global warming.

From my point of view, I felt little guilt in plopping down nearly eighty thousand dollars for the slightly used T-bird. Global warming was beyond the point of reversal, and I hadn't yet given up hope that someday the Krichard ship would return, allowing me the opportunity to complete my original mission, thereby preventing this warped reality from ever occurring.

Once I completed the transaction for my car—not an easy thing to do with just a debit card—I returned to the hotel and dyed my hair again. This time, I was more successful and eliminated the blue.

According to the clock in my motel room, I still had two hours before dinner. I used that time to take the T-bird out for a spin and to pick up some items I had forgotten to get earlier: a case full of prerecorded cassettes (apparently CDs no longer existed since music was available only on cassette), a prepaid cell phone (apparently smartphones no longer existed since I could buy only an old-fashioned flip phone), and a watch (available only in analog style). I carried my retro necessities to the car, feeling shopped-out but physically prepared for life in 2056.

Physical needs aside, I still had much to learn. That, however, would come mostly from interacting with people and seeing more of the country. I hoped tonight's dinner would be a positive start to that learning process.

* * *

With the bouquet in one hand, I knocked on the door of a midsized rambler with the other. Ray answered and looked at me with wide eyes. "Is that really you, Marty? You look so different!"

"It's Marty Smith, in the flesh."

"Smith? I thought you said your last name was Manfred, Mann, or something like that."

"I may have used one of my undercover names, Manning, yesterday, but now that we're friends, my real name seems appropriate."

As we shook hands, he said, "Come on in and meet my wife and daughter." I walked into a house that could have been a set for a 1950s television show, with club chairs, a boxy couch, and a dark wood dining room table. I could see into several rooms from where I was standing, and depending on the room, the color scheme consisted of mostly solid greens, oranges, or reds.

Sitting on the living room couch were two women dressed in long, shapeless housedresses. The younger one had bright red hair in a pixie cut, and the older one had ash brown hair styled in a conservative bouffant. Neither wore noticeable makeup.

"Hello. I'm Marty Smith," I said, holding out my right hand as I approached them.

We exchanged handshakes, with the older woman identifying herself as Lucinda, and the younger woman identifying herself as Nellie. I handed the flowers to Nellie. She accepted them with a warm smile and set them on the table next to the couch.

Small talk has never been my forte, but I did my best to avoid being awkward as we engaged in the traditional getting-to-know-you activity. And, thankfully, we never reached that moment when, after an uncomfortable pause, someone brings up the weather. Does talking about the weather ever improve a conversation?

After a bit, Lucinda excused herself to check on the food in the oven. Moments later she called out, "Supper is ready!"

Ray directed us all to the preset dining room table and indicated that I should sit across from his daughter. Despite her frumpy dress and apparent intention to appear plain, Nellie's bright green eyes and pale freckles betrayed that look and gave her a striking appearance. Why would someone with such natural beauty still be single in a society that put such value on marriage? I added that to my list of things I hoped to learn.

Once we were all seated, I raised my glass of sweet tea and said, "To new friends!" After we clinked glasses, I scanned the various dishes and picked up the closest one—a large bowl of mashed potatoes.

Ray cleared his throat.

I set the bowl back down.

"Marty, would ya like to offer the blessing?"

"Um . . . sure."

Nellie made eye contact with me and subtly smirked.

I hadn't said grace since I was a kid, and I somehow didn't think reciting, "God is great, God is good, and we thank him for our food. Amen" was going to cut it. A panicky feeling came over me as I tried to come up with something. Eventually, I began, "Heavenly father . . . thank you for this wonderful meal we are about to eat. I'm sure it will taste, um heavenly. And thank you for Ray, who gave me a ride when I needed one and found me a place to stay at his cousin's motel. Bless this house and family. And finally, bless our supreme leader, who, um . . . I-am-sure-is-as-great-and-good-as-he-says-he-is. Amen."

Nellie snatched a napkin to cover her mouth, her eyes widening.

"Well," said Ray, "that was different, but good. Shall we eat?"

We passed the food around, and I took a little of everything, including ham, which I wouldn't normally eat. Might avoiding certain foods—whether for health or for ethics—be considered abnormal, or worse, liberal? This was a time to blend in, not stand out.

Ray swallowed a bite of peas and looked over at me. "Are ya enjoyin' this wave of cool weather?"

Cool? It seemed rather hot to me. "Yes, this has been a nice break."

Ray continued. "When I was a kid, hot weather was seldom a problem, and Florida was a great place to live. Now it ain't easy livin' here. Damn those environmentalists! On the bright side, though, with so many folks movin' north, it's not as crowded as it used to be."

"How long have you lived in this house?"

"All my life. My father lived here too until he died. Before it started gettin' hotter, it was difficult to buy real estate in Immokalee. That's why years ago, when my neighbor passed away, I snapped up his house for Nellie. When I finally find the right man for her," he looked me straight in the eyes, "the two of them will have a nice place to start a family."

Nellie recoiled. "Daddy, stop it! I'm not interested in getting married now."

Ray clanged his fork on his plate. "Yer thirty-four years old. Are ya lookin' to become an old maid?"

"Thirty-four is not old!" She took a deep breath and let it out in a hiss. "You can't run my life."

"That's not what the law says."

"Screw the law!"

"Mmm mmm," I said, attempting to change the subject. "These sweet potatoes are delicious. Is this a special family recipe, Lucinda?"

"Yes. It was passed down from my great-grandmother."

"Well, you're a fantastic cook."

"Nellie is a great cook too," Ray added, still chewing his food. He swallowed and glanced sideways at his daughter. "Wouldn'tcha love to cook for a military hero?"

"Daddy!"

"You're moving a little fast here, Ray. Besides, I'm not a hero. In fact, I've decided to leave the Army."

"Why on Earth would you do that?" he asked. "There's not a more honorable profession."

"Actually, there are many. Imagine if everyone just laid down their arms and walked away. Without soldiers or people to operate all the killing machines, there could be no wars. Governments around the world do everything they can to convince their people that military service ensures peace, but it's really the opposite. What good are expensive weapons, ships, airplanes, and tanks if they're never used? Government leaders and military contractors need wars and continual fear of bad guys to keep the money flowing. The rest of us would be much better off without any of that. I never should have joined the Army in the first place, but like so many others, I got caught up in the hype."

Ray gasped.

"I guess I'm not such a hot prospect for your daughter after all."

"Ya got that right. I can live with ya not bein' in the military, but disrespectin' the men who fought to keep our nation safe and pure is another matter. Other than the church, the armed forces are our most sacred institutions. I didn't report you to the authorities as a Muslim, but now I'm half-tempted to call ya in as a liberal traitor."

"That won't be necessary. I got my car back this afternoon, and I've always wanted to see the country of California. I'm leaving for there in the morning and won't return." I pushed away from the table. "Lucinda, thank you so much for the delicious home-cooked meal. Nellie, you deserve better than me or anyone your father tries to choose for you. I wish you the best. And Ray, in spite of our differences, I'm still grateful for all you did for me." With that, I walked out the door and hopped into my car.

I was just about to start the engine when I glanced over my shoulder at the house. Nellie was watching me from the window. We exchanged waves as I drove away.

CHAPTER 6

Ogle All You Want

I awoke early the next morning, grabbed a coffee and some rolls in the motel lobby, loaded all my belongings into my shopping cart, and checked out. I hadn't really intended on going to California until the words came out of my mouth at Ray's house. Now the idea intrigued me. Part of me wondered if I should stay in Florida in case the Krichards returned. Then again, how long was I to wait? The information I found on the internet didn't give me much hope of a timely rescue. And, I reasoned, as long as my implant didn't malfunction, they still had a chance of finding me if they really wanted to.

As I pushed the cart toward my car, I noticed a woman sitting on the edge of the hood, with one foot on the bumper and the other on the ground. She was dressed in short denim cutoffs with a plaid blouse, its tails tied beneath her breasts. She smiled as I approached.

I tried to be cool and not look her up and down, but I couldn't help it. She was so damn beautiful. I returned her smile and said, "The scene with the barefoot girl drinking warm beer on the hood of a Dodge in Springsteen's 'Jungleland' has come to life before my eyes!"

She shook a finger at me and replied with just a hint of a Southern accent, "Except this is a Ford, I'm wearing sandals, it's not raining, and beer and Bruce Springsteen are illegal."

"Beer and Bruce Springsteen are illegal?"

"Where have you been!"

Oops! I changed the subject. "Nellie, what are you doing here? You look so . . . different."

"I don't often get the chance to get all prettied up because my father insists that I dress down. But after meeting you last night and hearing what you had to say, I decided I couldn't hide the real me anymore."

"Well I like it."

She looked me in the eyes and opened her mouth partway as if she were about to say something. Then she looked down. "Listen . . . dressing how I want is just part of it. I can't explain it, but you seem different from other men I've met. If I tell you something I've told only a few other people, can I trust you?"

"Of course."

"There's a reason I'm thirty-four and my father can't find me a husband. I don't want a husband. In fact, if I were ever to get married, I'd want a wife."

"Oh, my God! I'm so sorry for looking at you in such a lecherous way. I should have known better."

"Don't worry about it. No matter what sex the compliment comes from, a girl likes to hear she's pretty. Ogle all you want, but to quote Bruce Springsteen, 'You Can Look (But You Better Not Touch).'"

I tilted my head and gave her a puzzled look.

She started to laugh and covered her mouth with her hand. Speaking through her fingers, she said, "I'm sorry. That really sounded militant, didn't it?" She dropped her hand. "I'm not implying that I have an invisible barrier around me or that we can't hug or anything like that. Maybe I should have quoted the Tubes instead and said, 'Don't Touch Me There.'"

I chuckled. "I'd answer you with another song title, but I can't think of one that fits. So I'll just say, it's okay. I know how it works. I have several gay and lesbian friends. I'm comfortable being friends with you and not taking things further."

"It's not often that anyone who is gay or lesbian risks telling a heterosexual what they are. They must have sensed that same trustworthiness in you that I do. All it takes is one snitch and wham! You're in jail. But I just can't live life under my father's thumb anymore and—"

"You want to ride with me to California."

She flushed. "That sounds calculating, but yes. I also think we could be great friends."

I stepped around to the rear of the car and opened the trunk. "Did you pack any clothes? If so, you can throw them in here with my stuff."

She walked over between the next two cars and picked up a medium-sized duffel bag. "Will this fit?"

"I think you could fit half your house into this thing." I stowed her bag and the contents of my shopping cart, shut the lid, and lowered the convertible top. "California, here we come!"

* * *

I drove a short distance up County Road 29 and turned on my blinker to take County Road 82, which cut over to the freeway.

"Don't go that way," Nellie said. "They'll be looking for us there. Let's stick to the back roads, at least until we get out of Florida. Stay on 29 until you reach State Road 80. Then go west to State Road 31, and head north."

I glanced over my shoulder. "Who could possibly be looking for us?"

"You don't know my father like I do. Once he figures out that I'm not home, he'll piece things together quickly. He'll report you as a Muslim, a traitor, or a kidnapper—whatever it takes. And though he's never acknowledged it, I'm sure he knows I prefer women. He wouldn't hesitate to turn me in just to teach me a lesson."

"Swell."

"If you think this is too much, Marty, you can drop me off at the nearest bus station. I would understand."

I tightened my grip on the steering wheel. "How well do you know your American history? Specifically, two years before you were born."

"Wasn't that when Supreme Leader Handley saved us all from the aliens?"

"I'm sure that was what you were told, but it didn't actually happen that way."

She looked at me with a slight tilt of her head.

"You told me your secret. Now I'm going to tell you mine. Do you remember someone named Marty Mann from that same time period?"

"Hmm. . . ." She steepled her fingers over her nose as she thought.

"The person Handley wanted shot on sight."

"Oh! Now I remember. He colluded with the aliens to destroy Earth."

"He did no such thing! He was trying to *save* Earth."

"How do you know?"

"I am Marty Mann."

"That's impossible! He fled with the aliens. Besides, if you were him, you'd be in your seventies or eighties by now."

"Do you have any problem believing that aliens visited Earth?"

"No. I've seen pictures of their ship."

"Then you shouldn't have any trouble believing that aliens who could travel here from another solar system would also have the capability of time travel."

"You're a time traveler? Why come here?"

"I didn't have a choice. I'll fill you in on the details later, but the short version of a long story is that two aliens got into an argument, and one of them sent me here to spite the other. Perhaps someday I'll get back to my original time. For now, I have to assume I'm here to stay."

"That explains why you didn't know that beer and Bruce Springsteen are illegal." She pointed to her left. "We're coming up on State Road 80. Turn here."

"There's a lot I don't know, Nellie. I've learned as much as possible during the three days I've been in your time. If you can help me catch up the rest of the way, I will be eternally grateful."

She flashed a bright smile. "We're going to make a great team. The lesbian and the alien sympathizer—on the lam!"

"Let's put on some music. Every epic road trip in history has a soundtrack. I bought some cassettes yesterday. They're in a case behind my seat."

She reached back and grabbed the case. She scanned the cassettes and pointed. "Turn into that pullout!"

I complied.

Before the car even stopped, she opened the door, jumped out, and dumped the cassettes into the roadside trash can.

"Hey!" I yelled.

She hopped back into the car and tossed the empty case onto the back seat.

"Why did you do that?"

"You bought those at one of the shops near your motel, didn't you?"

"Yes."

"Do you have any idea what you really bought?"

"No. The only musician I know from your time is Billy Bob Jennings, and that's only because your father played him in his truck."

"Billy Bob is actually one of the better government-approved artists. It's all downhill from there."

"But isn't *any* music better than *no* music?"

"No epic road trip has ever featured a government-approved soundtrack. Our first stop is Gainesville. I know of a little back-alley shop that sells black market cassettes. We can even pick up some Springsteen there."

"That sounds great. In the meantime, I have some more questions for you."

"And I for you."

For the next four hours, I shared with Nellie my adventures

with the Krichards, and she shared with me what life was like as a closeted lesbian in 2056 America. The contrast was wide, with me having traveled as far as Neptune, and her having never traveled beyond Gainesville. Even so, her stories were just as interesting to me as mine were to her.

I couldn't help blaming myself for the world she now lived in. If I hadn't hyperventilated during my first time jump or if I had resisted crossing over from business to pleasure with Chrissie, this timeline might not even exist. Instead, the United States might now be a beacon for environmental leadership, free speech, and liberty.

One of the many depressing things I learned from Nellie concerned the ongoing battle between Christians in the United States and Muslims everywhere. America's Christian society had become more and more like the worst of the Muslim societies they professed to be better than. A small consolation was that at least the women here hadn't yet been forced into burqas.

Even more depressing was that global warming had hit much harder than scientists had predicted during my time. Landing in flooded Everglades City already told me that. Additionally, I wasn't surprised to learn that Florida was suffering more than most states. If it's possible for a state to earn its fate, Florida did so by steadfastly electing one global warming-denying politician after another. Iconic animals, such as alligators and manatees, were now extinct, and much of the land that wasn't underwater was brown and ugly. With little left to attract tourists or retirees, Florida's economy and population crashed. Once the third most populated state in America, it no longer even cracked the top ten.

* * *

By the time we reached Gainesville, Nellie and I had shared more secrets than most longtime lovers had. We both agreed that having sex off the table made it easier for us to be more open with each other. Yet I can't deny that her being gorgeous made me feel different about our relationship than I would have felt if she had been a male friend in a similar situation. Not only did I feel protective of her, but I also felt attracted to her. The first feeling was fine. The second was not, and I knew nothing good could come of it. Somehow I had to find a way to internalize that attraction without ripping my heart in two in the process.

We headed directly to the back-alley cassette store, which Nellie claimed was the only place in Florida that sold black market tapes. The store had some stock on hand, but for anything special, they'd have to download the music from a California satellite and record the cassette overnight. As it turned out, we had a long list of albums that required overnight service.

Our purchases included illegal music from Bruce Springsteen, the Rolling Stones, the Pretenders, Tina Turner (those four making me miss my Krichard friends), Collide, Joan Jett, Pearl Jam, Goldfrapp, Within Temptation, BoDeans, Garbage, Melissa Etheridge, and Grace Potter.

After paying for everything, I turned to Nellie and asked, "Why didn't you choose any music from your time period?"

She shrugged. "Rock and roll has been illegal for most of my life, and few new American artists will risk prosecution by recording something they can't even openly sell. Since older black market rock has always been easier for me to find, that's what I've learned to love. Unfortunately, most of my cassettes are muddy-sounding, multigenerational copies. Banning imports, confiscating the CD-manufacturing plants, and imposing heavy fines on companies offering streaming or digital downloads were three of the most effective things the government did to fight illegal music—both new and old. They knew that totally eliminating rock and roll would be impossible, so instead, they made sure it sounded shitty."

I smiled. "Since the music we bought came directly off a California satellite, it should sound pretty good—especially in a car."

"Yes! I have one first-generation cassette from this store, and the quality is so much better than the others in my collection."

We stepped outside and hopped back into the car. As I pulled away from the curb, I looked over and asked, "Wouldn't you love to hear real live rock and roll?"

"That would be something. I've heard rumors that a few underground clubs exist in New New Orleans."

I chuckled. *"New* New Orleans?"

"Yes. Old New Orleans had to move."

"Let's make sure we route our road trip through New New Orleans then."

* * *

The first day of our road trip ended one block away from the cassette store at an old mom-and-pop motel. Later we would try to stay in nicer places, but while in Florida, we agreed that a motel would be better than a hotel because we wouldn't have to go through an interior hallway first if a quick escape became necessary. We also agreed that registering as husband and wife and sharing a room with a single large bed was the safest thing to do until we reached California. The bed situation would be awkward for the first night or so, but neither of us was too concerned about it.

Just like the motels I remembered during my time, the one we checked in to was dreary. Rather than hanging out there for the evening, we found a nice Italian restaurant and opted to sit on the outdoor patio. Although the food was good, adjusting to a dry country was going to take some getting used to. How can anyone eat fettuccine Alfredo without wine? If a black market exists for rock and roll, surely a similar one exists for alcoholic beverages.

Since such places wouldn't be publicly advertised, we walked over to the cassette shop after dinner. Our reasoning that someone who sold black market music might also have black market alcohol connections proved true. The proprietor asked what we wanted, made a phone call, and an hour later a man carrying a box full of assorted bottles knocked on our motel room door. I handed him six hundred dollars, and we were set for a long road trip.

"Whatever you do," Nellie said, "don't get pulled over. Between the booze and the cassettes, neither of us would see the outside of a prison cell for years."

We sampled a bottle of whiskey—which was much better than expected—climbed into bed, and soon fell asleep.

CHAPTER 7

Taking One for the Team

I awoke before Nellie, took a shower, and loaded all my stuff and the box of booze into the trunk of the car. She was still asleep when I returned, so I left her a note that I was going to walk over to the shop and pick up our cassettes.

When I got back a half hour later, Nellie was just turning off the shower. I flicked on the TV and scanned the stations while I waited. Eventually, she strolled out of the bathroom in a new outfit. It was similar in style to what she had worn the previous day, yet somehow she looked even more stunning in this one. Despite her permission to ogle, now that we were becoming good friends, I didn't feel right doing it. Still I wouldn't be human if I didn't at least take a glance. Okay, fine—I stared at her as if she were an amazing work of art. But I most definitely averted my eyes before it became an official ogle.

As we stepped out the door of our second-floor motel room, I asked, "Where should we go for breakf—"

"Shh!" Nellie lowered her finger, and we both peeked over the railing.

Standing directly below us, next to the T-bird, were two police officers.

"How did they find us?" I whispered.

"Your car doesn't exactly blend in," she whispered back.

My instinct to protect my new friend kicked in. I started to say something, when she shushed me again.

"I've got this. Take my bag, give me the key card, and stay out of sight. Once I get the men into the room, start the car and lower the top. Be ready to rock and roll."

I stood back as Nellie strutted down the outside stairs and couldn't resist spying from above when she approached the cops—her entire body oozing with sex.

"Hi, boys! What's up?"

"Are you Nellie Dixon?" asked the older of the two policemen.

"Maybe. Did I do something wrong, Officer?"

"We have orders to return you to Immokalee and to bring the owner of this car in for questioning," said the younger man.

Nellie looked the fresh-faced officer in the eyes and purred, "Have you ever had a *reeeal* blowjob?"

"Uh, I—"

She turned to the older man. "How about you?"

"Well, um . . . y-yes," he stuttered. "We're cops."

She pursed her lips and blew a kiss. "With these?" She held up her key card and swayed up the steps with the two men in hot pursuit.

I hurried in the opposite direction, ran down the far steps, and raced to the T-bird. I fumbled with the keys before cranking the engine and dropping the top. Then feeling that I had a little time, I turned the car around for a quick exit, hopped out, and began letting air out of the left front tire of the police car. When I heard the motel room door slam, I jumped back into the front seat.

"Go! Go! Go!" Nellie yelled as she vaulted over the door and landed in her seat.

I squealed out of the parking lot as she leaned her head over the door and spit in rapid succession. I raced a few blocks in one direction before quickly turning in another. Nellie kept spitting.

"What are you doing?" I asked.

"Where's the whiskey?"

"In the trunk."

"Pull over!"

"I can't. This is the car chase scene in our epic road trip!"

"*Pull over!*" she screamed.

I swerved to the curb and tossed her the keys. She ran to the rear, opened the trunk, grabbed the whiskey, and threw the keys back to me. As soon as she landed back in her seat, I floored the accelerator. Then I remembered to start the car, and we were off!

We sped down the road with Nellie first gargling with the whiskey, then swallowing several mouthfuls.

When I looked in my rearview mirror and saw no one, I reduced my speed. "What happened back there?"

"I bit him!"

"You what?"

"I bit him hard!"

"Okay, take a deep breath and start from the beginning."

She inhaled and slowly exhaled. "Once I lured the men into the room, I knew I had to separate them. No way could I take on two at once. So after I unzipped the older cop's fly, I accused the younger cop of staring too intently at his partner. Since nothing is worse among male police officers than even the hint of being gay, I convinced the younger cop to wait in the bathroom, promising him the same privacy when it was his turn. Then I pushed a chair under the bathroom doorknob."

"He fell for that?"

"It's amazing what a man will do if he thinks it will lead to his helmeted eel getting its gills wet."

"Then what happened?"

"When I turned around, the older cop was lying on the bed with his pants already off and his little moray standing at attention. I thought I could be like an actor and just play the part. Get him excited enough that he couldn't walk, and get out of there. Anyway, I'm obviously not experienced at such things. So I just positioned myself between his legs, licked my lips suggestively, leaned over, and uh . . . bit him!"

I cringed. "Did you draw blood?"

"Oh, yeah. It wasn't my intention, but it turns out those things are much more fragile than I imagined they were."

"That's an understatement."

"When the man screamed, I let go and ran out the door." She took another swig of whiskey, swished it around in her mouth, and spit it onto the road.

I held out my hand, and she placed the bottle in it. I took a few swallows before handing it back. "Thanks for taking one for the team."

"Oh, you would have done the same thing for me."

I pondered that for a moment before erasing the image from my brain. "Hey, we haven't had breakfast yet. Keep an eye out for a diner."

"Gimme another hour. . . . And if you order anything that comes with sausages, I swear I will kill you."

"I wouldn't think of it."

* * *

Even though we doubted that the two policemen Nellie outmaneuvered would dare to tell anyone what happened, we didn't know if anyone else was looking for us. Rather than take the direct route to New New Orleans, across the Florida Panhandle, we continued north on the backroads all the way to Valdosta. From there, we headed west across southern Georgia and Alabama.

An extra benefit of leaving Florida was that the scenery greened up a bit, and with our nerves settling, we could actually enjoy the ride. The T-bird may have been an easy car to spot, but nothing beat cruising with the top down, the wind blowing through our hair, and rock and roll blasting out the speakers.

We spent most of the day driving, stopping only for bathroom breaks and the occasional interesting sight. By the time we reached Hattiesburg, Mississippi, Nellie and I were both exhausted and agreed that ten hours in the car was too much. Still, we felt relieved to have put some distance between us and Florida.

We checked in to a nice hotel, plopped down on the king-sized bed, and realized that neither of us had the energy to go out for dinner.

"Let's have something delivered to our room," Nellie said.

I hadn't had a beer since I lived in Montana, and Nellie had never had one. Our box of liquor included a couple liter bottles of homebrew. I put one on ice and ordered a pizza from a local shop.

"You're in for a treat, Nellie. No combination of food and drink goes better together than pizza and beer."

Once she tried it, she agreed wholeheartedly.

* * *

The next morning we slept in. Then, over breakfast, we planned our route to New New Orleans. The drive would take only two hours, and we were both eager to see the new city. Fifteen years earlier, rising sea levels had forced the state of Louisiana and the United States government to move the entire city of New Orleans to the opposite side of what was once Lake Pontchartrain.

The move took almost ten years, and it became one of the most expensive and controversial endeavors in U.S. history. The city devoured several small towns, creating local unrest, and millions of taxpayers objected to the cost of the project, stirring up massive nationwide protests. Of course, in a theocracy, dissent never lasts long. One by one, the loudest protesters disappeared, never to be heard from again. Or, as some claim, to become fill material for the swamps.

Nellie and I checked out of our hotel and carefully surveyed the parking lot before approaching my car. This time no one was waiting for us. We headed south and reached New New Orleans in time for lunch. A prime parking spot greeted us at the edge of the New French Quarter, and we took a walk from there.

The city appeared to be a mixture of old and new. Some of

the French Quarter landmarks, such as Preservation Hall (now dedicated to country music), the St. Louis Cathedral, and the ironworks balconies, looked just the way they did during the early twenty-first century. I even recognized some of the restaurants, including Antoine's, Arnaud's, and Broussard's.

One business I didn't expect to see was Pat O'Brien's Bar, the birthplace of the hurricane cocktail. We stopped in for two of their famous drinks and asked how they could legally serve alcoholic beverages in a dry country. The bartender told us that the United States government had given New New Orleans an exemption from the national liquor ban in exchange for a 25 percent tax on drinks. That tax would ultimately repay the enormous cost of moving the city.

Not everything was old and relocated, however, since new buildings occupied much of the city. On the off chance that someone was still trying to find us, Nellie and I decided to check in to a massive new hotel just off Bourbon Street. Blending in there wouldn't be a problem.

We unpacked and relaxed for a bit in our hotel room. Then we walked Bourbon Street and eventually ended up at Antoine's for dinner. There we enjoyed a scrumptious Creole meal, and our waiter gave us a great tip about where we could find some live rock and roll. We walked—or should I say waddled?—directly there after dessert.

Nellie and I never would have found Melissa's Rock House without instructions because it looked like a large, old, double-gallery home from the outside with no sign to indicate what was inside. One of the advantages of being in a new city was that Melissa didn't have to rip out the insides of an old house to turn it into a nightclub. Instead, she was able to build specifically for live music. That was evident even before we entered since the insulated outside walls prevented sound from escaping. After paying our cover charge, we stepped inside an elegant, chandeliered room with a wide stage and spacious dance floor. The acoustics were nearly perfect.

As the two of us weaved through the crowd, I was a little worried we might be stuck standing all night. Luck was on our side, however, and we managed to stake a claim on a table that was just being vacated near the dance floor. Soon we were sipping drinks—a daiquiri for her and a hurricane for me—and watching an outstanding band performing a mixture of covers and originals.

When Nellie heard a song she knew, she grabbed my hand and yelled over the music, "Let's dance!"

I wasn't sure how she learned to dance with such confidence, having had such a sheltered upbringing. But then, nothing about her now matched my first impression of her, four days before, in a housedress. She commanded the dance floor, and I did my best to keep up. As the band segued into another song, more eyes were on us than on the stage. And by *us*, I mean Nellie. She exuded sensuality and moved as if she were boneless. All the while, she smiled with such joy that my heart just melted.

When the band's next number was a slow song, we looked at each other awkwardly for a moment and started back toward our table. I sat down and glanced over to say something, but Nellie wasn't there. A tall blonde woman had waylaid her, and the two were heading out onto the dance floor.

As I watched the women dance close, my brain battled my heart:

Brain: "Did you expect that you'd have some magical power over Nellie that would change her sexual orientation?"

Heart: "She's funny. She's beautiful. She's graceful. I've fallen in love."

Brain: "Stop falling in love so easily. In less than a month, you've fallen in love with a woman who currently exists thirty-six years in the past and who-knows-how-many light-years away and a lesbian you've known for only four days. What is it with you and impossible love anyway?"

Heart: "I can't help it. I have as much choice in deciding whether to fall in love as you do in deciding whether to like or dislike chocolate."

Brain: "What are you, back in high school?"

Heart: "Shut the fuck up!"

Five songs later, the band took a break, and Nellie returned to our table. "Sorry to abandon you like that. Getting picked up was the last thing on my mind."

"Picked up?" Oops! I said that with way too much bite.

"What? Are you jealous?"

"Maybe a little."

"Damn you! You seemed like a smart, liberal guy, who understood. You can't change me to be attracted to men any more than I can change *you* to be attracted to men."

"I know that. I really do. But at the same time, who I fall for is just as uncontrollable."

Her face softened. "The truth is . . . Well, I've fallen for you too. And if you were a woman, we definitely would have been doing much more than just sleeping in the same bed these past few nights. Do you have a sister?"

"I did, but she died several years ago."

"Oh. I'm so sorry. Were you close?"

"Very."

She put her hand on top of mine. "Think about her and how much you loved her."

"I do, often."

"Now imagine having sex with her."

I yanked my hand back.

"Think of me as your new sister, and I will think of you as the brother I never had."

I returned my hand and gently squeezed hers. "I'll try . . . , *sis.* If I fall off the wagon, just give me a noogie or sit on top of me and let a long string of drool escape your mouth until it hits me in the face."

She chuckled. "Your sister did *that* to you?"

"Yes, at least until I grew bigger and stronger than she was."

"Now here's what's going to happen tonight." She took a sip of her drink and looked me in the eyes. "I haven't been laid in ages, and in a country like this, who knows when I'll ever have such a low-risk opportunity again? If you'd like to stay for the next set, I'd love to dance with you some more. But at the end of the night," she pointed, "I'm going home with the girls at that table."

"All three of them?"

She reached over and applied a weak noogie. "They're room-mates who share a house a few blocks away from here. I'm going to bed with the blonde I was dancing with—and her alone."

I smiled.

"And stop trying to visualize it. I'm your sister!"

During the next set, the blonde woman, Toni, and I took turns dancing with Nellie. I also danced with the other two although that was a bit awkward since they obviously preferred each other's company to mine. When the set ended, we all decided to leave.

Out on the sidewalk, my protective instinct kicked in. I motioned Nellie aside and said, "It's a beautiful night for a walk. If it's okay with you, I'd like to tag along just far enough to get you and your friends safely to the front door." I reached into my pocket and retrieved my cell phone and a card with the hotel's phone number on it. "Take these. When you're ready to return, call me, no matter the time, and I'll walk over to get you. Our room number is 973."

"That won't be necessary."

"Perhaps not. But if you don't call me, you'll be riding in the back seat for the rest of our road trip."

She rose on her tiptoes, kissed me on the cheek, and whis-pered in my ear, "Thank you for letting me have tonight. Tomor-row night is your night, and I promise it will be worth the wait." She winked and turned to follow her friends.

What did she mean by *that*? My heart and my brain resumed their battle.

Minutes later, we reached the house. The four women stepped inside, waved, and closed the door. Once again, I was the loneliest man on Earth. I spent a few minutes watching the house, just to make sure everything was okay, before walking back to the hotel and trying to fall asleep.

* * *

The phone didn't ring until late morning. Twenty minutes later, I was at the door looking at four smiling, surprisingly perky, women. Nellie said her goodbyes, and the two of us walked toward the hotel.

"Shall we hit the road a little after lunch?" I asked.

"Are we in a hurry to get somewhere?"

"No, but—"

"Let's stay another night then."

Even though Nellie and I had come to an understanding, mere logic couldn't extinguish my feelings that easily. Knitting needles in my eyes seemed preferable to another night alone in New New Orleans while she slept in the arms of another woman.

I forced an unconvincing smile.

"No! No! That was only a one-night stand. I'm going to make good on my promise. Tonight is *your* night."

"That's sweet, but I would never expect you to—"

"That's *not* what I'm talking about!" She rolled her eyes. "Tonight you're going to find out just what an advantage it is to have a smokin' hot lesbian best friend."

I considered pressing her for a less vague explanation of what she had in mind, but her devilish smile convinced me to keep my mouth shut. The mystery would be half the fun.

We reached the hotel a few minutes later and extended our stay. Then for the rest of the day, we played tourist.

First, we picked up lunch from a curbside food cart and enjoyed a picnic at a nearby park. While we ate, I took the opportunity to share with Nellie more details about my dinosaur adventure, including my rock-skipping world record and the fact that she was eating with the inventor of the picnic. She was suitably impressed.

Next, we spent a delightful few hours watching and interacting with the many characters that make the city unique: street musicians, mimes, artists, fortune-tellers, and people dressed in the most outrageous costumes imaginable.

Finally, we did some shopping and toured a few art museums.

At dinnertime Nellie said, "Okay, your special night begins now."

I wiped my brow with the back of my hand and feigned a look of pain. "Good. Because waiting to hear what you have in mind was fun for a while, but now it's killing me."

She smiled again, even more devilishly. "Tonight you are going to get laid by the best-looking woman in all of New New Orleans—excepting me, of course."

"I don't think I'm attractive enough to aim that high."

"Yes you are. And your smokin' hot lesbian best friend is going to make it happen."

I admired her enthusiasm. Yet did I even want to get laid? Some guys don't care what's between a woman's ears as long as they can get between her legs. I'm not one of those guys. On the other hand, I wasn't currently attached to anyone—at least on Earth—and Nellie seemed to need an equalizer to make up for the previous night. For the time being, I decided to play along.

We dined at an elegant Cajun restaurant, and Nellie made sure we sat at a table with an unobstructed view of the door. Whenever a woman entered, she surreptitiously pointed and whispered, "How about her? She's cute."

Eventually I asked, "Is there *any* woman you don't think is cute?"

"Compared to the choices in Immokalee? No."

I waited until our dessert and after-dinner drinks arrived before deciding to make things more interesting. When an attractive woman in her late forties entered, firmly attached to the arm of her husband or boyfriend, Nellie ignored her. Once the maître d' seated the couple, it was time to see if my smokin' hot lesbian best friend was as good as she claimed to be. I looked from Nellie to the woman and said, "Her. She's the one."

Nellie choked on her drink and buried her face in a napkin. "Be serious! She's too old for you."

"Are we selecting a woman *you* want to have sex with or a woman *I* want to have sex with?"

"Okay, if you insist." Then—either to gain confidence, put

on a show, or do a little of both—Nellie chugged the remainder of her drink and clunked the glass down on the table. Next, she stared at the woman until they made eye contact. After holding her gaze for several seconds, Nellie stood and swayed to the restroom. The woman followed moments later.

I cringed. Nellie had called my bluff. If she was successful, could I really follow through? While fidgeting in my chair and sipping my drink, I noticed out of the corner of my eye that the woman's companion was staring at me. When I looked over, he winked. *Oh, God!*

Nellie returned after several minutes and whispered, "She'll fuck you, but only if her husband can fuck me at the same time."

"That sounds fair."

Her shoulders stiffened, then relaxed. We had been through too much in the past few days for me to get a rise out of her. Instead, she smiled and said, "Would you like to go dancing?"

"I'd love to. But only if we can both take rain checks on getting laid tonight."

"You have a deal!"

I paid for our dinner and started for the door. When I turned to say something to Nellie, she was at the other couple's table, whispering in the woman's ear. As the husband watched, she applied a sultry kiss to his wife's cheek. He did a double-take from the women to me, and I winked. Then, without looking back, Nellie sauntered through the door I was holding for her. As soon as we were out of sight, we howled in laughter.

We spent the rest of the evening listening to music and dancing at Melissa's Rock House. The three women from the previous night were there as well, and they joined us for a few drinks.

When the band took a break just after midnight, Nellie leaned her head on my shoulder and said, "I'm tired."

We walked back to the hotel, both of us ready to continue west in the morning.

CHAPTER 8

How Do I Look in Orange?

The joy of our epic road trip diminished as we headed into Texas. Even though states in the Southeast had lost much of their coast to the rising ocean, at least large tracts of land still existed that were more or less green. Texas, on the other hand, was a depressing moonscape. Everywhere we looked, we saw dusty, cracked ground, and if we saw trees, they were either sickly or dead. Even the sky looked different with its sickening yellowish-brown tinge from all the dust and pollution.

If humans were the only ones paying the price for the devastation, I could have driven through Texas with the smug satisfaction of knowing that the state responsible for producing some of the most devious anti-environmental politicians in American history was now getting its just punishment. But humans aren't the only species on Earth. I wondered how many plants and animals had gone extinct in Texas during Nellie's and my lifetimes—all because greedy politicians shamelessly sold their souls and let dirty energy companies do as they pleased.

The one positive for anyone crossing Texas was that the state had eliminated speed limits on interstate highways. The speedometer on my T-bird went up to 140 miles per hour, but with the air conditioning on, the engine labored at 118. Ultimately, we opted to slather on sunscreen and go topless—the car, not us. With the air conditioning off, the T-bird cruised comfortably at

125. Although we had previously sworn off long, tiring drives, we both agreed that Texas wasn't a desirable place to hang out. We made the eleven-hundred-mile drive from New New Orleans to El Paso in just over twelve hours.

* * *

After an uneventful night in El Paso, Nellie and I awoke early and decided to check out the controversial Handley Wall. In my time, the American city of El Paso and the Mexican city of Ciudad Juárez had an easily climbable fence between them, and construction of the border wall was just beginning. Now, in Nellie's time, the completed wall was impressive looking but still climbable with a simple rope ladder.

We found a talkative border guard, and he told us that the only thing the wall did efficiently was block migration routes of animals, not people. To make the wall effective against Mexicans, the United States had to post guards like him every two hundred feet or so, with orders to shoot anyone who stuck a head above the wall. Eventually, as America became a less desirable country to live in, the flow of people over the wall slowed to less than a trickle.

"I haven't had to wing a Mexican since the government stationed me here eleven years ago," the guard said with a wink.

His candor surprised me until I noticed that he couldn't take his eyes off Nellie. She could have asked him to do anything, and he would have complied, simply to keep her in his sight. I stepped back and became invisible.

As the conversation continued, the guard smiled at Nellie's breasts and said, "For the first time in a long time, we've had an uptick in illegals coming over the wall, but most of the guards take pity on them and look the other way. They aren't coming to steal American jobs or pervert our culture anymore. They're just trying to get to Canada to escape the heat."

Nellie frowned. "That's what's so unfair about global

warming. It doesn't care about borders or who is responsible. Everyone pays."

"Not everyone. It does provide jobs for me and others who guard the border."

"How many guards work along the wall?"

"Along just the Mexican border or the Californian border as well?"

"Wait. Are you saying this wall continues all the way along California?" She glanced over at me and bit her lower lip.

"Of course! Hell, war could break out any day between our two countries."

"Over what?"

"Mostly water. Those liberal bastards in California still seem to think they're entitled to water flowing from America."

"Thank you. You've been most helpful."

"Any time, little lady," he said, looking her up and down once more.

Nellie and I didn't say a word to each other until we reached the car where I shouted, "You didn't tell me about the California border wall!"

"How was I supposed to know?"

"I don't know. Perhaps a news story."

"Have you *seen* the news in the last few decades?"

"Uh . . . I haven't exactly had the time."

"It's all government produced."

"And?"

"If it's not rah-rah, 'the supreme leader is on your side,' it's some glossy production to get us to believe whatever they want us to believe. The few underground news sources that exist on the internet get blocked as soon as the government censors discover them. They pop up elsewhere, but the continuous cat-and-mouse game makes it difficult for anyone but the most internet savvy to find unfiltered daily news."

"Okay, I forgive you. But we may not be able to get into California, and even if we can, we might not want to." I took a deep breath. "Since we drove such a long way yesterday, how about we make today a short drive?"

"I'm all for that."

"Let's head north to Santa Fe. In my time, it was a fun, artsy little town. Maybe it still is."

"I hope so. I didn't realize how much I enjoyed art until we toured those museums in New New Orleans. Living under my father's thumb in Immokalee has caused me to miss so much. For me, what is truly making this an epic road trip isn't the distance we travel. It's the new experiences."

"Will you be disappointed if we can't get into California?"

"A little. After all, it's a safer, more open place for someone like me. Then again, Canada is also an option."

"I was thinking that too. I was born in Duluth when it was still in the *state* of Minnesota. Back then it was a liberal town. Now, because of Lake Superior, it's likely surviving global warming better than most cities. After we check in to our hotel, let's do some research and decide once and for all where we're going."

* * *

We arrived in Santa Fe later that day and reluctantly removed California as our ultimate destination. Ports of entry existed to allow people to travel between the United States and California, but as a consequence of the severe water shortage, entry into California for nonresidents was restricted by a waiting list. Currently the wait was three months long, and even then, the maximum stay was only two weeks.

The Canadian province of Minnesota looked much more promising. Passports would be necessary to cross the border, though, and getting a passport in the United States was almost impossible, except for the very rich. Fortunately, we could acquire temporary Canadian passports at the border that would allow us to visit for up to six months. Additionally, we had the option of becoming permanent Canadian citizens through their refugee program. For that, all we had to do was fill out a form and check off at least one group on a long list of oppressed minorities, which included gays, lesbians, non-Christians, non-whites, scientists, and liberals.

Armed with what we hoped was accurate information, we planned our route. We would head north into Colorado, cut northeast through Nebraska and Iowa, and enter Canada at the port of entry just south of Albert Lea.

"That's enough research," Nellie declared. "Let's get out of this stuffy hotel and explore."

"I agree. How about we head downtown? We can check out museums, shops, and art galleries at the plaza. When we get hungry, we'll find a nice place to have dinner."

"That sounds wonderful."

* * *

We spent the next few hours working our way along the plaza. Eventually I whispered to Nellie, "Have you noticed that woman following us?"

"Yes. This is the fourth place I've seen her. She's smiled and made eye contact with me numerous times. I think she's flirting with me."

"Be careful."

"Don't worry. We're just having a little fun. I won't abandon you for another one-night stand."

"I'm not worried about that."

"Yes you are. And if it makes you feel any better, she's not my type."

We continued shopping and ended up at a gallery that featured Southwestern-style paintings. While I was staring at a piece that I particularly admired, Nellie moved into the next room.

When I followed minutes later, the flirty woman was there again. I stopped just inside the room and feigned interest in a painting since the two women were speaking softly to each other, and I didn't want to interrupt. Then, out of the corner of my eye, I saw the woman put a hand on Nellie's cheek.

Nellie reached up.

The woman slapped a handcuff on her wrist!

I wheeled around.

She twisted Nellie to the floor.

Nellie shouted, "What are you doing!"

The woman secured both of Nellie's arms behind her back. "Police! You're under arrest for the solicitation of homosexual activities."

"You've got to be kidding!" I screamed. "We were just admiring some paintings. *You* were the one doing the soliciting!"

"That's not how the law reads. Her flirting gave me probable cause. Reaching up to put her hand on mine confirmed her guilt." She yanked Nellie to her feet.

Nellie glared at the police officer. "I was reaching up to pull your hand down, not to initiate a sexual act."

"You have no case. I witnessed what happened and will testify on my friend's behalf."

"That's not how these cases work. My job is just to bring her in. Neither you nor I will be able to say a thing in court. It's all up to her to prove she's *not* a homosexual. If she's innocent, she'll be released. If she's guilty, and it's a first offense, she'll be sentenced to a year in prison followed by a year of intensive treatment."

"How can I prove . . . ?" Nellie spat. "What are you going to do? Attach electrodes to my genitals and show me videos of sex acts to see if I get aroused?"

"Oh, you've done this before."

"You bitch!" I lunged and a gun slammed against my face.

"Try that again, and you'll be missing the side of your head."

I raised my hands and slowly stepped backward.

Without taking her eyes off me, the police officer walked Nellie out of the gallery and down the street to her car. I followed as close as I dared.

When the officer opened the rear door, Nellie looked back at me and said, "Don't worry. I can pass the test."

"I know you can, but I *won't* let them violate you. I'm going for help."

The officer shut Nellie inside and sped off.

I stood frozen for a moment, wondering what to do. I knew virtually nothing about how theocracy law worked in 2056 America. Could I get her released on bail? Could an attorney file to stop the test or at least delay it?

If there was one constant in America, it was that money talked, and fortunately I was a debit card millionaire. I ran for my car, keeping my eyes open for an ATM or a bank. I found an ATM a block down the street. The machine limited me to one thousand dollars, but it was a start. I jumped into the car and headed for the hotel, scanning for more ATMs on the way. I found two more, but neither would give me any cash. Finally, I spotted a bank nestled in a cluster of buildings near my hotel. I thought for sure that getting my own money—well, actually Handley's money—there would be easy, but even the bank limited me to seventeen thousand dollars, and I had to argue for that. I hoped it would be enough.

Next, I returned to the hotel and searched the internet for legal help. I called several attorneys, but because it was late in the day, none were accessible. I switched to bail bond companies and reached a man named Vern, who invited me to meet him at his office in twenty minutes.

I was there in fifteen. Vern greeted me with a smile and walked me into his inner office. He was a stout man in his sixties, with black-rimmed glasses and a curly gray beard. As I recapped the events of Nellie's arrest for him, he nodded occasionally while twirling a finger in his beard.

When I stopped talking, he said, "The Streamlined Homosexual Act of 2038 is clear in cases like this. So are the local procedures. In the morning, two police officers will escort your friend from the Santa Fe County Adult Correctional Facility to the

Municipal County Court Lab. There, a technician will administer the test—*accidentally* attaching everything just a little too tight—and a judge will witness the test. If she passes, she will be released later that day, but I have to tell you that few people pass."

"Oh, God."

"Assuming your friend isn't one of the lucky ones, the judge will then enter an immediate conviction order and have her transferred to the corporate Women's Penitentiary in Albuquerque. Once incarcerated there, she can repent, and an attorney can file an appeal. If that appeal is successful, she'll be able to take a more sophisticated test that's easier to pass. Unfortunately, the entire process is deliberately slow, guaranteeing that the prison will profit from having her in their care for a minimum of six months."

"So there's no way to get her out on bail?"

"I'm afraid not. Especially when cases are determined by *science*," he said, making air quotes around the word. "Now if she had shot someone with an assault rifle or got caught poaching what little wildlife we have left, I might be able to do something."

"What has this country become?"

"I don't like these scientific convictions any more than you do. I'm sorry. I truly wish I could help."

"Perhaps you still can." I pulled all the money out of the bank bag I was carrying and placed it on his desk. "I have eighteen thousand dollars. It's all yours if you can do three things for me."

"Name them."

"Get me in to see Nellie tonight, rent me a storage garage near the court lab—one the police don't regularly visit—and arrange for a few people to *accidentally* get in the way at the proper time tomorrow morning."

Vern picked up the money and counted it. "Okay, I'm in."

"Here's my phone number. Call me tonight with the location of the garage and the hiding spot for the key. How soon can I see Nellie?"

"Give me fifteen minutes. It's past visiting hours, so I have to call in a favor and forfeit a hunk of the money you just gave me. In the meantime, help yourself to some coffee in the lobby. It shouldn't be too horrible."

* * *

I paced outside Vern's office until he had everything in order. Then we jumped into his car for the ten-minute drive to the Santa Fe County Adult Correctional Facility. As he drove, I explained my plan in detail. He nodded, fiddled with his beard, and offered a few modifications. Since he knew the process and where Nellie and her escorts would most likely be at specific times, I was relieved to have his input.

"You will still most likely get yourself arrested or killed," he said, "but at least you'll have a slim chance of success."

"A chance is all I'm asking for."

As we pulled into the correctional facility parking lot, I was shocked by the sight. Although the brick-walled prison wasn't tall, it spread out as wide as a city block. The main building was shaped like a blocky X, and a separate, rectangular administrative building sat beside it. Surrounding everything was a razor wire-topped fence. I got nervous just looking at the facility from the outside and could only imagine how terrified Nellie felt inside.

Having Vern with me was probably the only thing that kept me from visibly shaking. He had obviously been inside many times, so I hung back and followed his lead. First, a guard searched us. Then we passed through a body scanner and numerous doors that shut behind us with loud, metallic clanks.

Several minutes later, I entered a room, where I sat face to face with Nellie, separated by a security window. We both picked up our handsets.

"It's good to see you," I said.

"It's good to see you too. How do I look in orange?"

"Hmm. It kind of clashes with your hair."

"That's what I told them. I asked for something in green, but the lady with the fat fingers said they were fresh out."

"Fat fingers?"

"Oh, that's been the best part of my day so far, getting strip-searched by a woman prison guard who could have played nose tackle for the Miami Dolphins. And they're worried about *me* being a dyke!"

I gripped my handset so tightly that I thought I might crush it. "I've been getting legal advice. The law isn't on your side as I'm sure you already know, but sometimes you just need to duck and roll."

"Duck and roll?"

I straightened my head and looked deeply into her eyes, "Yes, you never know what obstacles life will throw at you, so my philosophy of life has always been to *duck and roll.*"

Nellie nodded. "I like that philosophy."

"The crime the state has accused you of doesn't allow for bail, so I'm afraid you'll be stuck here for the night. I'm sorry, Nellie. I tried."

"Don't worry about it. They'll just lock me up with a bunch of women who are suspected of wanting to have sex with other women. It ought to be a real party."

"Tomorrow some cops will escort you over to the Municipal County Court Laboratory for your test and judgment. Know that even if you don't see me, I will be there."

A guard opened the door behind Nellie and barked, "Time's up!"

Nellie put her hand against the window. I did the same on my side.

"I love you, Marty."

"I love you too, Nellie."

As I walked out, my entire body vibrated with anger.

* * *

Vern drove me back to his office. As I stepped out of his car, I thanked him profusely for his help and said, "I need to get to a store tonight that sells tools. Do you know of any open this late?"

He looked at his watch and thought for a moment. "Most stores are already closed for the night. There's a big-box store three blocks down on your left." He pointed. "If they're still open, they close in four minutes."

"Thanks. And don't forget about the garage."

Vern waved as I jumped into my car and sped down the road.

I reached the parking lot just in time to see the lights dimming inside the store. I ran to the door and opened it as a pimply faced man approached from the other side. "Sorry, mister," he said. "We're closed."

"You can't close on me! . . . Please."

"I'm not allowed to—"

"I'll buy you any item in the store. Just put it in my shopping cart, and it's yours. I only need ten minutes, maybe less than that if you help me. *Please!* It's very important."

"I suppose if you already had . . ." He dashed down an aisle and returned seconds later with a vacuum cleaner. "this in your basket, I can't officially turn you away."

"Now that's great customer service! Can you show me where you keep your bolt cutters?"

My after-hours shopping trip took a little longer than planned, but when I let the man add another item for himself, he was perfectly happy with our arrangement.

My next stop was an all-night grocery store. I hurried inside and stopped to take a deep breath. Here, I wouldn't have to rush so much. I loaded my shopping cart with more supplies, and, conveniently, just as I was checking out, Vern called with the garage information. Finally, I had everything I needed, or at least I hoped I did. I returned to the hotel and worked late into the night, preparing for the following morning.

CHAPTER 9

Down, Boy!

I can't really say what time I woke up because I tossed and turned more than I slept. But once I was out of bed, I took a shower to make sure all my makeup was off, slipped into a T-shirt, and put a knit cap on my head. Then I grabbed a cup of coffee and a roll in the lobby, packed up the car, and checked out of the hotel.

Nellie's test was scheduled for nine thirty. I reached the Municipal County Court Lab parking lot a few minutes past eight. I needed to be early, so I could find the perfect parking spot and get a feel for the traffic flow. I lowered the windows and the convertible top and waited. Time slowed to dentist chair speed.

By nine, every police car that approached on the road paralleling the parking lot set me on edge. Was Nellie inside? Finally, at twenty after nine, the car containing my friend pulled into the lot and parked in the space facing the "Reserved for Lab Patients" sign.

I started the car and sat low in my seat as one of the officers helped Nellie out of the back. Her hands were cuffed in front and secured to her waist. A short chain ran between her ankles. My plan wasn't to run over the police officers, but if I had ever been tempted to commit murder, this was the moment. Instead, as Nellie shuffled, flanked by a man on each side, I quietly pulled my car alongside and said, "Hello, Officers. Duck and roll!"

Nellie ducked.

I emptied a can of pepper spray into the men's faces.

They screamed.

I yelled, "Time to roll!"

Nellie rolled into the back seat of my car, and we squealed out of the lot.

I chanced a look in my rearview mirror and saw two cars simultaneously entering the two parking lot exits. Although I doubted that either of Nellie's escorts could see well enough to drive, I knew Vern's assistants would get in the way just enough to make sure we got the head start we needed.

"Stay down! We're almost there." I made a quick left and a quick right, then slowed to blend in with traffic. Minutes later, I spotted the sign for the storage garage company, turned down the second row, and pulled into the one open garage with a light on inside. I jumped out of the car and yanked down the door. "We're here!"

Nellie sighed. "That was quick."

"Would you have preferred an extended chase—flying over hills, crashing into food carts, and racing through shopping malls—with half the police force behind us?"

"Isn't that kind of a requirement for an epic road trip chase?"

"Hey, we've tried twice. It's not our fault that the cops haven't come through on their end. Besides, I kind of enjoy getting away without a scratch on my car . . . and living."

"Come here, you. Let me give you a big hug."

"This, I've got to see."

"Yeah, I guess I am kind of tied up at the moment. What are we gonna do about that?"

I opened the passenger-side door and helped Nellie to her feet. "Never fear. Your mildly hunky heterosexual best friend is here, and he has come prepared." I removed the bolt cutter from the trunk, wondering if it was sturdy enough for the job. I inspected her restraints. "We need some chairs and more light." I pulled two folding chairs out of the trunk, helped Nellie onto one, and set up a battery-powered lantern. "That's better."

First, I cut the chain between Nellie's ankles. Next, I cut the chain around her waist and the one between her handcuffs. Yay, bolt cutter! She was free but still wearing ankle and wrist bracelets.

"Have you ever picked a lock with a bobby pin?"

"No."

"Me neither. Now we have a choice. I can either try to cut through the metal cuffs, or we can try to pick the locks. The bolt cutter will be faster, but if I slip, you're going to get a nasty cut."

"I assume we don't plan to leave here anytime soon."

"No, I expect we'll hole up here for a few days. Vern, the bail bondsman who helped me pull this off, will let us know when the police scale back their search efforts."

"In that case, let's entertain ourselves by attempting to pick the locks first. If we're hopeless locksmiths, we'll defer to the bolt cutter."

I reached into the glove box and grabbed some bobby pins. "Vern says to pull off the plastic tip and bend the very end of the pin twice: first straight forward and then straight down. Both bends must be close to each other, so stick the tip into the lock, and use the lock as a vise when bending. Finally, once the pin is the correct shape, stick it into the top part of the lock, push up, and twist toward the chain I just cut—or something like that."

"Can you explain that again?" She winked.

"While you start on that, I'll set up our apartment." I pointed. "The bathroom is over there, the kitchen is there, and since neither of us will be able to sleep in the bucket seats, somehow we'll have to contort our bodies enough to make the back seat work as our bedroom."

"Anything is better than sleeping in a prison cell."

I pulled our supplies out of the trunk along with what I had stashed under the seats, between the seats, and on the front passenger-side floor. One of my best finds at the big-box store was a collapsible toilet, complete with a dozen deodorizing waste bags.

When I showed the toilet to Nellie, she let some air whistle through her teeth and said, "Thank God. It would get unbearable in here quickly if we had to pee and shit on the floor. Did you remember toilet paper?"

"Yes, one roll for each of us. Plus somewhere in all this stuff is a container of moist towelettes for hand and face washing. Later, when it gets dark, I'll sneak out and fill this water bag. I'll also see if I can find a restaurant within walking distance and bring us back some dinner."

"Won't that be too dangerous, Marty? Every police officer in the state has to have a description of you by now."

"They'll be looking for a dark-skinned man last seen wearing a knit hat. I'll reapply my makeup before leaving. Tonight I'll be just another blond-haired white guy."

"What about your car? I assume we'll eventually have to drive out of here."

I reached under the front passenger-side floor mat and pulled out two license plates. "Last night, as a precaution, I borrowed the plates from a Cadillac in the hotel parking lot. We made such a clean getaway that it probably wasn't necessary, but who knows if any surveillance cameras captured us? I'm going to remove the Cadillac plates and put mine back on. As for my car standing out from the crowd, I spotted a few red Thunderbirds in town, so at least it's not a one of a kind. I could buy another car, but that comes with risks as well. When we leave, we'll do so in the middle of the night, take the backroads, and cross our fingers."

* * *

That evening, I slunk out of the garage and returned with two gallons of water, some ice, and an extra-large pizza.

As I set down my treasures, Nellie proudly held up a complete set of successfully picked ankle and handcuffs. "The one on my right wrist was a bitch since I had to use my left hand to do the picking. I got it open just a few minutes ago. Let's celebrate!"

We set the open pizza box on the trunk lid and climbed into

the back seat. I leaned against the wall on the driver's side, while she leaned against the wall on the passenger's side, and our legs alternated in the middle. The arrangement worked great for grabbing pizza off the trunk, though we had to be careful to make sure the toppings didn't slide off the crust and into our laps.

Since we were going to be stuck in a hot garage for an indeterminable amount of time, we had no reason to remain sober. We drank our last liter of homebrew without even waiting for the ice to cool it and chased that with multiple shots of rum.

We also had no reason to stay up late, especially since neither of us had slept well the night before. Unfortunately, buying an inflatable mattress didn't cross my mind during my late-night shopping spree. We tried several positions in the T-bird, and ultimately agreed that the person who designed the back seat had never actually tried to lie down on it. Spooning was the best option, with me curled around her. Despite our intimate contact, we kept everything brother and sister.

I was just dozing off when Nellie trembled and sucked in air through her nose. I repositioned my arm under her head and felt something wet. "What's wrong?"

Sniff. "Nothing."

"That's obviously not true, or you wouldn't be crying. I'm here for you."

Her body shook, and she sniffled again. "Do you know what it's like having to spend your entire life hiding who you are, like some kind of freak?"

"No, I don't. But these last few days have helped me to understand a little better."

"I got fucking arrested for just being who I am! What's with these people?"

"They're incredibly insecure and blinded by an archaic belief system."

"I can't ever go home again." *Sniff.* "Not that I'd want to. But why the fuck should the government or anyone else care who I fuck?"

"Everything will be different in Canada."

"But my own father . . . my own country. They won't have me!"

I kissed the back of her head, doing my best to console her. "We will always have each other."

She wiggled in closer to me. "You're such a good friend—my hero. You saved me."

Strands of Nellie's short, soft hair covered my face. "You would have done the same for me." I inhaled her light floral scent. *Oh, shit! No! Not now. Down, boy!*

"Mmmm. We really do make a good . . . What's that?"

"Nothing."

"I may be a lesbian, but I'm not that naïve about men. You have a hard-on!"

"I most certainly do not!"

She reached back and grabbed me.

"Okay, maybe I do."

"Is that what you want? To fuck me?"

I bit my tongue, not sure what to say.

Nellie took a deep breath and let it out slowly. "If I spread my legs and we do this. *Just this once.* Will that ease the tension between us?"

"No."

"No? Do you expect me to give up women and just be with you?"

"No, Nellie. If we have sex, I will never forgive myself for taking advantage of you during a vulnerable moment. And you'll never forgive yourself for giving in."

"Then what's with the erection?"

"It's totally involuntary. But I'm also a man. Thousands of years of evolution never anticipated that someone like you would be spooning with someone like me in the back of a T-bird—and all we'd do is sleep! The brain in my head grasps and accepts the nature of our relationship. My auxiliary brain, down there, not so much—at least not yet. As time goes on, I'm sure that lower brain of mine will realize who's in charge, and embarrassing moments like this won't pop up again."

She chuckled and said, "You're the best, Marty Mann" before turning and kissing me lightly on the lips.

"That wasn't helpful."

"Sorry."

* * *

Nellie and I spent another day and another night in the garage. By the time Vern called late on the third day, our cabin fever was almost unbearable. "A cop just got shot in the leg while attempting to apprehend a suspected Buddhist on the south side of town," he said. "The suspect got away, and half the police force is headed there to join the manhunt. If you head north, you should be able to get out of here without being noticed."

Rather than leave immediately, we waited until after midnight. Once we were sure no one was milling about, we removed all evidence of our stay, raised the top on the T-bird, and departed for Colorado. We didn't speak until we were well out of the city.

"I don't care how cute she is," I said, finally breaking the silence. "Neither of us will even glance at another woman until we reach Minnesota."

"Neither of us? Why not you?"

"Consider it my show of solidarity."

"Okay. Women are poison."

"Until Minnesota. Then I may have to cash in my rain check."

"Rain check?" She paused for a moment to think. "Oh, that's right! I still owe you a date with a beautiful woman."

"I think I've earned a free upgrade to smokin' hot. Don't you?"

"There are limits to my matchmaking talents, you know." She looked over at me, clearly hoping for a reaction. When I gave her none, she took a deep breath and said, "Okay, fine. Smokin' hot it is."

Rather than cut over to the interstate highway, we stuck to

the backroads and followed a lonely two-lane road over the San Juan Mountains. When we finally pulled into a hotel parking lot in Alamosa, we both breathed sighs of relief. If we could avoid trouble in Colorado, we had only two more states to go.

We checked in and carried our bags to our room. "Do you feel like going out for breakfast?" I asked.

"No."

"Do you want to take a shower?

"More than I've ever wanted to in my entire life."

"It's all yours. Go for it."

While Nellie made a valiant attempt to use up the hotel's entire hot water supply, I went in search of some cash and some food. A local bank allowed me to withdraw ten thousand dollars from my account. I doubted I'd need that much, but I decided that from now on I was going to hoard as much cash as possible. If I needed it for a bribe or any other reason, I'd have it.

When I returned to the hotel with takeout from a local café, Nellie was brushing her hair, and her skin was still red from the hot shower.

"That smells delicious!" she said.

After we enjoyed the food, I took my turn in the shower. When I stepped out of the bathroom, I found Nellie fast asleep on our king-sized bed. I covered her up and crawled under the blankets with her. When she began twitching through a dream, I resisted the urge to open my eyes and watch. I was a strong modern man. I was master of my emotions! I rolled over to the far edge of the bed and fell asleep.

* * *

Nellie and I woke up a little before five and forced ourselves to get dressed and head out for dinner. We chose a restaurant just down the street from the college. The parking lot was packed, which we took as a sign that the food was good.

As we entered, an enthusiastic hostess greeted us. "Welcome

to ladies night! All women eat for half price."

Nellie grabbed my elbow.

"It'll be okay," I said with a smile. But, of course, now she had planted the idea in my head. After we sat down and ordered, I had to play it for all it was worth: "What do you think of her? . . . Did you see how she looked at you? . . . She's cute. . . . Have you ever seen so many beautiful women in one place? . . . Oh, my! Look at—"

She kicked me in the shin.

I totally deserved it.

CHAPTER 10

Smokin' Hot and Spunky

Three days later, we reached the Canadian border. Having lived in Minnesota through college, I had traveled on Interstate 35 many times. Back then, the border between Minnesota and Iowa was little more than a simple sign. Now, we encountered a short line of traffic that branched into multiple lanes, each of which led to a booth occupied by armed customs agents. We stayed to the far right and entered through one of the lines for visitors needing temporary passports.

Overall, the process was relatively painless, and we were on our way in less than an hour. I had to laugh at the first Canadian road sign we saw: "Welcome to Minnesota: Land of 10,000 Lakes, Modern Automobiles, Equal Rights, and the 2055 Grey Cup Champion Minnesota Vikings." Having grown up as a Vikings fan, my heart had been ripped out by more last-second losses than I could remember. It was nice to see that my beloved team had finally found a football league where they could win a championship.

One thing I had noticed as we traveled north from New Mexico was that the land gradually began to look less parched, or at least the land that wasn't fire-scorched looked that way. Global warming was still a serious problem, but the states to the north hadn't been hit quite as hard. Of course, the warmer temperatures still moved north, and they didn't stop at state, province, or country borders. They continued all the way to the North Pole. When the United States abandoned virtually all conservation measures, numerous other industrialized countries followed their lead. So just like alligators and manatees had become extinct in the South, polar bears and wolverines had become extinct in the North. Even so, at first glance, Minnesota still looked like the Minnesota of my teenage years—beautiful and green. Then I remembered it was late November.

We drove straight to Duluth and reached the city early in the evening. We selected a hotel on the Lake Superior waterfront, Fitger's Inn. The hotel got its name from the old Fitger Brewing Company, which occupied the building until 1972. Now the renovated structure contained the hotel and a variety of restaurants and shops.

As we walked into the lobby, I said, "We don't have to pretend we're married anymore. If you want, we can get separate rooms."

"Is that what *you* want?"

"Not necessarily."

"Then let's share a room. We only have each other in this world, and I don't want to be all alone."

"I don't want to be alone either."

Since we planned to stay in Duluth until we figured out what to do with our lives, I reserved the penthouse suite for an entire week. I was surprised it was available, but a last-minute cancellation worked in our favor. Eventually, I'd have to conserve my money and find a job, but for the time being, we planned to live it up, and live it up good.

We started this new phase of our lives by calling room service and having our dinner—complete with an expensive bottle of legal wine—outside on our private balcony, which overlooked Lake Superior. The evening was perfect, with the bright moon reflecting off the lake and the waves gently lapping the shore. And us, the odd couple, enjoying each other's company, laughing about our adventures, and being totally unromantic in the most romantic setting imaginable.

* * *

In the morning, I did some research and confirmed that I had been largely correct in my assumption that Duluth was doing okay in a climate-changed world. Some people enjoyed the notoriously cold city's warmer temperatures, and Lake Superior prevented it from suffering the water shortages so many other cities were suffering. Still, severe storms had increased, and many of the bird species that used to stop at Hawk Ridge during their migrations hadn't been seen in years.

As for technology in 2056 Minnesota, it wasn't retro, like in the United States, but it wasn't as advanced as I had anticipated either. If I had been asked to guess what year it was, I would have said 2030. My theory was that when the United States headed backward, it stunted the advancement of other countries as well. After all, the United States had led the world in so many things for so many years. Eventually, countries like Canada grabbed the reins of leadership and began moving technology forward again. So while many items looked sleeker, shinier, and smaller than they did in 2020, there were still no flying cars or android servants.

* * *

After breakfast, I was eager to tour the city, both to see how it had physically changed and to show Nellie places that were once my favorite haunts. First, we headed to Park Point, a seven-mile long sand peninsula with a road down the middle. There, we took off our shoes, played on the beach, and waded in Lake Superior. Everything seemed the same as it had been during my time, except that Park Point in late November back then was a place to freeze your ass off, not a place to enjoy warm sand squishing between your toes.

As we departed Park Point, I glanced to my right and said,

"I can't believe it! Grandma's Saloon & Grill is still in business. I wonder if their food is still as good as it used to be."

"Shall we go there for lunch?"

"Why don't we make it dinner? I doubt that all November days in Duluth are going to be this perfect. Tomorrow might be rainy and cold. Let's take a drive past my old house and old high school and continue up the North Shore. I have a lunch idea you're going to love."

I was pleased to see that the house I had grown up in was still there—albeit with bright blue siding instead of white—and disappointed to see that my old high school had been torn down and replaced with an apartment building. Visible changes continued as we drove northeast out of town. Most noticeable were housing developments that added a few more miles to the city. At one time, Duluth was losing its population. Now it was a trendy place for up-and-comers to relocate to.

Ten minutes out of town, I found what I was looking for: a store that sold cheese and smoked whitefish. I purchased an ample supply of both, along with a box of crackers and a bottle of wine. "I'm going to take you on a classic northern Minnesota picnic," I said with a smile. "And remember, I'm the inventor of the picnic."

Minutes later, we found a place to park along the North Shore Drive, a two-lane road that parallels Lake Superior. We climbed over a line of boulders and walked down to the lake. Unlike the sandy shore at Park Point, the shore here consisted of wide, densely packed, wave-worn rocks and outcrops interspersed with occasional bands of smaller rocks.

We walked the shoreline, looking for agates and watching the gentle waves roll in. Eventually, we found a secluded spot that was perfect for our picnic.

Nellie licked her lips. "Mmm. I've never had smoked whitefish and cheese on crackers before. You're right. I do love it!"

"Minnesota has many special foods, both native and adopted. Another favorite of mine is smelt. They're a small, silvery fish that lives in the lake. Every spring they go up the local rivers to spawn. People used to be able to just stick nets into the water and pull out dozens at a time, but even during my childhood, their numbers were a fraction of what they used to be. I'd be surprised if the smelt run even exists anymore. One other *delicacy,* and I'm being extremely loose with the word, is lutefisk. It's dried codfish soaked in lye."

Nellie cringed. "Ew!"

"I know. I feel the same way. To make it edible, the lye is removed via more soaking, and then the fish is baked, steamed, or boiled. The result is a fish that jiggles on your plate and slides down your throat. It's definitely an acquired taste."

"Minnesota is kind of quirky, but I like what I've seen so far."

"Having lived in both Minnesota and Montana, I used to have a difficult time deciding which I liked better. Now, of course, since they're under vastly different governments, there is no comparison. Minnesota is the place to be."

"Do you think we should live here?"

"We?" I laughed. "Our relationship could get quite complicated."

"We could do it!" She smiled mischievously. "We'll buy a special house together. It will have a large middle section where you and I will live, a wing on the left for the lesbian women, and a wing on the right for the heterosexual women."

"Ha! I'll have to remember that. Maybe in this new life, I'll give up being a travel writer and become a men's magazine writer instead. With a little tweaking, your suggestion could become an excellent first story. Hmm. . . . Can we steal women from each other's side?"

"Good luck with that! Perhaps we'll need a bisexual wing too."

"Are we ever going to actually sleep?"

"Well . . . maybe my idea needs some more thought."

"Here's what I think. You and I have known each other for two weeks. Granted, they've been fun, intense, adventure-filled weeks, but we have no reason to rush. We have the hotel suite for six more nights and can extend our stay if we want. If we both like it here, we can find an apartment with a short-term lease, look for jobs, and apply for Canadian citizenship. From there, let's see what happens."

"I can go for that."

"One more thing."

"What?"

"The last time I had sex with a woman was before you were born. Okay, that sounds worse than it really is, but it's time."

"Does that mean you're calling in your rain check tonight?"

"Hopefully, I can still remember how to woo a woman without help, but yes."

"Oh, this is going to be so much fun!"

We packed up the remains of our picnic and started back toward the car. "Wait! There's the perfect skipping rock." I picked it up and let it rip.

Nellie looked out over the lake. "Eight skips. Is that good?"

"Well, as you know, I did hold the world rock-skipping record for sixty-seven million years."

"Can you show me how?"

"Sure. First, you find a flat rock . . . like this one. Then you lean over, like this, and—"

She let loose with a ten-skipper and grinned from ear to ear. "Hmm. Beginner's luck, I guess."

I'd been had.

* * *

We returned to the hotel and relaxed for a bit before readying ourselves to go out for dinner. Nellie also took the opportunity to do a little shopping in a boutique housed in the same building as our hotel. There, she found a dress that looked smashing on her. As for me, my dyed skin had lightened up considerably in recent days, and for the first time in a long time, I felt as if I looked like myself.

Nellie clutched my arm as soon as we reached the entrance

to Grandma's Saloon & Grill. When the hostess led us to the table we had reserved, heads turned to gawk at us as if we were a celebrity couple.

"Don't do that!" I whispered. "I'm never gonna get laid if people think we're attached."

"I'm just narrowing down the field for you. The smokin' hot woman you want will appreciate the challenge."

Once we were seated, I glanced over the top edge of my menu and pointed with my eyes. "I kind of like that blonde behind your right shoulder."

Nellie looked. "No. You're the wrong sex for her."

"How can you tell?"

"I'm pretty good at sensing these things. Unless she's an undercover cop, of course."

We both laughed.

When our dinner arrived, we stopped looking around and savored the restaurant's upbeat ambience, our eclectic meals, and the company of each other. Later, we moved outside to the big top where a band was playing.

From what I had heard through the walls while we were eating, the band had a danceable electronic sound with a definite rock and roll edge. I had no idea if their songs were originals or covers from after my time, but that didn't matter. I was just pleased to know that legal rock and roll was still thriving in my old hometown.

"Let's dance!" Nellie shouted.

Our dancing went pretty much as it did in New New Orleans, with Nellie becoming the main attraction. After a few songs, a beautiful woman with shoulder-length auburn hair, bangs, and a narrow nose walked onto the floor to dance with a couple other women. Nellie made eye contact with me and mouthed that she was going to the restroom. I took the opportunity to introduce myself to the woman, and soon we were dancing.

Part of me, I suppose, was looking for a one-night stand, but in reality, that's not what I'm about. I'd much rather find someone

I can mentally connect with, so the initial night has the potential to lead to something long-term. For that reason, when the band took a break, I bought Alison a drink and invited her to my table with the intention of getting to know her. When Nellie joined us, I gave her a *what-are-you-doing-here?* look, which she simply ignored.

She reached out to shake Alison's hand. "Hi. I'm Nellie, Marty's friend. I just want to let you know that he's a great guy, and I'm not competition in any way." Then she put a hand beside her face and stage whispered, "Of course, I could be competition for the blonde-haired woman who is talking to the brunette over there."

"Hi Nellie. I'm Alison, and I'm not worried about any competition."

Nellie's eyes shot toward me. "Ooh! She's spunky. I like her, Marty."

"I might like her too. . . . If I ever get the chance to talk to her."

"Oh! I'm sorry. Why don't you give me the key to our hotel room? I'll take a cab back and wait for you there. Just knock loud when you return."

"Wait. You two are sharing a hotel room?" Alison asked.

"Yes, at Fitger's Inn," Nellie said with exuberance. "We have the penthouse suite with an *amazing* king-sized bed."

"A *single* king-sized bed?"

"That's the one!"

I buried my face in my hands.

When I looked up, Nellie stood, put her fists on her hips, and said, "My work here is done. I'm sure you two have lots to talk about." She winked. "Good night, y'all."

I handed the key card to her along with some cash for a taxi. Then I turned back to Alison, fully expecting to find her hurrying away in the opposite direction.

Instead, she gave me a half-smile and said, "I don't know why I'm still sitting here. Am I curious? Or am I just waiting for the proper moment to pour this drink into your lap?"

"Oh, you don't want to waste that. There's high-quality alcohol in there. Just think of all the thirsty people in the United States who would love to have your drink."

She laughed, and our eyes locked for a moment before she looked down and stirred her drink with a finger.

I continued. "This isn't what it looks like. Let me start from the beginning. . . ."

I told Alison about Nellie and our road trip adventures, but of course left out everything about the Krichards and time traveling. That information could wait until I knew if our relationship was going to last more than a single night. For now, I was just happy that Nellie's little performance didn't totally freak her out. In fact, perhaps as Nellie intended, Alison and I had something in common to talk and laugh about, thereby avoiding much of the awkward getting-to-know-you small talk.

When the band kicked into their next set, Alison and I hit the dance floor again. She couldn't move like Nellie, but then few people exhibited that kind of grace and allure. Instead, we were more or less equals as dancers—paying attention to each other, rather than being the center of attention.

After several songs, Alison said, "Would you like to go someplace quieter? I have a house up on Skyline Parkway with a porch that has a breathtaking view of the lake."

"That sounds nice. I'll follow you in my car."

She grabbed my hand and led me out to the parking lot. My T-bird really stuck out, especially since it was one of the few gas-powered vehicles in the city. Her car, on the other hand, looked much more appropriate for 2056. It was a sporty, solar-powered two-door, made in Canada. According to Alison, the manufacturer built solar cells into every inch of its exterior. Those cells not only powered the vehicle during the day, but they also charged an efficient battery that could keep it moving from dusk to dawn.

Skyline Parkway had been a favorite of mine in high school. Much of Duluth is on a hill, and the parkway runs along the side of that hill, overlooking both downtown and Lake Superior. Back then, the road's most important feature was that it had several spots where you could take a date and park in relative privacy. I had to laugh that once again I was heading to that parkway to be with a woman.

Our drive didn't take long, and soon I was following Alison into a small, single-story house that appeared to be about fifty years old.

"I'm going to open a bottle of wine," she said. "Do you prefer red or white?"

"Red, if that's okay with you."

"I was hoping you'd say that." She popped the cork, filled two glasses, and handed one to me. "C'mon. I'm going to show you why I live on the hill."

She slid open the screen door, stepped onto the back porch, and motioned for me to sit next to her on the padded wooden porch swing. We set our wine on a side table, and she snuggled under my arm.

"Isn't this view amazing? When this house became available, I was ready to buy it the second the real estate agent took me out here."

Of all the nighttime cityscapes I'd seen in my life, none could beat the twinkling lights of downtown Duluth framed by the night sky and its reflection off the lake. We glided in the swing and talked for at least an hour.

When our conversation slowed, Alison slid her hand under my shirt and kissed me deeply. "Shall we move to someplace more comfortable?" she asked.

"I'd love to," I said.

We kissed our way to the bedroom, leaving a trail of clothes in our wake. Once inside, we paused just long enough for Alison to light a few candles. A great idea, I thought, as I admired her nude body. When you're lucky enough to have a date who is truly smokin' hot, the last thing you want is to lose sight of that person in the dark.

We met on our knees in the middle of the bed and softly kissed. Each touch of our lips made her breathe deeper, and just listening to her breathe was erotic. When she pushed me onto my back, the anticipation was almost unbearable. She kissed me on my earlobe, on my lips, on my neck, on my left nipple, on my right nipple, on my navel, on my—

"Marty, it's Chrissie! Are you there?"

"Chrissie!" I jerked out of bed and poked Alison in the eye. "Oh! I'm so sorry!"

"For what?"

"Not you, Chrissie! I'm talking to someone else. Are you okay?"

"Of course I am. How about you? It took us forever to find you."

"No! No! Hold on for a few minutes. I think I just hurt someone. You'll know I'm talking to you when I begin the sentence with *Chrissie*."

Alison scowled at me with one hand clutching a blanket to her chest and the other covering her eye. "Are you on LSD or hallucinogenic mushrooms or something?"

"No. I'm talking to someone on a spaceship through an implant in my head."

"*Spaceship?* Oh, God! Why do I always attract the nutcases? You need to leave, right now."

"This isn't what it looks like."

"Yeah. I've heard that before!"

"I'm so, so sorry." I backed out of the bedroom, gathering my clothes along the way. When I reached the foyer, I quickly dressed and tried to think of something to say to Alison that would sound rational, but it was hopeless. I opened the door and stepped out into the night.

CHAPTER 11

The Patron Saint of Lesbians

Rather than start up a conversation in Alison's driveway or risk crashing the car in my distracted state, I drove about a mile down the road to a pullout I'd used as a teenager. "Chrissie, I'm alone now. We can talk."

"What was that all about?"

"Just, uh . . . a meeting that didn't go so well. Anyway, I'm so excited to hear from you. I thought you were gone forever."

"We would never abandon anyone on a time jump."

"But I saw several news stories on the internet that claimed your ship had disappeared, never to be seen again."

"We did leave, for almost two weeks. We're now hidden on the opposite side of the moon. No one on Earth knows we're here other than you."

"Where did you go?"

"First, we just got out of the way. Then we headed fifteen light-years from here to a space station. There, we got our time-travel attachment replaced with a newer model and picked up another Chromosphere Cruiser—a prototype we're supposed to check out and report on after this mission is complete. Everyone was fed up with time-travel mistakes, whether caused by equipment failure or operator malfunctions. Hopefully that's all behind us now."

"I can't wait to see you and everyone else."

"We should be ready to bring you back in twenty-four hours.

We would've contacted you sooner, but we didn't expect you to leave southern Florida. We kept widening the search until we located your implant. Some of us feared that you had drowned or been swallowed by some aquatic animal that isn't yet extinct. Now that we know where you are, Tina is busy working on pinpointing an exact time and place to pick you up."

"Tina! How can she still have her job?"

"Oh, she apologized and promised to never, ever send someone on an unauthorized time jump again."

"That's all? If she had done something similar on an Earth ship, she would have been court martialed and sentenced to life in prison—at minimum."

"Obviously, we're a more forgiving species. If it makes you feel any better, the captain also docked her the equivalent of a week's pay."

"Actually, I forgive Tina too. After all, if it hadn't been for her, I wouldn't have met a very special woman here."

"A woman?"

"Yes. Her name is Nellie."

"And just how special is she?"

"Are you jealous?"

"I don't know. Should I be?"

"No. Chrissie, my feelings for you haven't changed one bit. It's just that . . . Well, the United States Tina sent me to is even more extreme than it was under President Handley. Nellie is a lesbian, and that's an imprisonable offense in 2056 America. We're in Canada now, but I think she'll be happier if we take her with us."

"Why?"

"Once we make the correction to history we've been trying to make, she'll have a much more accepting planet to go back to."

"She'll disappear from existence."

"What! . . . Why?"

"Remember our conversation near the end of your first time jump?"

"Um . . . Do you mean about making sure I came from a stable family line?"

"Yes. We can't send anyone back in time to correct an error if that correction will cause that person not to exist in the first place. In Nellie's case, I'm afraid that even a stable family line can't save her because—"

"The timeline she was born in won't ever exist."

"Exactly!"

"Then I won't do it."

"Think about this carefully, Marty. Is one person more important than preventing the millions of deaths caused by religion-inspired wars? Is one person more important than preventing the global warming-induced extinctions, droughts, and famines that have already started and will only get worse? Is one person more important than preventing the United States from enduring President Handley's reign and ultimately becoming the country you've witnessed during the past two weeks?"

"Oh, God. I have to do it."

"If it's any consolation, she won't feel a thing."

"Maybe *she* won't, but *I* sure as hell will."

"Is she really that special to you?"

"She's the closest thing I've had to a sister since my real one died—and then some."

"Let me think for a second. . . . It's not much of a compromise, but we can bring her up on the ship with us. She'll still disappear when you correct the past, but at least you'll be with her until the last moment, and the rest of us will make sure she gets the best of everything we have to offer. Her final days will be happy ones."

"I need to talk this over with Nellie."

"If you are uncomfortable jumping back at this time tomorrow, I can delay things up here and give you an additional day."

"Thank you, Chrissie. . . . Oh, two more things."

"Sure."

"You have to take Nellie first. I'll wait for the next cycle. I won't risk getting back on the ship, having something go wrong, and Nellie ending up all alone in Duluth waiting to go poof."

"That won't be necessary. Our new time-travel attachment features our latest technology. We can now transport two people at a time as long as they are in a tight embrace. Also, we need only three hours between recharge cycles."

"Wonderful."

"And what is the second thing?"

"Is there any way I can temporarily turn off my communications implant? It will be much easier for me to talk with Nellie if I know the entire ship isn't listening in."

"You can't turn it off on your end, but I can on mine. It's common practice on our ship to respect each other's privacy. That's why neither of us had to worry about anyone listening in when we were space camping. I'll mute communications for twenty hours. Just know that if you get into any unforeseen trouble, the implant has a safety feature that will override the mute."

"How do I activate that?"

"Extreme pain. Just have Nellie drop a brick on your foot or slam one of your fingers in a door, and we'll be in touch in seconds."

"Hmm. I think I'll stay out of trouble. Talk to you tomorrow night."

"Goodbye, Marty. I miss you, and I'm so sorry for all of this."

"I miss you too, Chrissie."

* * *

I knocked on the hotel room door, and Nellie let me in.

"I didn't expect you back so soon. Don't you believe in fore—" She stopped short when she noticed the somber look on my face. "Oh, dear. What happened?"

"Let's pour some stiff drinks and sit down."

Once we made ourselves comfortable, I told Nellie everything. Naturally, she thought my jump-out-of-bed, poke-in-the-eye maneuver was hilarious. Someday, I suppose, I will too. Then

I moved on to time travel and the effect it would have on her and the rest of the world.

"What are you so upset about?" she said. "The last two weeks have been the best of my life. Except for, of course, that little bondage incident in Santa Fe. If not for time travel, I'd still be back in Immokalee wearing a housedress and dodging the next man my father tried to force on me. Sure, I'd love to avoid going *poof,* as you called it, but if you pass up the opportunity to correct the toxic course of our planet on my behalf, I'll have to live with that knowledge for the rest of my life. Ultimately, I'd end up killing myself, and then you. Okay, maybe not in that order."

I reached over and grasped Nellie's hand. "You're taking this really well."

"Hey, I've lived a lifetime since I met you. Now I get to visit a spaceship and become the Patron Saint of Lesbians. It doesn't get any better than that."

"Do you want to head up to the ship as soon as they're ready for us, or should I have Chrissie delay our pickup?"

"That depends. Are there any single lesbians up there?"

"Hmm. I've never had any reason to ask. Eleven of the nineteen Krichards are women, and I've noticed only a few serious male-female relationships. So I'd be surprised if there aren't several of them."

"Then I'll be ready to go tomorrow night."

* * *

A knock on our door woke us both up shortly before eight.

I yelled from the bed, "We don't need housekeeping today. Please let us sleep. Thank you."

Nellie hit me with a pillow.

"Hey! What was that for?"

"That's our breakfast."

"Breakfast?" I mumbled. "I didn't order any breakfast."

"You didn't, but *I* did."

She slipped into a robe and hurried to the door to retrieve our meal before the room service attendant departed. Then she set the tray between us, and we propped ourselves up with some pillows. Neither of us said a word as we downed our breakfasts and sipped our coffees.

When we finished, I felt much more awake. I moved our breakfast tray over to the table by the couch, then rejoined Nellie on the bed and gave her a weak smile.

She returned my smile with one of enthusiasm and said, "Today is my last day on Earth, so I get to call the shots. First, we're going to have a pillow fight. Then, while you're in the shower, I'm going to call my mother and cry my eyes out. After that, I'm going to take a shower and give you that flash of skin I know you've always wanted to see. And finally, we're going to rip this town apart until it's time to leave."

"Um. . . . Can we change the order of that so you flash me the skin *before* I jump into the shower?"

"Oh, you dirty boy!" She pummeled me with a pillow, and the fight was on.

I hadn't enjoyed a proper pillow fight since I was a kid battling my sister. The difference now was that we had a lot more pillows in our arsenal, and we both figured out that we could make the down-filled artillery explode if we swung them just right. And that was half the fun. Even stubborn pillows that initially refused to explode were doomed because we'd give them artificial help until they did.

Within minutes, our room was totally trashed—feathers flying everywhere—with us sprawled on the bed, breathing hard, and laughing. We looked into each other's eyes, and an aura of seriousness overtook the room.

I kissed Nellie on the forehead and said, "My phone is on the table by the couch. You should call your mother." I walked to the opposite side of the room, pulled my clothes for the day out of the dresser, and stepped into the bathroom.

"Marty!"

I stepped back out to see Nellie grinning at me—totally naked. She was the most beautiful creature I'd ever seen. I held out my right hand—fingers splayed, palm to the ground—and wiggled it from side to side. "Meh," I said. As I turned to reverse course, the last remaining pillow flew past my ear.

* * *

Nellie stood on our hotel room balcony with her post-shower coffee, watching boats go by. She looked back through the open door. "Sailing! I wanna add that to our list of things to do today. I used to go out in the Gulf of Mexico with my dad when I was a kid."

I joined her on the balcony carrying a coffee of my own. "Do you still remember how?"

She arched an eyebrow. "Enough to keep us from capsizing."

"Finding a sailboat on short notice may be a challenge."

"That's what the concierge is for. Just hand him a big wad of bills, and let him do the work."

"Great idea. And while he does that, we can go to the bank and see how much more cash I can get out of my debit card."

"Why?" She lifted her cup, inhaled the steam, and sipped.

"At one time it was President Handley's money, and I want to give away as much of it as I can before we go."

"What good will that do? Won't all of it disappear when you change the timeline?"

"If that happens, the money will give only a fleeting boost to whoever receives it. But should my mission fail, who knows how long that boost will last?"

"That sounds fun. We'll be Robin Hood in the morning, Magellan in the afternoon, Fred Astaire and Ginger Rogers in the evening, and Picard and Janeway after midnight."

"Picard? Look at all my hair. I want to be Kirk."

She reached over and mussed up my hair. "Okay, you can be Kirk."

We packed a bag of extra clothes and took the elevator to the main floor. There we found the concierge and gave him eight thousand dollars to cover his efforts, the damage from our pillow fight, and a six-hour sailboat rental with a spectacular catered dinner.

Next, we drove down the street to a local bank and spoke directly with the president. At first, she was going to limit me to twenty thousand dollars. Then we came to an understanding: The bank would give me one-half million dollars cash if I gave them a twenty-five-thousand-dollar management fee. For that fee, they would take possession of my debit card and distribute the remaining funds to the list of environmental, human rights, and women's organizations Nellie and I wrote down. It was a win for everyone.

An hour later, some bank employees helped us carry bags of money out to my T-bird. Since we were looking for volume, we requested a variety of small and large denomination bills. Consequently, we had enough bags to cover both the back floor and the back seat.

As we pulled away from the curb, I said to Nellie, "Just in case something goes wrong, and we end up stuck here longer than anticipated, take out ten thousand dollars for each of us, and throw five thousand into the glove box."

While she divvied up the money, I drove west toward Morgan Park. Although a lot had changed since I resided in Duluth, I remembered Morgan Park as an impoverished neighborhood. Originally, it was a thriving, planned community, built by U.S. Steel in the early 1900s, but when the company departed, so did the jobs. Whether or not the people there were still experiencing tough times, it seemed like a good place to start.

I parked at the corner of 88th Avenue West and Idaho Street and lowered the top. Nellie positioned herself in the back with her feet on some of the bags and her buttocks on the trunk. After she lined up several open bags within easy reach, she practiced her wave and giggled, "I feel like Miss America!"

"By the time this is all over, you may be more famous than she is. Are you ready?" I started the car.

"Commencing Operation Robin Hood!" She threw a handful of cash into the air, only to watch it flutter onto the empty street. "Oh. . . . I assume this will be more fun when there are actually people around to catch it. Should I get out and pick it all up?"

"No. Someone will find it."

Several blocks later, we spotted our first prospects.

Nellie shouted, "Happy New Year!" and tossed some money into the air. That got their attention.

I pushed in a Garbage cassette and cranked the stereo, blaring "Only Happy When It Rains." We continued north on 88th Avenue West, a one-car parade followed by an ever-growing crowd running behind us eagerly scooping up cash.

By the time we left Morgan Park and turned onto Grand Avenue, several hundred people were in tow, including a police officer flashing his lights for us to pull over.

I looked back at Nellie and tilted my head.

She shrugged. "I didn't make a pass at anyone. I swear!"

When the police officer approached, I asked, "Did we do something wrong?"

"I could write you up for a number of things, from being a traffic hazard to . . ." he looked back and leered at Nellie, "riding without a seatbelt."

"Officer," Nellie said, accentuating her Southern accent, "we have all this money we don't need. We're just trying to help people. Surely that's not a crime." She leaned down, both to grab a stack of bills and to give the man an eyeful. "I'd be happy to donate one thousand dollars to your local police charity if you'd be so kind as to be our escort."

The officer took the money, then noticed the crowd staring at us. He cleared his throat and handed it back. "Just give it to the kids, ma'am. Now . . . where to?"

"Take us to Superior Street and follow it through downtown," I said. "I'll honk my horn and flash my lights when we run out of cash."

The officer sauntered back to his car and began leading us toward downtown.

"Male cops are so much more predictable than female cops," Nellie said.

"For you, maybe."

We proceeded slower than the news of our money storm spread. By the time we reached downtown, Superior Street was lined with cheering people, and television news crews were already filming from the roofs of their vans.

Nellie yelled above the fray, "This money isn't gonna last forever. How much farther?"

"We'll pass our hotel in about twelve blocks," I yelled back. "See if you can make it last until then."

Traversing downtown was more hazardous than we anticipated. A few people tried to climb into our car, claiming they merely wanted to help. Fortunately, others came to our aid and yanked them back. Only once did Nellie have to give someone a swift kick. She tossed her last handful of cash into the air three blocks short of our hotel.

When I honked the horn and flashed my lights, the police officer flicked on his siren and waved us around. As soon as we passed, he pulled his car sideways to block traffic so we could escape.

Nellie climbed back into the front seat. "That was so much fun! Now let's go sailing."

* * *

Once I was sure no one was following us, I pulled into a church parking lot and turned off the engine. I handed Nellie my phone and said, "Please call the concierge while I put up the top. We'll have a better chance of getting to the sailboat unmolested if we don't stick out so much."

Minutes later, Nellie completed her call and said, "The boat is ready, and the caterer will deliver our dinner in a half an hour. We're supposed to go to the marina on Park Point. It's on the bay side, a short distance beyond the Aerial Lift Bridge."

We headed there and soon found ourselves crossing Superior Street. People were still milling about, and our top-up trick fooled no one. Even so, rather than pursue us, everyone elected either to wave or flash a thumbs-up. Apparently, *Minnesota nice* was still in vogue after all these years.

A man was waiting for us when we pulled into the marina parking lot. He introduced himself as Phil and handed me a clipboard with our rental agreement. I initialed and signed everything without bothering to read it. Then he took us to our boat and started to explain the basics to me.

I held up an open hand to stop him. "Nellie is the sailor, not me."

If Phil was embarrassed, he didn't show it. He simply turned to face her and continued with the rest of his instructions. I listened and tried to absorb as much as I could, but when our caterer arrived with our dinner, I extracted myself from the nautical conversation and took care of loading our food onto the boat.

Soon we were on our way in a beautiful twenty-seven-foot sloop with a twenty-eight-foot mainsail, a small but comfortable cabin, and a battery-powered inboard motor. Since we were on the sheltered bayside of Park Point, we used the motor to travel through Superior Bay and around the tip of the peninsula. Once we hit open water, we hoisted the sails and headed northeast toward the town of Two Harbors.

Even though I had sailed a few times in my youth, I remembered very little that was useful. Nellie, on the other hand, had been overly modest about her sailing abilities and handled the sloop like a pro. My duties were relegated to trimming the sails, as instructed, and getting out of the way when necessary.

Neither of us was hungry yet, so we decided to sail for roughly two hours, then reverse course and have dinner on the way back. We weren't concerned about our food getting cold since it was packed in insulated containers. There was also a stove in the cabin if anything needed warming up.

Lake Superior is a beautiful lake to view from the shore. It's even more stunning to view from a boat, with rugged cliffs and rocky shoreline on one side and sky-blue water as far as the eye can see on the other. Nellie stood back at the rudder with her hair blowing in the wind and her face beaming with contentment.

Sunset happened around six o'clock, so we made sure Duluth was in sight before it got too dark. Then we lowered our sails, unpacked our dinner, and drifted.

Our caterer had prepared a meal fit for someone living her last day on Earth. From Canadian lobsters to stuffed pastries to smoked salmon to strawberry cheesecake to an amazing salad, there was more food than we could ever hope to eat. And best of all, no calorie counting was allowed.

We opened a bottle of fine wine and toasted to everything we could possibly toast to as we watched Duluth light up before our eyes. Eventually, we turned on the motor and let the GPS guide us back to the marina. This time we took the shortcut under the Aerial Lift Bridge, the famous landmark that joins Duluth to Park Point. The bridge rises high enough for seven-hundred-foot-long *salties* and thousand-foot-long *lakers* to pass underneath it. It will also rise to accommodate a mere twenty-seven-foot-long sailboat occupied by two people too full to move.

"Are you ready for some serious dancing?" Nellie asked after we docked the boat.

"As long as you don't get embarrassed if I throw up on the dance floor," I said.

"Grandma's again?"

"Duluth has changed too much for me to suggest anywhere else."

Since the marina and Grandma's were less than a mile apart, we soon had drinks in hand at our table inside the big top. We were glad to see that the band from the previous night was there again. And I might be wrong, but I think they were glad to see us—or at least Nellie—as well. The two of us danced for several songs before I retired to our table and watched Nellie dance with just about everyone who asked her, male and female alike.

I jotted a note on a piece of paper. When the band took a break, I walked up to the stage and handed it to the lead singer, along with a thousand dollars.

The singer's eyes lit up. "I haven't heard that song in years! I'll go over it in the dressing room with the guys. It may not be perfect, but we'll play it next set."

As long as I was on my feet, I decided to head to the men's room. Many of the other male patrons obviously had the same idea because I ended up in a line that started just inside the door. When a urinal finally opened up, I assumed the position, unzipped my fly, and—

"Marty, it's Chrissie! Are you there?"

I jerked back. "You have the worst timing!"

"Oh? Another meeting?"

"No. I'm in a restroom standing at a urinal with a line of men behind me, and now they all think I'm talking to myself."

She laughed. "I'll give you a second. . . . Hey. While you're doing that, there are a bunch of people here who would love to say hi to you."

"Hi, Marty!" several female voices shouted in unison.

"Ladies!" Clarence boomed. "What are you doing? Let the poor man pee."

"Oh, sorry," Chrissie said. "I wouldn't want you to freeze up."

I zipped my fly. "It's a little late for that. Hold on." I worked my way through the crowd and stepped out into the parking lot. "Okay, we can talk now."

"We'll be ready to pick you up tonight at one thirty. Will that work, or do you need another day?"

"Tonight is fine."

"Great. Tina will lock on to the coordinates beside a place called Enger Tower. Do you know where that is?"

"Oh, yeah." A flood of memories washed over me. Enger Tower overlooked the city, about two miles from Alison's house. The cylindrical eighty-foot-tall structure looked more like it belonged in medieval Spain than twenty-first-century Duluth, and it was another favorite hangout of mine in high school.

"Wonderful. We'll see you soon."

"I'm looking forward to it. In the meantime, can you mute communications again?"

"Consider it done. I'll unmute at one twenty-five."

After stopping at the less-crowded inside bar to grab a drink, I returned to the big top. The band had resumed playing, and Nellie was already dancing.

Several songs later, she joined me at the table for a rest. "I've been looking all over for you. Where were you?"

"In the parking lot, speaking with Chrissie. They're picking us up at one thirty."

"This is really happening, isn't it?"

I nodded.

The band wrapped up their current song, and the lead singer raised his hands to hush the crowd. "We have a special request. It's a golden oldie, from Marty to Nellie."

Nellie looked at me with a huge smile of anticipation. When the keyboardist ripped into the long organ intro, she recognized the song immediately and let out a scream, "Oh, my God! This is perfect!"

She grabbed my hand and pulled me onto the floor. We danced—or should I say *partied?*—like it was 1999.

* * *

At a quarter past midnight, we said goodbye to all the temporary friends we made at Grandma's and walked out to the car.

"We'll be on the Krichard ship in a little over an hour. How much of your ten grand do you have left?" I asked.

"A little more than half of it. I only bought a few rounds of drinks for the house."

"There's no reason to bring it with us. Give me everything you've got, plus the five thousand in the glove box."

After she handed me the cash, I ran back into Grandma's, found the manager, and asked for two large envelopes and two pieces of paper. I pocketed one of each. Then I wrote a note that said, *In memory of Prince* and placed it and the money in the envelope I kept out. When the band finished their current song, I handed it to the lead singer and returned to the car.

"All set?" Nellie asked.

"Almost. We have one more stop to make."

Ten minutes later, I parked the car just down the street from Alison's house and quickly wrote another note: "Dear Alison, My deepest apologies for last night. As unbelievable as it seems, I really was talking to someone on a spaceship. I'm going there now. And since I can't take my possessions with me, here's all my cash, the title to my T-bird, and a set of keys. You'll find the car at Enger Tower with the other set of keys locked in the glove box. I thoroughly enjoyed the few hours we spent together. Had we met at another time, perhaps . . . Marty."

I sealed the note, the title, the keys, and roughly nine thousand dollars in the remaining envelope. Then, like a kid playing Ding Dong Ditch It, I slipped the envelope between the screen door and the front door of her house, rang the bell, and high-tailed it back to the car.

From there, we headed directly to Enger Tower and reached the parking lot a little after one. A bright green beacon illuminated the top of the tower, but it was pitch black inside. I opened the trunk and grabbed the battery-powered lantern I had purchased in Santa Fe, then tossed the keys into the glove box and locked both it and the car.

"We still have a few minutes," I said. "Let's climb to the top."

I held the lantern in front of us as we walked the paved path to the tower and continued up the short flight of stairs to the open entrance.

"It looks haunted," Nellie said.

"That's what I used to tell the girls I brought up here."

"Some date you were!"

"Well, if you ask Alison, I'm not any better as a date now."

We followed the spiral stairway to the top and looked out over Duluth.

"This is just stunning, both the view and the tower. Is this where you used to kiss the girls?"

"I tried to, anyway," I said, pointing. "Over there, across the bay, is Superior, Wisconsin. I used to joke that Enger Tower was used as a lookout during the great Duluth-Superior War. Now that Superior is in a separate country, I suppose that old joke isn't as farfetched as it used to be."

"Marty, it's Chrissie! Are you there?"

I pointed to my head. "Yes, Chrissie, I'm here."

"The captain has moved the ship into position. Where are you?"

"I'm with Nellie at the top of Enger Tower."

"Tina doesn't want you in the tower. Go down and stand just outside. We'll grab you in exactly four minutes."

"We're on our way." I looked at Nellie. "It's time."

As we descended the stairs, I glanced out one of the wall openings and spotted the headlights of a car entering the parking lot.

Nellie spied the lights too and said, "Ah, I see you're not the only one who brings dates here in the dead of night."

"Yes, and we're getting out of here just in time."

We continued our downward spiral and were soon back outside and in position. I set the lantern on the ground and said, "We're ready Chrissie."

"Twenty seconds. Don't forget to hold each other tight."

Suddenly, a dark figure came running up the path and shouted, "Marty!"

I recognized the voice immediately.

"Ten seconds."

Our eyes locked as she neared. "Stay back, Alison!" I hugged Nellie as tight as I could.

Whoosh!

Everything went white.

Everything went colorful.

CHAPTER 12

Smarter Than a Krichard Scientist

Holding Nellie in my arms calmed my claustrophobia. In fact, when Tina opened the hatch and pulled us out, I felt a twinge of disappointment.

"Welcome back, Marty Mann," Tina said aloud before whispering in my ear, "I'm so sorry."

"Don't worry about it," I whispered back. "All is forgiven."

Tina tilted her head. "And who is this?"

"Hi. I'm Nellie. You must be Tina." As the two shook hands, Nellie's eyes widened to take in all the strange and colorful sights of being on a Krichard spaceship, including a second colorful woman.

"Welcome aboard, Nellie. I'm Chrissie." She reached out a hand. "Marty has told me wonderful things about you."

"Likewise, and thank you. It's so nice to finally meet some of the voices in his head."

"Oh, you're funny!" Tina said, her eyelashes flickering pink. "I'm sure Marty and Chrissie are just dying for a moment alone together. Come with me. I'll give you the grand tour of the ship, introduce you to the crew, and show you to your quarters."

"I'd love that." She gave Chrissie and me a quick wave and smile and followed Tina into the hallway.

"She's beautiful!" Chrissie said, her eyelashes twinkling green.

"I'm pretty sure Tina thinks so as well."

"You noticed that too."

"Tina's heterosexual. Isn't she?"

"Marty, you should know us well enough by now to understand that we don't follow the same rules as humans do. Close to half of our population is bisexual, and most have at least experimented with the same sex once or twice. How do you know what you like or dislike if you don't try it?"

"Although I don't personally need to experiment with men to know that I prefer women, I'm open-minded enough to appreciate what you're saying. In fact, many humans are right there with your people. Still, how can a species like yours be advanced in so many ways and still support the archaic concept of unclaimed males?"

"That tradition dates back thousands of years. We all know it's archaic, and if the males complained, we'd undoubtedly abolish it. I guess we just keep it because it's fun."

"Do you have a similar tradition for unclaimed females?"

"Certainly not!"

"So do you think—"

Chrissie put a finger to my lips. "What I think, Marty, is that you're doing way too much talking. You haven't even kissed me yet."

"Hmm. Well, let's take care of that right now."

As we kissed and I once again tasted her soft, sweet lips, my brain and heart finally called a truce and properly compartmentalized the love I felt for Nellie under I-would-do-anything-for-you platonic and the love I felt for Chrissie under some combination of you-literally-light-up-my-life and you're-so-fucking-hot-I-can't-stand-it.

"That was a pretty good start." Her eyelashes flashed pink. "Would you like to come to my cabin and see where it leads?"

"This claimed male will follow you anywhere."

* * *

I woke up the next morning in Chrissie's bed. A wave of guilt washed over me for leaving Nellie to the sole care of Tina. Then again, Nellie was a natural with strangers, and we had arrived so late. She had probably fallen asleep long before I did. I slid out of bed and padded to the bathroom.

When I returned, a pair of eyes peered at me over the edge of the blanket. "Come back to bed. We have all afternoon to change the world."

Who could argue with that logic?

Unfortunately, logic also dictates that nothing good will ever last as long as you hope it will. As such, the two of us eventually had to pry ourselves apart and out of bed. She had a staff meeting to get to, and my stomach was growling. Hey, I was hungry. The last time I had anything to eat was thirty-six years from now.

I walked down the hall to the cafeteria and found Nellie sitting by herself. "Feeling lonely?" I asked.

She looked up from her plate and smiled. "This is the first time I've been alone since I arrived. Everyone here has been tending to my every need, especially Tina."

"It sounds like you two have really hit it off."

"Oh, we have." She paused to consider her words. "When you might go poof on a moment's notice, you don't have the luxury of time to carefully cultivate a relationship."

"I agree. No rules for you. I bet Captain Jagger will even let you fly the ship if you ask."

"What's with all these names anyway? Jagger, Bruce, Clarence, Chrissie, Tina . . . They can't be real, not for aliens anyway."

"They're not. You couldn't pronounce most of their real names if you tried, or at least I couldn't."

"So you named them after rock stars?"

"Uh-huh. They were very accommodating."

She laughed.

I pointed to her plate. "How do you like Krichard food?"

"I'm not sure yet. Some of it's really good, and some of it stings when it hits my tongue."

"They will serve Earth food if you ask for it."

"Oh, no, I like the adventure."

"Marty, Nellie," Captain Jagger summoned over the intercom, "please come to the conference room in ten minutes."

"We'll be there, Captain," I said.

I grabbed a light brunch and wolfed it down. As we stood to head to the conference room, Nellie looked me directly in the eyes. No words were necessary.

* * *

When we arrived, the usual crew was already there, and everyone gave Nellie an over-the-top welcome. She had become, without a doubt, the ship's celebrity.

As soon as Nellie and I took our seats, the captain began. "We've now set a record for the longest time-correction mission in our history. My superiors have grown impatient and ordered me to complete it and move on. Marty, you must make your jump to AD 31 tomorrow afternoon. Tina and Chrissie, please make all the necessary preparations and double-check everything. No screw-ups this time. Nellie, I'm so sorry this has happened to you. If there is anything I can do to make your remaining time on this ship more comfortable, just let me know. If no one has any questions, this meeting is adjourned." He stood as if heading for the door.

Everyone else remained seated.

Tina slapped her palms on the table in rapid succession. "I have a question. When did our superiors become such assholes?"

The captain stared her down as he returned to his chair. "Tina, be careful. I've already forgiven you once on this mission."

Tina's eyelashes flashed fire yellow. "I—no, make that *we*—can't let anyone on our ship cease to exist, at least not without a fight."

"I concur with Tina," Chrissie said. "This isn't what we are about."

Bruce and Clarence nodded in agreement, and Nellie slouched to look small in her chair.

"With all your technology and time-travel experience, there must be *something* you can do," I said.

"Our experience is precisely why further delays are unacceptable. This certainly isn't the first time a problem like this has occurred. Our best scientists have tried everything—from moving the subject to another solar system to impenetrable isolation chambers to moving the subject forward or backward in time—to no avail. We don't know why, but we can't fool time. Once a timeline disappears, so does everything that was created within it."

I ran my fingers through my hair and looked over at the captain. "Your species has studied this. Mine hasn't. And one thing I've learned over the years is that fresh eyes and fresh ideas can sometimes solve what seem to be insurmountable problems."

"No offense, Marty," the captain said, "but your species is technologically far behind ours, and you aren't even a scientist. If we can't come up with a feasible solution, I highly doubt your fresh thinking is capable of doing anything other than delaying the inevitable."

"Let's try anyway." I turned to face Nellie. "When we met in 2056, you were thirty-four years old. Is that correct?"

"Yes."

"Currently, we're in 2020, which is the present as we know it. So from our perspective, you haven't even been born yet."

"I never thought of that!"

I turned back to the captain. "What if we go forward in time and kidnap Nellie's mother just before she gives birth? Nellie could be born right here on the ship, in present time, then we could return her and her mother to where we got them. Nothing would change, except Nellie would now belong to *our* timeline."

No one said a word as the Krichards considered my proposal.

Eventually, Tina flashed an eyelash and said, "Marty's idea just might work."

Bruce looked up from rubbing his temples and added, "We'd have to create a room on the ship that looks exactly like the delivery room on Earth and make sure the mother is so high she can't remember a thing."

I grinned at my human friend. "This could be fun, Nellie. You could be the first person ever to witness your own birth. Live!"

"Hmm. I'll have to think about that."

"I hate to be a pessimist," Chrissie said, "but time-travel departures are so perplexing that it's almost as if some godlike referee is watching to make sure no one cheats time. While Marty's idea seems logical, what if it's conception, not birth, that determines the time Nellie belongs to?"

"Oh, don't say that. Every conservative in America would pounce on that theory. Soon they'd have armed guards around every womb."

"I'm not in any way making a political statement, Marty. I'm just saying we should prepare for both possibilities."

"Kidnap my parents at the moment of my conception?"

My smile widened. "It will be great, Nellie. Not only can you watch your own birth, but you can also watch your own conception."

Nellie glanced around the table as if looking for something to throw at me. When nothing was in reach, she shot me a sisterly glare and playfully stuck out her tongue.

Bruce leaned back in his chair. "So in addition to the delivery room, we will also need to construct a replica of the conception room."

Nellie and I both giggled before she said, "I've never thought of my parents' bedroom as a conception room, but I know their prudish lifestyle made sex anywhere else unlikely. I also know I will be born at the Gulf Coast Medical Center two days earlier than expected."

Everyone turned to the captain, who was cradling his head in his hands. Finally, he looked up. "You're all going to get me fired and this ship recycled. However, Tina is correct about our superiors becoming assholes, and Marty, you may have just out-thought our best scientists."

"And if this works, we'll have come up with a solution that will benefit time-correction missions everywhere," Tina added.

"Captain, what can I do to help?" Clarence asked.

"As security officer, you can conjure up some fathomable reason why I'm temporarily incapacitated and must delay the completion of our mission. Relay that to whoever is working the nightshift at the Department of Time Corrections."

"And the rest of us?" Bruce asked.

"You and Chrissie need to put together a team to construct rooms identical to those in which Nellie will be conceived and born. Also, consult with Ann and Nancy to come up with some sort of drug that will allow Nellie's parents to do what they need to do without remembering anything. Tina, you'll need to do your magic and figure out when, where, and how to accomplish the necessary kidnappings. You'll also need to rig up a portable transporter to move the subjects directly from the airlock to their respective rooms and back. Nellie, please make sure we have as many accurate details as possible about everything. As for you, Marty . . . Hmm. Would you like to learn how to fly the spaceship?"

* * *

After the meeting broke up, I returned to my cabin and realized that for the first time in weeks I had nothing to do. Sure, I could have taken the captain up on his offer to fly the ship, as long as I kept us hidden behind the moon. That, however, seemed too much like sitting on my father's lap as a child and *driving* the car. I considered visiting the euphoria dispenser, but that seemed inappropriate with Nellie's past and future still very much in doubt. Eventually, I decided to check on the two projects while doing my best to stay out of the way.

First, I checked with Tina. She and Nellie had already gone

over the likely dates and locations for the kidnappings. The toughest part would be getting precise enough to make the grab at the right time and to grab the right person. She finally decided the only way to do that was to send a robot disguised as a housefly to each location. Those robots would send back video feed and serve as homing devices for time travel. The process bordered on breaking the Krichard rules for respecting privacy, but we were well beyond worrying about such things.

Next, I checked with Chrissie and Bruce. They, along with Nellie and some other crew members, were working on converting two of the cabins that were previously used by the humans who had been sent back to Earth. Nellie's eyes were closed in deep concentration as she described her parents' bedroom to Bruce.

As for Chrissie, she was tapped into Earth's internet, trying to find photos of delivery rooms at Gulf Coast Medical Center. Once she had what she needed, she turned to me and said, "We forgot something very important."

"What's that?"

"Someone has to deliver the baby."

"Can't Ann or Nancy do that?"

"Even with surgical masks, Nellie's mother will recognize them as non-human. The fact that she'll be drugged makes it worse. One flash of an eyelash could send her into a panic. It's just too risky. A human has to make the delivery."

I looked over at Nellie. "How do you feel about doing that?"

"Deliver myself? No way!"

Chrissie smiled mischievously and flashed an eyelash. "We already know that the obstetrician who will deliver Nellie is a man, Dr. Kelty. And since you're the only human male on the ship—"

"You get to be Dr. Kelty," Nellie finished.

"Don't worry, Marty. Ann and Nancy will monitor the entire birth and give you instructions through your implant. You'll do just fine."

I looked back to Nellie. "You know that flat spot on the back of your head?"

She instinctively reached back to feel, then smiled. "I don't have a flat spot."

"You will after I faint and drop you!"

CHAPTER 13

Girls Rule Mars!

By the end of the day, everything was ready except for the deployment of the first robotic housefly. That part of the operation would require extra concentration, so Tina wanted to start fresh in the morning after a good night's sleep.

We were all hungry and on our way to the cafeteria when I whispered to Chrissie, "Rather than eating on the ship, why don't we take Nellie and Tina on a double-date in the Chromosphere Cruiser? We can go someplace close, like Mars."

"I like that idea," she whispered back.

"But what about Bruce and the others? I don't want to be rude."

"Hey Bruce," Chrissie called out in a full voice. "You and the rest of the crew go ahead and eat without us. Nellie, Tina, Marty, and I are going on a double-date to Mars." She then turned back to me and whispered, "Sometimes you just need to be assertive."

"A double-date?" Tina asked.

"Oh, Tina," Chrissie said, "don't be coy. Marty and I have seen how you and Nellie look at each other. We both think it's great."

"Mars?" Nellie asked.

"You'll love it, Nellie," I said. "Remember the story I told you about Chrissie and me camping on Enceladus? We'll take that same Chromosphere Cruiser."

We split up to go to our respective cabins and change into whatever we felt like wearing for the evening.

When I walked into the cruiser bay thirty minutes later, Nellie was already there, beaming. "This is amazing, like something right out of a science fiction novel!" She ran her hand down one side of the cruiser. "I really love this shade of pink."

"Yeah, I kind of think of Chromosphere Cruisers as the Krichards' answer to Earth's four-wheelers, but without all the noise and environmental destruction."

I didn't realize that Tina was inside the cruiser until she stepped out to do a visual preflight check. "Nice dress," I said, noticing she'd changed into a tiny garment that accentuated her long legs. "I'm glad to see you're getting into the spirit of things."

"Oh, this?" she said dismissively. "I don't get off the ship often. I'm tired of always having to wear work clothes."

Just then, Chrissie showed up in a colorful little dress that rivaled what Tina was wearing. In her hands were temperature-controlled containers with our dinners.

Nellie was wearing jeans and a casual, deep blue, button-up shirt. She looked at the two dressed-up Krichards and then at me in my jeans and a casual, deep green, button-up shirt. I shrugged and said, "I think they've been holding out on us."

"Most definitely. I had a choice of three outfits in my closet," she said, looking hungrily at Tina, "and not one thing like *that*."

Tina flashed an eyelash. "No one expected you to be around for more than a few days. I'll have some more clothes fabricated for you in the morning."

"Shall we go?" Chrissie asked.

"Who's piloting?" I asked.

"I am," Tina and Chrissie said in unison.

I took Chrissie's hand into mine. "This is Nellie's first ride. Let's take the back and give her the better view." Our eyes locked. "Well, at least from *her* perspective."

We climbed in as eyelashes flashed, front and back.

Tina pushed a series of buttons, grabbed the floor-mounted control stick, turned to everyone, and said, "Hold on!"

We shot toward the door. It opened just in time, to the sound of Nellie screaming in delight.

I turned to Chrissie and said, "I see you and Tina went to the same flight school."

She just smiled.

I smiled too as Nellie began asking Tina all the same questions I had asked on my first cruiser ride. Soon Mars filled our view. Even though I had previously experienced Krichard space travel, the speed at which we reached the planet surprised me. It didn't seem any longer than taking a drive to the mall back home.

Once we landed, I asked, "Are we going to get out or just eat in and enjoy the view?"

Nellie looked over her shoulder with wide eyes. "I want to get out!" She turned to Tina. "Can we? Please?"

"There's not much out there, and the spacesuits are a hassle to deal with, but sure."

"Thank you. We don't have to go on a long hike or anything. Just a few minutes on the planet will be enough for me."

Chrissie reached forward and put a hand on Nellie's shoulder. "Come into the back with me. Let's see if we have a helmet with a communications unit and a suit small enough to fit you. Last time, Marty had to wear a women's medium."

"Oh, you just *had* to bring that up. Didn't you?" I said, feigning annoyance.

The four of us got dressed, and despite a women's small being baggy at Nellie's knees, we were soon ready to go. Having experienced plenty of firsts since I met the Krichards, I suggested that Nellie enjoy the honor of being the first humanoid ever to set foot on Mars. Tina and Chrissie seconded my suggestion.

Nellie stepped onto the planet and turned back to face us, grinning from ear to ear. She did a little dance and shouted, "Woo-hoo! Boys can have the moon. Girls rule Mars!"

We laughed and applauded before heading away from the cruiser. For a while, we walked in silence, taking in the vast landscapes around us.

Eventually, I stopped and asked Tina, "Do you think anyone from Earth knows we're here?"

"Perhaps. But it's not as if they could do anything about it even if they wanted to."

As I shuffled my feet in the loose red dust, an idea struck me. "Then let's blow their minds!" I dragged a foot sideways and spelled out in thirty-foot-tall letters, *Marty was here!*

Everyone else joined in the fun, and before long Mars sported an impressively large and somewhat artsy graffiti field featuring our names and hearts with arrows through them.

"You know, the next windstorm will just blow this away," Tina said.

"That's okay," I said. "We're living for today."

We turned and started walking back toward the cruiser.

Chrissie stopped after a few steps. "Hey, Nellie. Have you tried jumping yet?"

"No. Why?"

"Gravity here is only 38 percent of Earth's. You'll be able to jump almost three times higher than you've ever jumped before."

"Oh, my God!" Nellie squealed when she gave it a try. "Where's the basketball hoop?"

"Someday when we have more time, we'll take you to a small moon where you can really fly."

We completed our Mars hike and climbed back through the airlock. Once everyone was safely inside, Tina pushed the button to drop the outside opaque surfaces and put the cruiser into bubble mode, Chrissie stored our spacesuits, Nellie put dinner on the table, and I opened two bottles of wine. As the four of us relaxed over a delicious meal, we agreed: not only were we on the best and most unusual double-date on Mars, but we were also on the best and most unusual double-date in the history of the entire solar system.

We returned to the ship hours later, happy to let the autopilot do all the work.

CHAPTER 14

That's My Mother He's Riding

Even though we had two separate rooms prepared for our kidnappings, we decided to do one each day, in biological order. For tomorrow's job, Tina would be able to find the correct time and room for Nellie's birth via medical records downloaded from 2022.

For today's job, we assumed the location of the bedroom, but had the much more difficult task of figuring out when the Nellie-producing copulation was going to take place. In our favor was that sending a robotic housefly on a time-travel journey required much less energy than sending humans, so at least the delay between jumps would be minimal.

Nellie, Chrissie, and I all met in the hose room after breakfast to observe Tina's fishing expedition on a wall-mounted computer monitor. Because of the sensitive nature of what was about to happen, others on the ship agreed to refrain from watching unless their talents were required. At Nellie's suggestion, Tina would begin at eleven in the evening and work back to earlier hours:

11:00 p.m.: Lucinda and Ray Dixon in bed, sleeping.

10:30 p.m.: Lucinda and Ray Dixon in bed, sleeping.

10:00 p.m.: Lucinda and Ray Dixon in bed, watching television.

"Go fifteen minutes later," Nellie said.

10:15 p.m.: Lucinda and Ray Dixon in bed, watching television.

9:30 p.m.: Bedroom empty. Bed made.

"I'm going to split the difference again," Tina said.

9:45 p.m.: Lucinda and Ray Dixon, getting ready for bed. Ray looks disappointed.

I glanced over at Nellie. "It appears as if your father is destined to go to bed frustrated on that night."

"That can't be. My mother told me several times that I was born two days early."

"Maybe they'll enjoy some early evening delight," I said. "Will both of your parents have jobs outside the house in 2021?"

"No, only my father."

"What time will he get home from work?"

"At five fifteen."

"Try forty-five minutes after that," I said.

6:00 p.m.: Bedroom empty. Bed made.

"Is this a weekend or a weekday?" Nellie asked.

"Weekday," Tina said.

"That doesn't make any sense. Perhaps he'll have this day off. Try a few hours earlier.

4:00 p.m.: Bedroom empty. Bed unmade.

"Now we're getting somewhere," Tina said. "I'm going an hour earlier."

3:00 p.m.: Lucinda and Ray Dixon in bed, having sex.

We all exchanged high-fives and quickly turned away from the screen out of respect for the couple's privacy.

Okay, I snuck a peek. "When your father was younger, he had beautiful red hair just like you do now."

"What? He's had brown hair all his life." Nellie reluctantly turned back toward the monitor as the bed emptied.

Tina changed the picture to the duplicate room on the ship. Then, after a brief shot of an empty bedroom, the amorous couple appeared on the bed.

"Uh-oh. He stopped," I said.

"He probably knows something is wrong," Tina said. "We injected hallucinogenic drugs into the hose, but he's just had quite a ride."

I snorted. Nellie whacked me. "Ow! You hit hard."

"That's my mother he's riding. Be respectful."

"Okay," Tina said. "They're at it again."

"Leave it to a man to never pass up an opportunity to get laid," Nellie said.

I gave Nellie a playful whack back. "Now *you're* being disrespectful. That's your dad you're talking about."

"He may be my biological father, but he's not my dad. That's Otis, my next-door neighbor."

"Otis? . . . Really?"

"It's a good Southern name."

"Is Otis the neighbor, dead in 2056, who owned the house your dad bought for you?"

"Yes."

"What will he die from?"

"Why do you ask?" Her confusion turned to understanding when she saw my expression. "Oh. No, his death won't be suspicious at all. He'll get throat cancer."

"Well, that's good. I mean bad. I mean, at least we know where you got your red hair."

She put a hand on mine. "I understand what you're trying to say."

I glanced back at the screen. "Hey, the man has staying power."

"It's nice to know I won't come from a quickie."

"This is really weird. Live sex is going on behind us that hasn't even happened yet."

Nellie tilted her head. "Or has it? I'm so confused."

I turned to face Tina, who was now the only one watching the screen. When she saw me out of the corner of her eye, she said, "Don't mind me. I'm only doing my job. I don't want to mess up and return them too early or too late."

"Yeah, whatever you do," I said, "avoid premature ejection."

Group snort.

Minutes later, Lucinda and Otis successfully climaxed, and

they were on their way back to Immokalee, 2021. The first of our two kidnappings was a success.

I turned to give Nellie a hug, only to see a pile of clothes on the floor. She was gone.

CHAPTER 15

Misbehaving Sperm

"Oh shit! Oh shit! Oh shit!" I screamed. "What happened?"

"I'm checking," Tina said, her fingers moving frantically on her computer keyboard.

Chrissie grabbed another computer and worked just as frantically. As the minutes dragged on, all I could do was sit there helplessly, flogging myself for coming up with such a stupid idea. I should have known better than to think I could be cleverer than all those Krichard scientists.

"Is Nellie an only child?" Chrissie asked.

"Yes."

"I found a Dixon family photo on a social media site. I'll move it to the wall monitor."

We all inched closer for a look at what appeared to be a picture taken after a college graduation ceremony.

"That's definitely Ray and Lucinda," I said, "and the younger redhead certainly resembles Nellie. Perhaps he's a cousin or something."

"Or perhaps the wrong sperm fertilized Lucinda's egg," Tina said.

"Could that happen?" I asked.

"We tried to re-create everything exactly as it would occur on Earth, but the hallucinogenic drugs, the time travel, even the brief moment when Otis stopped thrusting could have changed things. Two hundred million or more sperm cells were all racing for the same goal. This time, it appears that Nellie's sperm lost."

"I'm looking at more family photos," Chrissie said, "and the same redheaded male is in all of them. There's no sign of Nellie."

"If that's the case, why do we all remember her?"

"We're remembering her, like we would a dream," Tina said, "and just like a dream, those memories will fade fast."

"Do you have another computer I can use? I want to record as much as I can before I forget."

"Use mine," Chrissie said, handing it to me. "It's set to English. I'm going to the medical lab to discuss an idea with our doctors." She dashed out of the hose room.

While I keyed in my memories, desperate to hang on to them, Tina and Chrissie searched for solutions. An hour later, my brain fogged over, and I forgot everything except Nellie's name and that she was very important to me. I gritted my teeth in frustration, fighting without success to snatch a memory back of her face, her laugh, her voice—anything.

Chrissie returned and walked directly to Tina's station. "Can you retrieve Nellie?" she asked.

"Sure. But unless we want to rerun what we did before for an incalculable number of times, she'll keep disappearing."

"How can you get her back?" I asked.

"That part is simple," Tina said. "We'll just do what we did before. Only this time, we'll grab Otis and Lucinda a few seconds earlier, making our original transport a failure since no one will be in the bedroom for us to grab. Then, in theory, Nellie will come back. At least until Otis's sperm successfully fertilizes Lucinda's egg again."

"Do it!" Chrissie said.

Minutes later, we were watching the amorous couple back at it again in the replica bedroom. A second or two after that, Nellie appeared by my side.

"Here." I handed Nellie her clothes and looked away.

"Why am I naked?"

"Now, Ann!" Chrissie shouted over the intercom.

The bedroom filled with gas, and Otis and Lucinda collapsed.

"Tell me what's going on!" Nellie demanded.

I stared up at the ceiling. "Our plan failed miserably. The wrong sperm cell fertilized your mother's egg. She gave birth to a boy, and you poofed off the ship."

"Ew! I had a penis?"

"Well, technically he wasn't you."

"Yeah, I guess he'd be more like the twin brother I never had. How'd you get me back?"

"Tina grabbed Otis and your mother from the bedroom again, just before she grabbed them the first time."

"Now what?"

Chrissie sat down next to Nellie. "You need to go to the medical lab. Nancy is waiting there for a tissue sample. Instead of having Tina snatch Otis and Lucinda an impossible number of times, the doctor is going to make a copy of your DNA. She can't use your actual DNA because it might disappear. Once she has that, she will extract your mother's ovulated egg, make a clone using the copied DNA, and insert the egg back into your mother."

"So I'm going to be a clone?"

"Yes, but our cloning process is more advanced than what you have on Earth—even in 2056. You'll be physically identical. And since you, as a clone, will live through all your experiences precisely the same way, you'll be mentally identical as well. The only difference is that you will most likely be immune to any timeline corrections Marty makes in AD 31."

My face brightened. "Does that mean I get out of delivering the baby?"

"I talked that over with the doctors. No one has ever successfully fooled time before. They feel it's just too risky to take a shortcut."

"That makes sense. I will happily be terrified to deliver Little Nellie."

* * *

Over the next three days, the doctors kept Otis and Lucinda asleep while they worked on cloning Nellie. Everyone was in high spirits because we were confident our solutions would work. The captain even let both Nellie and me fly the ship, and they weren't sit-on-Dad's-lap flights either. Sure, we couldn't go full throttle, but we did get to take the ship for a spin outside the solar system, cruising at more than seven times the speed of light. The captain, of course, took over the controls at the end of the ride to precisely park us "just so" behind the moon.

On the morning of the fourth day, the cloning process was complete. Nellie, Chrissie, Tina, and I met back in the hose room to return Otis and Lucinda to Immokalee. Rather than send them to the time she originally took them, Tina planned for them to arrive fifteen minutes later. Ann would coordinate with her and give Otis and Lucinda a stimulant just before they departed. We needed them to believe they had fallen asleep right after sex, but not sleep so long that Ray came home from work and caught them in bed together.

Chrissie and I sat on opposite sides of Nellie, each holding one of her hands. We all knew that if time took her again, she'd slip right through our grasp. Still, the effort made us all feel better. Time needed to know it was in for one hell of a fight.

"Five . . . four . . . three . . . two . . . one," Tina counted down. "Now!"

We held our breath as Otis and Lucinda disappeared. Tina switched the screen to the robotic housefly, and we watched them reappear. We exhaled and continued watching until the two woke up.

Finally, Tina said, "My computer is still scanning the time-line. So far, everything looks good. Most importantly, Nellie you are still here!"

"Does anything feel different?" I asked.

Nellie wiggled her fingers, her arms, her legs, and her head.

"Hmm. Everything seems to work just as it did before. Do I look the same?" She stood and slowly turned.

I beamed. "You look exactly as you did before."

"Wait. Something just doesn't feel right. Hmm. . . . Have I always been attracted to men?"

"What!" Tina and I blurted in unison.

Nellie smiled devilishly. "I got you!"

Tina smiled with relief. I smiled, hoping Chrissie hadn't read anything into my over-eager response. And Chrissie smiled, either because she appreciated a well-played gag or because she was going to enjoy interrogating me the next time we were alone.

No matter why we were smiling at that moment, we were all breathing a little easier and feeling proud of our accomplishment. We had, perhaps, become the first humanoids ever to fool time.

"We should have a party," Tina suggested.

"No!" Nellie and I shouted in unison.

"Why not?"

"One thing the vast majority of humans have in common is a superstition about celebrating too early," I said.

"We call it a *jinx*," Nellie added.

"Or if you live in Minnesota, it's called a *Favre.*"

"That's totally illogical," Tina said.

"Nellie and I both know that, but trust me. If we celebrate now, we'll be picking up another pile of clothes off the floor."

"Let's all watch Marty deliver a baby," Nellie said. "*Then* we can celebrate."

"Every obstetrician needs a nurse. And since that nurse must be a human, and, correct me if I'm wrong, I believe there is only one other—"

"Yes, Marty, I will be your nurse."

"Oh, goodie!" I said with a cheeky grin. "We're going to make such a great team."

Tina shook her head and pushed the intercom button. "I'm happy to announce that Otis and Lucinda have been successfully returned to their proper place and time, and that the cloning of

Nellie was successful as well. Congratulations, everyone! That said, Nellie and Marty have asked us all to respect an Earth superstition known as a jinx."

"Or a Favre," I stage whispered.

"Or a Favre," she continued. "No one is to celebrate until after we deliver the baby tomorrow."

"Then we can party like it's 1999," Nellie stage whispered.

"Then we can party like it's 1999. Whatever that means."

CHAPTER 16

I'm Never Having Sex Again

After Nellie and I spent the next morning in the medical lab going over the basics of childbirth with Ann and Nancy, we reported to Chrissie and Tina in the hose room.

I leaned back in what had become my usual chair. "I think I've got the delivery down, but how am I going to pull off cutting the umbilical cord—which I assume we must do to have Nellie officially born on the ship—without the doctor on Earth getting suspicious?"

"So what if he gets suspicious," Chrissie said. "Tina will release a little gas into the delivery room to render everyone unconscious for a few minutes. When they wake up, they'll wonder who delivered the baby but be relieved that someone did it successfully."

"And Lucinda will tell Dr. Kelty and the nurse that they did a wonderful job," Tina added.

"Okay, I'll try to live up to that." I paused for a moment to think. Did we have any more obstacles to overcome? I looked over to Nellie. "What about Ray? Doesn't he need to be in the delivery room?"

"Because I wasn't due for two more days, he thought it was safe to make a quick run to Orlando for business. By the time he got back, I was already born."

"I bet that went over well."

"He never heard the end of it." Nellie closed her eyes and

smiled to herself before turning to Tina. "When are you bringing Mom up?"

"In a half-hour. You two should change into your medical costumes and scrub up."

* * *

Twenty-five minutes later, Nellie and I strolled into the ship's delivery room with her most definitely looking better in her costume than I did in mine. The delivery room was a convincing replica—from the fetal monitor to the birthing bed to the IV pole to the little private bathroom off to the side—or at least I assumed it was since I had never actually been in one myself.

Tina spoke over the intercom, "We're almost ready to go. One small complication is that Lucinda has an IV in her arm. When we transport her, the tubing will get cut. We have an identical IV set up in your room."

"Do you want one of us to reattach the IV?" I asked, hoping she wouldn't assign the task to me.

"No. That's too advanced for either of you. Nancy will come in and do it. She'll be wearing makeup and a surgical mask, but you two need to make sure Lucinda looks in the opposite direction."

"That we can do," I said with relief.

Tina continued. "We will coordinate the transport to be as close to the actual birth time as possible. Once Lucinda is in place, expect the baby in less than five minutes."

"Isn't that a bit risky?" Nellie asked.

"We're taking every precaution. Nancy will be right outside the door if there are any major complications."

"Good luck, everyone," Chrissie said. "And remember that after the countdown, all communication from us will be through Marty's implant. Nellie, if anything unexpected happens, just follow his lead."

Nellie and I pulled up our surgical masks and stared into each other's eyes.

"Five . . . four . . . three . . . two . . . one," Tina counted down. "Now!"

Lucinda materialized in mid-scream. Nellie and I hurried into position, she on the right, holding her mother's hand, and me—oh, God—feeling like a catcher in a baseball game, waiting for a ninety-five-mile-per-hour slider.

"It's okay, Mrs. Dixon," Nellie said in a comforting voice. "Remember your breathing."

"Who are you!" Lucinda shrieked. "Where's Kim?"

Nancy snuck in to reattach the IV.

"I'm Nel . . . er, Nadine. Kim had to step out, but she'll be back soon."

"We are almost there, Mrs. Dixon," I said.

"*We?* What are *you* going to do? Push it out your asshole?"

Ann spoke in my head, "Don't take it personally, Marty. You're bound to hear worse before this is all over."

The next contraction hit, and Lucinda bellowed.

"That's it, Mom! You're doing great."

"Mom?" Lucinda asked.

"Yes, I know you're going to be a wonderful mom."

"I see the top of the head."

"Tell her to pant, not push," Ann said.

"Mrs. Dixon, I need you to stop pushing. Just pant."

Slowly, Little Nellie's head appeared—*I'm never having sex again.*

"Your baby's head is out."

"Okay, Marty. I want you to feel around the baby's neck for the umbilical cord. If it's there, nod."

I took a deep breath and nodded.

"Now I want you to slip your fingers under the cord, and slide it over the baby's head."

I gave it a try, but everything was slippery, and my finger slid over the top. I tried from a different angle, and carefully pulled the cord over Little Nellie's head. I nodded again.

"Reassure the mother," Ann said.

"Everything looks perfect, Mrs. Dixon."

Soon, Little Nellie's shoulders appeared, followed by the rest of her.

"Mrs. Dixon, you have a beautiful baby girl!" *Or is it a giant salamander? At this point, who could tell the difference?*

I gently set Little Nellie on her mother's belly and began cleaning her off with a sterile towel.

"Remember, you still have to cut the umbilical cord," Ann said. "Just clamp it in two places and cut between the clamps. You'll find everything you need on the tray beside you."

I did as she said, even though I was terrified that the clamps wouldn't hold and that the baby's innards would shoot out like the contents of an overfilled, untied water balloon.

From there, Nurse Nellie took over, putting on socks and a hat and wrapping her little self in a blanket. She then handed herself to her mother. "Here you go, Mrs. Dixon. She looks perfectly healthy. And I must say, she's the most beautiful baby I've ever seen."

"Beautiful and smart," I added. "I can tell just by looking at her that she's going to go places."

"Who knows? She might even be the first person to walk on Mars."

"Or someday she might escape police custody and travel back in time. You just don't know."

"Stop it you two, before you screw things up!" Ann shouted. "Just deliver the afterbirth and get out of there."

I looked at Nellie and subtly pointed to my head. "Mrs. Dixon? We're now going to help you deliver your placenta. Then we'll clean you up and give you some privacy to bond with your baby."

She offered a tired smile and looked lovingly at Little Nellie.

Nurse Nellie and I completed our tasks without getting yelled at even one more time. In fact, other than almost losing the contents of my stomach when I had to handle the afterbirth, and Nellie's little snort, we performed just like a real doctor and a real nurse.

"If you need anything, just push this button, and someone will help you right away," Nellie said before we slipped out the door.

On the other side, everyone working behind the scenes congratulated us with smiles, hugs, and eyelash flashes.

Tina stood face to face with Nellie and grasped both of her hands. "What was it like to hold yourself?"

"It wasn't nearly as weird as I expected. Sure, I could see some similarities in our facial features. Still, I don't think my brain totally processed what I was doing."

I put a hand on Tina's arm and asked, "When are we sending the mother and child back to Earth?"

Before she could answer, the captain leaned in. "Not until we all get to hold Little Nellie. This is a first. None of us has ever seen a human baby in anything other than pictures. In fact, we've never had a baby of any humanoid species on our ship."

"The mother will need to sleep soon," Ann said. "We'll sneak Little Nellie out then."

* * *

After Lucinda had time to bond with Little Nellie, Nurse Nellie returned to the delivery room to check on her mother and inform her that she was going to take the baby to the nursery for an exam and a nap. She also suggested to her mother that she take a nap as well. Then, with herself bundled in her arms, Nellie stepped out of the delivery room.

All nineteen Krichards greeted her on the other side of the door.

At the sight of the eager Krichards, most with their eyelashes flashing and hands clasped just below their chins, Nellie broke into a wide smile. "If you're all here, who's running the ship?"

The captain, who was first in line, looked at Little Nellie and cooed. He brushed the back of a finger against the baby's soft cheek and cooed again. Then, realizing no one had answered Nellie's question, he said, "To use an Earth term, I put the ship in park."

I stood back to observe the baby lovefest. Each crew member took a turn holding, or at least touching Little Nellie, and it seemed that the bigger they were, the more easily they melted. Clarence was so nervous about holding the baby, he was shaking. Then he cradled her in his arms with a gentleness that belied his massive size.

At the end of the line were the doctors, Ann and Nancy.

"We're the lucky ones," Nancy said. "We get to take the baby back to the medical lab for a health checkup."

Ann glanced around the room for Tina and spotted her off to the side talking with Nellie. She stepped closer to get her attention. "You should make preparations to return the mother and baby. I'd like to get them back to Earth within the next hour."

Tina frowned. "So soon? I've barely had a moment to hold her." She flashed an eyelash and sighed. "Yes, we'll be ready."

* * *

Once again, Nellie, Chrissie, Tina, and I met back in the hose room. This time, however, we were all quietly confident that returning Lucinda and Little Nellie to 2022 would cement the adult Nellie to the 2020 timeline with the rest of us.

Earlier, Nurse Nellie gave her mother a sedative and returned Little Nellie at the same time. After the doctors were sure Lucinda was fast asleep, Nancy disconnected the IV. She also made sure Little Nellie was secure in her mother's arms.

Now that all the preparations were complete, Chrissie and I sat on opposite sides of Nellie, each holding one of her hands. As the two humans in the room knew, jinxes (or Favres) have difficulty interfering with precisely followed routines. So we did everything exactly as we had when returning Lucinda and Otis to 2021.

"Five . . . four . . . three . . . two . . . one!" Tina counted down. "Now!"

We held our breath as mother and daughter disappeared.

Tina switched the screen to the robotic housefly, and we watched them reappear. We exhaled and continued watching until Dr. Kelty and Nurse Kim woke up from their gas-induced blackouts.

Finally, Tina said, "My computer is still scanning the timeline. So far, everything looks good. Most importantly, Nellie you are still here!"

"Does anything feel different?" I asked.

Nellie wiggled her fingers, her arms, her legs, and her head. "Hmm. Everything seems to work just as it did before. Do I look the same?" She stood and slowly turned.

I beamed. "You look exactly as you did before."

"Wait. Something just doesn't feel right. Hmm. . . . Have I always been attracted to men?"

We all cracked up.

"Can we have that party now?" Tina asked.

Nellie and I looked at each other with wide smiles. I knew what she was going to say, so I waited until she blurted out, "We can party like it's 1999!"

"Why that number?" Chrissie asked.

I raised a finger to indicate I had the answer. "As the Year 2000 approached on Earth, people feared everything from massive computer crashes to accidental nuclear war to you-name-it that would end the world. A musician named Prince sang a song about it called '1999.' Later, on our last night on Earth in 2056, '1999' became Nellie's and my song."

"We should play it for them," Nellie said.

"We will. In anticipation of this night, I downloaded a bunch of songs to play over the ship's sound system. I doubt many of the crew have researched where I got their names from, so I think it's about time to introduce Chrissie to the Pretenders, Tina to Tina Turner, Captain Jagger to the Rolling Stones, Bruce and Clarence to Bruce Springsteen and the E Street Band, Ann and Nancy to Heart, and on down the line. I didn't name anyone Prince, but we can make '1999' our song in 2020, just as it was in 2056."

CHAPTER 17

It All Depends on the Housefly

That night, the Krichard ship became a party ship. Chrissie opened several bottles of wine and other Earth-based alcoholic beverages, and I showed Nellie how to use the euphoria dispenser. As music rumbled throughout the ship, we experimented with different styles of dancing. We started with some line dancing and do-your-own-thing at standard gravity in the halls and eventually moved to the bridge where we turned off the gravity and made use of the much larger space.

Although no one could match Nellie's moves at standard gravity, the Krichards excelled at zero gravity. The best part of the night was when I introduced all the Krichards to their name-sakes and played a representative concert video clip for each over the large bridge screen. Then I repeated the songs without the videos while the Krichards named for those artists re-created the concert scene. Their performances were hilarious, and since Krichards were new to Earth alcoholic beverages, the impersonations grew wilder as the night progressed.

While I emceed, Nellie sat in the captain's chair and judged the action. In last place, because of his awkward performance, was Captain Jagger. In his defense, the Mick Jagger strut just didn't work in zero gravity. Nellie and I both agreed that he looked more like a bug struggling to walk on water in a toilet bowl than anything else.

Among those I was closest to on the ship, Ann and Nancy did an accurate imitation of Heart—especially Nancy floating in the air, playing air guitar. Chrissie only superficially resembled Chrissie Hynde of the Pretenders, yet she masterfully pulled off the tough girl persona as she rocketed around the bridge, lip-syncing "Bad Boys Get Spanked." Without a doubt, every male on the bridge wanted to be her bad boy at that moment. As for Tina, she was a natural as the Queen of Rock 'n' Roll and executed all the moves to perfection—even while she was floating upside down.

Still, despite all the great performances from the women, Nellie declared Bruce and Clarence the winners—and rightfully so. The highlight of their performance was their rendition of the legendary knee-slide where Bruce Springsteen ends up playing guitar between the legs of saxophonist Clarence Clemons. The difference here was that at zero gravity, Bruce could air-slide all the way across the bridge. The danger, of course, was that without a solid surface to slide on, Bruce could easily end up too low or—God forbid—too high. We were all relieved—especially Clarence—when Bruce nailed his slide.

After all the Krichards performed, our hosts demanded that Nellie and I do the same. I cranked up "1999," and we did our best at zero gravity, with both of us playing Prince. The Krichards loved our dueling air guitars, but there was no way I could keep up with Nellie when she did the air-splits.

When I realized the party was about to end, I set the song on repeat, and the two of us led a conga line through the halls, dropping everyone off at their respective cabins. When only Tina and Chrissie were left behind us, Nellie ducked into Tina's cabin, and I ducked into Chrissie's cabin.

* * *

Late the next morning, Nellie and I met with our Krichard friends in the conference room to go over plans for another attempt to send me to Galilee in AD 31.

"Marty," Captain Jagger commenced once everyone was seated, "please have either Ann or Nancy dye your skin and hair again. Tina, please provide Marty with a new first century-appropriate wardrobe since his last one came back in tatters. Also, is there any way we can improve the accuracy of the drop-off? I'd like to get him in and out as quickly as possible."

"I've been thinking about that, Captain," Tina said. "We had great success using robotic houseflies for Nellie's conception and birth missions. We've never tried a housefly outdoors before, but since we have a couple that work really well, I recommend using them to scout the area."

The captain nodded. "Good idea. That may prevent Marty from having to traipse around searching for Jesus."

"Captain, is anyone going with Marty?" Nellie asked.

"No. All time correction missions are solo."

"Why?"

"Because that was all we could send—" the captain began.

"Until we got our time-travel attachment replaced," Chrissie finished.

"Hmm. Technically, I suppose we could now send—" the captain began.

"Two people," Nellie finished.

"Can I complete a sentence around here?"

Nellie leaned forward and looked down the table to the captain. "I want to go."

"It's too dangerous. Women in AD 31 had no rights or legal protections."

"I grew up in a backward, male-dominated theocracy. I even got arrested for being a lesbian. Other than the lack of technology and a natural environment that humans have yet to fuck up, AD 31 probably isn't all that different from AD 2056."

The captain looked over at me with questioning eyes.

"It's her world too, Captain. She's tough. She's resourceful. She'd double our chance of success."

He closed his eyes in thought for a moment, then opened

them to address Nellie. "Fine. When this meeting is over, go with Marty to get your hair and skin dyed. You should also get some contacts to hide the green in your eyes."

"And she should get a communications implant," Bruce added.

"How do you feel about that?" the captain asked.

"I can't say I'm thrilled about it. What if a voice in my head startles me and I accidentally poke someone in the eye?" She looked at me and winked. "That said, I'm all in, no matter what."

"Okay, Nellie," the captain said. "Have one of the doctors install an implant when you get the other work done. The operation is painless and takes less than twenty minutes." He glanced across the table and asked Tina, "How soon can we initiate the time jump?"

"It all depends on the housefly. If we're lucky, we'll know when and where to send Nellie and Marty in a few hours. If we're not so lucky, that time could stretch to several days. Let's shoot for tomorrow at this time and be ready to adjust if necessary."

"Does anyone have anything else to add?" the captain asked, looking around the table. "All right then. Let's get to work."

* * *

Nellie and I went straight to the medical lab. Sometimes I wondered if having two doctors on the ship was overkill. After all, Captain Jagger didn't make it his practice to beam down to strange planets with a bunch of red-shirted crewmen. On this day, however, the extra doctor was a nice convenience. Ann immediately got to work on Nellie, and Nancy did the same with me.

Because of the implant and Nellie's natural talkativeness, her conversion took an hour longer than mine did. When we were both finished, we stood and looked at each other, amazed by the transformation.

Although she had seen me with dark skin before, she had never seen me with black hair or a fake beard. As for Nellie, I always thought her best physical features were her green eyes, freckles, and bright red hair. Her transformation took all of those assets away. Still, in my opinion, a woman's true beauty comes from the life behind her eyes and the energy behind her smile. Even if she were totally green, she would still be gorgeous.

Now all that was left was the waiting. We stopped by the cafeteria for a meal, then wandered to the hose room to check on Chrissie and Tina. Both were staring at their computer monitors when we entered.

"Have you found Jesus?" I asked.

Tina turned away from the flow of images from the robotic housefly just long enough to shoot me a frustrated look. "No. In fact, I'm now glad your first mission was so far off target. Had you successfully reached Galilee in AD 31, only an extremely lucky landing would have saved you from a long, fruitless hike."

"Is there a better time in biblical history you can send us to?" Nellie asked. "I'd hate to get all dressed up with no place to go."

Chrissie swiveled around in her chair to face Nellie. "I'm checking on that now. Life on Earth was incredibly primitive back then. If you think about it, Jesus's entire world existed within an area he could reach on foot or by donkey. He couldn't possibly have imagined the long-term, widespread impact his preaching would have. Whether you and Marty actually meet him isn't nearly as important as finding a way to eliminate the major negative side effects that sprouted from the religion his life inspired."

"What about other religions?" Nellie asked.

"In a perfect world, all religions—or at least those used to justify controlling or harming others—would become extinct. To accomplish that would require more heavy-handed intervention than our moral code allows. Since Christianity is Earth's largest religion, we've made it our target. Our hope is to throw it off enough that critical thinking can become the norm and eventually dominate supernatural thinking everywhere."

"I was really hoping to meet Jesus," I said.

"You still might," Tina said over her shoulder. "No one today really knows what Jesus looked like, so the best I can do is find the person in Galilee who seems to be preaching to the largest crowd, preferably from an elevated location."

"The Sermon on the Mount," Nellie added.

Tina nodded and returned her gaze to her monitor.

"I'm confident you two will get us to wherever we need to go." I put a hand on Nellie's shoulder. "We should probably quit interrupting, and let our friends work. Let's go to the observation lounge and brainstorm. I'd like to bounce some ideas off you."

CHAPTER 18

Nellie Gets Stoned

Shortly after breakfast on the following day, a harried Tina summoned everyone to the hose room. Once we arrived, she showed us a fly's-eye view of a crowd gathered around a man who was preaching from atop an oval rock that appeared to be at least eight feet high and fifteen feet wide. "If there was indeed a Sermon on the Mount in AD 31, this must be it."

"It looks more like the Sermon on the Potato," I quipped.

Captain Jagger studied the image on the monitor. "Good job, Tina. Can you send the fly higher?"

Tina entered a command, and after a short delay, the picture zoomed out.

The captain pointed to a cluster of boulders in the upper right-hand corner of the screen. "If we drop them off there, no one will notice their arrival."

I pointed to where the man was preaching. "Captain, now that the ship has a more advanced time-travel attachment, can you pick us up there?"

He looked at Tina, who nodded. "Of course," he said.

"I'll be ready to send Marty and Nellie right after they change into their period clothing," Tina said.

"We'll get dressed right now." I handed Chrissie a piece of paper. "Nellie and I did some brainstorming yesterday. Here are a few items we'd like to bring with us. They should be small enough to fit into our pockets."

Chrissie scanned the list. "Not bad, but I'll need a little extra time to get all this together." She turned to the captain. "We'll have them on their way in an hour."

* * *

Even though I did pretty well in the airlock when Tina picked us up in Duluth, I stopped by the euphoria dispenser for a little something to take the edge off. Nellie, who didn't mind tight spaces at all, joined me, declaring, "Our partnership on the mission starts here." Choosing for both of us, she concocted a euphoria, which she called "Puppies, Wine, and Chocolate."

From there, we headed directly to the hose room. Tina quickly rechecked all her settings, and Chrissie inspected our clothing for accuracy and inserted the items from our list into our hidden pockets.

"Good luck to both of you," Chrissie said as we exchanged hugs.

Tina also embraced us both. "I'll drop you off about an hour before the crowd gathers for the sermon. Don't forget that I can't bring either of you back for at least three hours."

We nodded our understanding, then stepped into the airlock and assumed the required position, holding each other tight as Tina sealed us in.

"Mmm. I smell chocolate," Nellie said.

"Mmm. I smell puppy breath," I said.

We giggled.

Whoosh!

Everything went white.

Everything went bright.

"Ow!" I shouted, shielding my eyes. "Chrissie, do we have any historically accurate sunglasses hidden in our pockets?"

"Sorry. You'll have to wait a while. Sunglasses won't be invented for at least another thousand years."

"Maybe that's the problem. People during biblical times were running around half-blind. Let's tell them that if they wear sunglasses, they'll be just as powerful as the sun god. We'll give them a few thousand pairs in return for promising to treat women as equals and never, ever starting another war. They'd go for it in a second."

Chrissie ignored my comment and asked, "How are you doing, Nellie?"

"It's going to take a while to get used to having voices in my head. Other than that, I'm ready to kick some misogynistic ass."

I peeked around some boulders before saying, "Chrissie, we're going to go check out the area. I see a few people milling about, so we may not be able to respond if you or Tina say anything to us."

"Understood."

Nellie and I walked ahead about fifty feet and climbed onto a large rock that sat atop a cluster of even larger ones. The hilly area was full of boulders framed by dry, scraggly trees. The *potato pulpit* was about sixty feet in front of us, and anyone who stood up there to preach would face away from us. It was a perfect forum for public speaking because in front of the potato-shaped rock was a wide, flat area strewn with pebbles, sand, and grass. People could sit there in relative comfort. Off to the sides were more boulders that onlookers could lean against or sit on, and behind the potato pulpit was a shallow pit that shielded the backstage area from view. Finally, off to the right, someone had stacked numerous large rocks to create steps to the top of the pulpit.

I whispered to Nellie. "We should hang out here and observe for a while."

"I was going to say the same thing."

Our rock was just wide enough for both of us to sit on with our legs hanging over the edge. Nellie pointed. "That man approaching from between those trees over there looks like the preacher we saw on Tina's monitor."

"I think you're right, and his entourage is right behind him."

Nellie chuckled. "They called them disciples back then."

"Same difference."

One of the men was leading a donkey saddled with a set of baskets and what looked like a primitive crutch lashed between them. He led the animal to the backstage area, removed the crutch, and unloaded the baskets.

The preacher gathered his entourage backstage. Although we were too far away to hear any words, he was obviously giving everyone instructions. Soon, all but three of the people dispersed, including a man carrying the crutch as if it were a briefcase. The preacher and the man with the donkey stayed behind, along with a woman who was carefully applying brown clay to her face from a ceramic pot she had pulled from one of the baskets.

"Tina, Chrissie," I whispered, "are you watching this?"

"See the fly that just landed on your knee?" Tina asked.

"Yes."

"Don't slap it."

Nellie covered her mouth to repress a laugh. Then, talking through her fingers said, "Keep that away from us. Swatting flies is pure instinct for me."

The fly took off and hovered several feet away.

"Is that better?"

"A few more feet," Nellie said. "I can still hear the wings. It's giving me the creeps."

"Okay, now that we know you can see what we see," I said, "what do you think?"

"I think the preacher is a flimflam man," Chrissie said.

"I agree. And for us to pull this off, we're going to have to out-con the con man."

"Or out-god the god," Tina said. "That's why I gave you the butane lighter the first time we tried this."

"We've seen this before with religious leaders on other planets," Chrissie added. "Which is why you must not underestimate your competition. The most pious-looking person could slit your throat in a second."

Nellie pointed at the gathering crowd. "This place is going to fill up fast."

"It's almost show time. Chrissie, Tina, unless you see something from your housefly view that we absolutely have to know about, please stay out of our heads. We need to concentrate. Nellie, I'm glad you don't have a shy bone in your body. Let's be over-the-top on this and play off each other."

"Hey, I'm the only one here who is truly born again. What do I have to be bashful about?"

When the stream of spectators slowed, the preacher made his final preparations backstage. While he was doing that, Nellie and I descended from our rock and worked our way into the crowd. When I realized that I couldn't understand what anyone was saying, I said, "Psst. Tina, I don't think my implant is working. All I hear is gibberish."

"That's because I haven't activated the vocal translator function yet. Once I do, any words you say in English will come out in Aramaic. Since you don't have a hind brain, the process will tax the Broca's area of your single brain. If you talk too much, your speech may become temporarily slurred."

"How much is too much?"

"We don't know. You and Nellie are the first humans we've tried this on."

Nellie and I looked at each other. I smiled nervously, and she comically dropped the lower lip on the right side of her face.

"Okay, we're ready," I said.

"Activating now."

Suddenly, the clutter of Aramaic voices around us became a clutter of English voices.

"Can you understand me, Nellie?"

"Yes. Can *you* understand me?"

"Yes. But it's weird. I'm hearing English while your lips are speaking Aramaic. Have you ever watched a foreign film dubbed into English?"

"Sure."

"That's exactly what this is like. We'll have to be careful and remember that we can't read each other's lips."

We sat off to the side as the show began. Whether or not we were watching the actual Sermon on the Mount, I can't say. Even if it was the real thing, the words couldn't possibly match any Bible since primitive writing techniques wouldn't allow for someone to blend into the crowd with a reporter's notebook to record the words. Also, at least fifty years would pass between the time of the sermon and the writing of the Gospel of Matthew.

One thing that did strike me, however, was that the preacher introduced himself as Yeshua. Many historians believe that Yeshua is the true Hebrew name for Jesus. If those historians are correct, perhaps I was indeed looking at the man we had hoped to find. Then again, Yeshua was a common name at the time.

No matter what, I had to chuckle to myself at how closely the proceedings resembled tent revival services in modern times. After the sermon, it was time for the miracles. First up was the man with the crutch. Workers made a big show of helping him up the steps. Then after Yeshua looked up to the heavens and shouted a prayer, he grabbed the man's crutch and threw it into the backstage area, so he could reuse the prop later. To conclude the illusion, the injury-faking actor took a few steps before crying out, "I've been healed!" and bounding around on the pulpit.

More healings followed, including the woman who had covered her face with clay, claiming to have leprosy, and a man from the entourage, claiming to be blind. Others taken directly from the audience had ailments that were not visible. Yeshua declared most of those people possessed by demons, which he—after much showmanship—exorcised from their bodies.

The service concluded with Yeshua announcing that he'd be back in three days for another sermon and more healings. In the meantime, he needed donations to continue God's work. As men walked through the audience, collecting whatever people brought to give, I nodded to Nellie, and the two of us bounded up onto the stage.

I looked out over the audience and yelled, "Yeshua has deceived you! The man with the crutch wasn't really injured. I saw him walking just fine before the sermon. I also saw the woman apply clay to her face to trick you into believing she had leprosy." I reached down and picked up a glob of clay that Yeshua had tossed on the pulpit during the mock healing and squeezed it through my fingers.

The crowd roared in anger as Yeshua and his entourage slinked away.

"That's right!" Nellie yelled. "He's—"

"Woman!" the audience bellowed.

Nellie and I looked at each other in confusion.

She tried again. "The demons—"

"Woman!" they roared. This time several in the crowd pelted the pulpit with stones, one of which caught Nellie in the shoulder. Fortunately, she wasn't seriously hurt, and just as fortunately, no one in the crowd knew what Nellie meant when she flipped them off.

Chrissie entered our brains. "Marty, Nellie, in AD 31, it wasn't proper for a woman to speak to men like that, especially in public."

I reached into a hidden pocket, grabbed my butane lighter, flicked it on, and turned the flame all the way up. "My name is Marty Mann! I can instantly make fire and hold it in my hand, yet I am not a god. The woman next to me is Nellie Dixon, and she is not my wife. In fact, she is not any man's property, nor will she ever be. The next time she speaks, you will show her respect. You will not yell at her. You will not throw stones at her. If you do, you will regret it." I nodded for Nellie to continue.

"We are here today bec—"

"Woman! Woman! Woman!"

I calmly pulled an oversized firecracker out of my pocket, handed it to Nellie, and lit it. She lobbed it at a man who was just about to pitch a stone.

The man smiled, thinking Nellie had made a weak, girlie throw. Then it exploded!

The firecracker didn't hurt anyone, nor had we wanted it to. The noise was all we were after. Nellie glared down at the man, who was now cowering behind others in the crowd. "When I speak, you will show me just as much respect as you show a man, or the next one goes down your tunic!"

The man, his face full of fear, bowed his head and moved off to the side.

"Now, I know everyone has already had a long day," I said, "so we won't keep you here much longer. We have two messages for you today. First, don't be fooled by miracles. Everything Yeshua did up here was a sham. No one was actually healed, and demons do not exist." I leaned in close to Nellie's ear and whispered, "Women."

She nodded and picked up where I left off. "Second, women are not inferior to men, and you should never consider them ritually unclean. Would anyone like to challenge me on that?"

A man moved through the crowd to approach the pulpit.

Nellie held out her hand, and I placed another firecracker in it.

The man, his eyes wide, retreated as quickly as he could.

"Wise move," Nellie hissed.

"Come back here in three days and bring everyone you know. Tell them Marty Mann and Nellie Dixon will do something amazing. Something that is real. Not just a trick."

Nellie's scowl transformed into a bright smile. "Until then, how about a group picture?" She pulled a digital camera out of a hidden pocket and snapped one from the pulpit. No one, of course, had any idea what she had done, so she hurried down the steps to show the image on the screen to those closest to the pulpit. When they still didn't understand, she started taking individual photographs. At first, people were fearful of the images, but eventually, after a little patient coaxing, they grew braver. Before long, both men and women were pointing and howling in laughter, thrilled to see themselves on the screen.

As Nellie worked the crowd, making sure she took everyone's picture, I stayed close, making sure she stayed safe. I also pulled up anyone who tried to kneel or bow to us, each time saying, "We're not gods. We're just showing you what humans can accomplish on their own."

The crowd stayed for hours and even grew in size as word spread. When Nellie noticed that the camera battery was running low, she started requiring people to pose in small groups. In all, she took more than seven hundred shots.

By the time the photo shoot ended, we had our own entourage. Somehow, we had to figure out how to ditch them, so we could communicate with Tina and Chrissie without looking like we were out of our minds. Walking away or saying we had to go home didn't work because they followed us like adoring groupies. We finally achieved success by giving them all jobs in our promotions department and reframing what we had already asked the crowd to do.

"Go to every village within walking distance and spread the good news," I said.

"Tell them Marty Mann and Nellie Dixon will return with more amazing non-miracles in three days," Nellie added.

Once we were sure we were alone, we returned to the potato pulpit.

"Scotty, beam us up," I said.

"Who's Scotty?" Tina asked.

"Never mind. It's just something from an old TV series that goes through my head every time you suck me back up to the ship. I think we're done here for now, but as you obviously heard, we need to come back to the same place in three Earth days."

"We can send you there directly, and you'll arrive in seconds, or you can come back to the ship, get a good night's sleep, and go back in the morning."

I looked at Nellie, and she pointed skyward. "I hate to whine, but I've just mingled with hundreds of people on a planet where antiperspirants and deodorants have yet to be invented." Her voice slowed, and she began to slur. "I would really like to take a long, . . . hot shhhowweer."

"Get into position. I'll have you back on the ship in an instant."

Nellie and I embraced.

Whoosh!

Everything went white.

Everything went *aah*, civilization!

CHAPTER 19

The Ultimate Selfie

After Nellie and I indulged in showers, we headed directly to the conference room for a progress report. Chrissie, Tina, and Captain Jagger were already seated at the table when we arrived.

Chrissie spoke first. "Congratulations! I have been examining Earth documents, and you've already made progress. In the New Testament, Marty Mann, spelled M-a-r-t-y-m-a-n has replaced Jesus, and Nellie, with no last name, has replaced Mary. Unfortunately, the names are the only words that appear to have changed so far."

"Nellie, you're my mother? I was just getting used to you being my sister."

"Now that we've established that, once we're done here, you need to take out the garbage and clean your room."

"You can't tell me that! You may be my mother, but I am the Son of God!"

While Nellie and I laughed and Tina and Chrissie chuckled, Captain Jagger frowned. If I hadn't spent so much time with the Krichards, I would have worried that our kidding around upset him. Instead, I knew it was only that, being the captain, he felt obligated to put on a serious front. I also knew that if I stared at him long enough, either his eyelashes or lips would betray him.

Seconds later the captain broke into a smile and asked, "Do

you think you two, as the Son of God and the Holy Virgin Nellie, can—"

"No! No!" Nellie interrupted. "The *virgin* part is not going to work."

"She prefers *smokin' hot*," I added.

"Okay, do you think that you two, as the Son of God and the Holy Smokin' Hot Nellie, can successfully make the necessary timeline changes on your next visit?"

"Yes," I answered. "Look at the effect we had in just one day. Now that the locals are out promoting for us, we should have an even bigger crowd the next time. To ensure success, though, we need to give them something in writing that will last."

"Like a new and improved Ten Commandments?" Nellie asked.

"That's exactly what I was thinking."

Chrissie entered something into her handheld computer and looked up. "Obviously, we can't send you down with stone tablets. What we can do is print something on a deterioration resistant scroll."

"Can you make multiple copies?" I asked. "I don't want to trust the fate of the world to just the one person we hand it to."

"Absolutely. I will create as many copies as you can safely transport."

"Do you have a list of commandments in mind?" the captain asked.

"I have some ideas. I'm sure Nellie has some too. We will work on the list over the next several hours and give it to Chrissie."

Nellie looked across the table to Tina and asked, "Can we bring some sort of weapon for protection just in case the crowd turns on us again?"

"I'm sure Chrissie can give you some more firecrackers. Also, in the storage bay, on the lowest level of the ship, you can grab two small canisters of pepper spray from the Earth artifacts compartment. While you are there, please do not attempt to unlock and remove any of the guns or knives. We are a nonviolent species.

Even this ship has only defensive weapons. Imagine if we gave you something deadly, and someone stole it and used it against you."

"Oh, I hadn't thought of that. I suppose we could get ourselves into a lot of trouble, couldn't we?"

The captain stood. "Okay, now that we have that sorted out, let's get moving. I'd like to get Marty and Nellie back to AD 31 tomorrow after breakfast."

I pushed back from the table. "We'll be ready, Captain."

Later that night, Nellie and I hashed out an updated version of the Ten Commandments and gave it to Chrissie for printing. We were proud of our list, but also nervous about it. If we were successful, those commandments would influence decisions on Earth for thousands of years. What if we left out something significant? And who were we to author such an important document, in a single night, over a couple glasses of wine?

* * *

In the morning, we took a pass on the euphoria dispenser and headed straight to the hose room. After loading up our pockets with small items we hoped would benefit our mission, Chrissie handed us each five copies of the commandments.

As Tina sealed us in, she said, "You will arrive two hours before the crowd shows up. That should give you ample time to get organized."

"Hmm. You smell like Chrissie," Nellie said.

"Hmm. You smell like Tina," I said.

We giggled.

Whoosh!

Everything went white.

Everything went Pffft!

"Ow! Bad landing," I said as I spit sand out of my mouth. "Are you okay?"

Nellie stood, leaned over, and shook her head. "Every girl loves to wash her hair with sand now and then."

I pointed to a nearby pile of dung. "It could have been worse."

We brushed each other off and checked the ground to make sure we had all our possessions.

"Chrissie, Tina," I said, glancing skyward, "we have landed safely and are heading to the potato pulpit."

"Your entourage is waiting for you," Tina said.

"How do you—"

A fly buzzed my head.

"Never mind."

Wide smiles greeted us as we arrived backstage. Soon people were telling us what big news we had become and that we should expect a huge crowd. Then while I shook some hands, Nellie gave two men and two women small digital cameras and showed them how to use them. She also told them they could keep the cameras, as a reward, if they promised to stay afterward to take photos of everybody in the crowd who wanted to pose for one.

Since we were changing the timeline, leaving the cameras wouldn't contaminate anything. Still, ensuring that they would eventually become worthless plastic boxes seemed like the prudent thing to do. With that in mind, after our previous jump, one of the Krichard technicians made two adjustments to the cameras. First, to make sure they retained power long enough to impress the entire crowd, she upgraded the batteries to last for roughly two thousand pictures. Then, to lessen the chance that they would be used for anything other than what we intended, she programmed the internal memory on each one to retain only the five most recent shots. Giving the people of AD 31 encouragement to advance using their own brainpower was one thing, but yanking them two thousand years into the future was quite another.

Nellie and I hung out backstage, talking to our entourage and trying to make sure we were somewhat organized. Occasionally one of us would peek around the rock to check out our audience. As the crowd grew, I started to get nervous. So many things could go wrong.

I felt a tap on my shoulder, turned, and recoiled. "Jesus Christ! You scared me."

"Sorry. I mean you no harm," Yeshua said.

For a moment, I was speechless. Since Martyman had replaced Jesus in the Bible, I had no doubt about who I was looking at. Though the man may not have been divine in real life, he was still the most well-known figure in Earth's history—at least until Nellie and I screwed that up for him.

I reached out a hand. "It's a pleasure to meet you, Yeshua."

He shook my hand and tilted his head inquisitively. "You are not from around here, are you?"

"No, I'm not." I looked up, hoping someone watching from the robotic housefly would provide some guidance.

"It's all right," Chrissie said. "Tell him."

"I'm from roughly two thousand years in the future, and my associate . . ." I glanced behind me and spotted Nellie in conversation with one of our helpers. "Nellie, come here. There's someone you should meet."

As she approached, she looked at me, then at Yeshua, then back at me.

"It's okay," I assured her. "Nellie, meet Yeshua."

She held out her hand. "Nice to meet you."

This time, Yeshua kept his hands at his side. "A man should not touch a woman that way."

"She is also from the future," I said.

Nellie shot me a surprised look.

"Where we come from, both men and women shake hands."

Yeshua looked around, then timidly offered his hand. "That is some future you come from."

"Do you actually believe we're from the future?" I asked.

"At first I was very upset about what you said the other day. You embarrassed me. Then people tell me about the miraculous things you did. Things I cannot do. I am here to learn your tricks. Perhaps you tell the truth."

"I'm sorry if I embarrassed you," I said, "but you were cheating people."

"Was I? Yes, I used some tricks. Without them, no one would

come. I am a good man, but I need people to listen to my message and gifts to support my work."

"You may be good now," Nellie said, "but in the future, people will use writings about you and the god you follow to justify horrible things like war, torture, bigotry, and slavery. And the masses will go along with them because their leaders will teach them not to question. Many of the worst things people will do will happen not because of actual writings about you and your god, but because of self-serving interpretations of those writings. I will even be thrown in jail because people will believe those writings give them permission to hate."

"This is confusing for me. I am just a simple preacher. Now two people from the future tell me that I am a bad man in their world."

Nellie reached out to put a comforting hand on his shoulder, then remembered where she was and pulled it back. "You are not a bad man, Yeshua. You . . . Your legacy will become a victim of others who are bad."

"That's why we are here," I added. "We want to make clear changes now, so the world will be better in the future. What we plan to do shouldn't affect the quality of your life, although I strongly advise that you change occupations—you'll live longer."

"I just want to serve my lord."

"That's honorable," I said, "but if there is a god worth serving, surely he doesn't need humans to act as his personal recruiters, and surely he would not want anyone harmed by sinful people claiming to act on his behalf."

"So can I serve him by helping you?"

Nellie and I looked at each other, not sure what to say.

She spoke first. "Yes. What god wouldn't want the best for his people? We likely won't need your help today, but you'll be able to improve more lives than you can imagine if you help when we're gone."

"Gone?"

I nodded. "That's correct. If everything goes as planned, after today we're going back to the fut . . . I mean back to our own time forever."

Nellie took a few steps and picked up one of the scrolls we had stashed behind the pulpit. She handed it to Yeshua. "Here's a copy of the New Ten Commandments. These are not from any god, and even though we call them *commandments,* they're really just requests from normal people in the future who need your help."

Suddenly everything became clear for me. "Yeshua, I believe that no matter which way Earth's history goes, you are destined to be the most important man in that history. Nellie and I were just sent here to point you in the right direction. Spread the word about the New Ten Commandments, and you will truly be a savior."

I reached into my pockets and pulled out a box of stick matches and a miniature telescope that Chrissie had given to me. I also pulled out two items I grabbed from the Earth artifacts compartment in the storage bay: a small, squished roll of duct tape and a pair of sunglasses.

"What are these?" Yeshua asked as I handed them to him.

"Gifts to you from the future we hope you will protect."

He was obviously unsure of what to do with the items, so I demonstrated the first three, spending a little extra time on duct tape—one of the most underrated inventions of all time. As soon as I finished, Nellie slid the black-rimmed, dark-lensed sunglasses on his face, and we stepped back to take a look.

"Pretty cool," Nellie said.

I dug out a camera, snapped a picture, and showed it to Yeshua and Nellie. We all cracked up at the sight of the first person ever to wear sunglasses. Then I reached out and shot a photo of the three of us together, and we laughed again. I returned the camera to my pocket and vowed to save both it and the photos. Someday, perhaps, I would be able to present Nellie with a framed copy of the ultimate selfie.

* * *

While we were talking with Yeshua, a steady drone of voices accompanied us from the other side of the potato pulpit. Now some people were beginning to shout. We had made our audience wait long enough. It was show time.

We hurried onto the pulpit, carrying the remaining nine copies of our New Ten Commandments, and gazed out at a crowd of several thousand.

I shouted to Nellie, "Even if we yell at the top of our lungs, there's no way even half the people will hear us!"

When a fly landed on my thumb, I raised my hand closer to my eyes and shot my Krichard friends a panicked look.

"Wrong fly," Chrissie said, "but don't worry. I'm already on it."

Nellie and I stood awkwardly on the stage, waiting and waving, as the cacophony of voices grew louder. To the left and to the right, I saw soldiers armed with shields and spears, and they certainly weren't there for our protection. I reached into my pockets to make sure I could easily grab the pepper spray, lighter, and firecrackers in case I had to defend myself.

Eventually, two wireless headset microphones and a small speaker appeared next to us. "Sorry for the delay, Marty. We had to program our computer to put this together from scratch. The battery-powered speaker looks small, but I think you'll be impressed with the sound."

"More importantly, our amplified voices will impress our audience," I said.

"After it scares the shit out of them," Nellie added.

We slipped the microphones on and pushed the power buttons.

"Hellooo, Galilee!" I said, with all the gusto of a rock star.

The audience shrieked and recoiled.

Nellie shot me a playful, open mouth look before turning and saying, "We are here to help. Do not fear us."

"Woman!" shouted half the audience.

"Oh, are we going to do *that* again?" Nellie reached into a pocket and pulled out a firecracker. She held her arm straight out from her side with the back end of the firework between her thumb and forefinger. When I lit the fuse, she watched it burn halfway before tossing the firecracker high into the air. It exploded above the pulpit and echoed through the hills. "Now, please, everyone listen to me. Marty and I have come from two thousand years in the future to talk to you. And in the future—at least the one we hope to create—women and men are equals. So while I'm up here, I ask you to treat me with the same respect you'd give to a man. If you can't do that, leave now."

We both looked over the audience, and when no one departed, I continued where Nellie left off. "I know it's hard to believe we're from the future. That's why we've brought a few items from our time to show you. For instance, this thing by my cheek is called a microphone. It sends my voice over to that yellow box, called a speaker, which makes my voice loud enough for all of you to hear me, even those of you in the back."

Hoping that giving each other breaks would keep our translated voices from slurring, Nellie and I eased into a rhythm of speaking for a short time, then nodding for the other to continue. Soon, we were like an old married couple picking up from where the other left off.

After a nod from me, Nellie said, "Please do not think of us as gods. We eat, bleed, and get sick just like you do. The difference between you and us is that we have had the benefit of countless amazing discoveries that others will make during the next two thousand years. Curiosity is a great thing. Instead of believing that a god must be responsible for things we don't understand, humans will endeavor to figure those mysteries out for themselves. Where we come from, people can swallow something smaller than a pebble to eliminate pain, place their dirty clothes into a machine that makes them come out clean, and even travel at speeds faster than the fastest bird."

She nodded, and I said, "The discoveries Nellie mentioned

will all come from science, not religion. People will also learn through science what makes the wind blow, the causes and cures for countless diseases, better ways to grow crops, that the Earth is round and it revolves around the sun, how to fly through the clouds, and so much more."

"But as amazing as that all seems, we still need you because what you do now will determine much of what happens in our time. Marty and I have traveled to the heavens, and we have friends who have traveled to the stars. Never has a god shown himself to anyone. Even if there is a god, we can only assume he chooses to hide and encourages us to make it on our own. With that in mind, we have a New Ten Commandments for you, meant to replace those Moses brought down from Mount Sinai. Although these commandments come from a place higher than any mountain, no one will punish you if you don't follow them. Instead, they are an appeal to the human decency that already exists inside each of you. If you follow them, I promise that your lives will be better, and so will the lives of all the generations to come, including ours."

I held up one of the scrolls and began to read, or at least recite since the writing was in Aramaic, and the language translator in my head was worthless for reading comprehension.

"One: Thou shalt have no gods. Find your answers through observation, experimentation, and testing.

"Two: Thou shalt be free to make images of anything. The arts are important.

"Three: Thou shalt be free to speak your mind, to use the words of your choosing.

"Four: Remember to be kind, generous, and honest.

"Five: Honor another person's right to choose whom they love and the sex of whom they love.

"Six: Thou shalt not kill. This includes wars, poisoning the Earth, and rationing health care.

"Seven: Thou shalt not dictate what others can do with their own bodies. This includes a woman's right to terminate her own pregnancy and the right of both sexes to practice birth control.

"Eight: Thou shalt not steal, cheat, take slaves, or pay your workers unfairly.

"Nine: Thou shalt not put any race or sex above the other.

"Ten: Thou shalt protect and preserve the animals, land, water, and air of all the Earth."

When I finished, the audience stared back at us with blank faces. In developing our New Ten Commandments, Nellie and I had tried to use words the people of AD 31 would understand, and we trusted the translator to help us. Still, we expected that some of the concepts might take generations for people to understand completely. In fact, for me, one of the true signs that the Bible wasn't written by or with the guidance of a supreme being was that it didn't mention any concepts that only later generations could understand. But I digress.

"We would love to give you all copies of the New Ten Commandments," Nellie said, "but we were limited as to how much we could bring here from the future. Some of you know Yeshua. Come up here, Yeshua!" She waited until he walked onto the pulpit and waved before continuing. "He has a copy of the New Ten Commandments and will be a great teacher for you from this day on. In addition, we have a few extra scrolls to give to any village leaders in the crowd. I would also like to personally hand a copy to that handsome soldier right there." She pointed to a man who had been eyeing her with a look that was more than just that of a soldier doing his job.

Nellie handed scrolls to the people as they approached. When the soldier's turn came, she smiled brightly and said to him in a breathy voice, "If you would deliver this to a respected scribe, I would be eternally grateful."

That he didn't melt right there on stage was a tribute to his training. I wasn't sure if Nellie's little sex kitten act was a good idea, but then again, men throughout history had done extraordinary things for the women of their dreams. Having a soldier willing to do anything to please the Holy Smokin' Hot Nellie certainly couldn't hurt.

I looked out over the crowd. We hadn't talked for long, but we said what we needed to say. What else could we do? Lead them in a song? I laughed to myself at the thought of teaching everyone "1999," complete with hand gestures for the numbers, but we had already pushed things as far as we dared.

Hoping that Tina was ready for us, I announced, "Nellie and I must leave you now. Although anything is possible, we don't expect to be back. We know that when we were here three days ago, you loved having your picture taken." I pulled out my camera and shot a photo of the audience. "We have given cameras just like this one to four of our helpers, and they have promised to remain after we leave to take more pictures of you. Please be courteous, and do not grab the cameras from them. If you behave poorly, one of these," I held up a firecracker, "will explode at your feet when you least expect it."

Nellie grabbed Yeshua by the hand and pulled him back to center stage. "I know some of you just gasped that an unmarried woman and a man touched like that. Get over it. The Ninth Commandment says, 'Thou shalt not put any race or sex above the other.' Please memorize that now, and remember that Yeshua will be here long after we're gone to help you learn and follow each and every commandment."

After Yeshua stepped off to the side, Nellie and I moved to the spot where the speaker and microphones had arrived, and waved.

"Goodbye, everyone!" I yelled.

We embraced for our dramatic exit.

Nothing happened.

I continued holding Nellie, partly because I wasn't sure what else to do and partly because well . . . it was Nellie.

Just when our pose started feeling a bit weird, Tina spoke in our heads, "Sorry. You must stall for a moment. Your timing would have been perfect if we hadn't had to send down the microphones and the speaker."

We let go of our embrace. The crowd stared at us in silence.

Nellie cupped a hand over her microphone and whispered, "What should we do?"

I did the same with my microphone and whispered back, "We could teach them 'Y.M.C.A.' The song is always a hit at sporting events."

"Yeah, but they won't know what a YMCA is. Also, the hand gestures won't mean anything to them unless we do them with whatever the equivalent letters are in the Aramaic alphabet. How about '1999'?"

"I thought about that earlier, but the lyrics will confuse them, and the gestures would be just as problematic." I paused for a moment and looked out over the sea of people. "Hey, why don't we just teach them the wave?"

"That would be hilarious!"

We walked to the front edge of the pulpit.

I uncovered my microphone and announced, "Even in the future, things don't always go as planned. Our ride back isn't quite ready yet."

"So Marty and I were thinking. It might be fun to—"

"Nellie, Marty, the recharge cycle is complete. It's time to go."

"Never mind," Nellie said. "The future is now ready for us."

We both alternated leaning over, performing a two-person wave from the stage, before returning to our embrace.

"Goodbye, everyone," I yelled again.

"Goodbye, y'all!" Nellie shouted. "And don't forget to be nice to the women!"

Whoosh!

Everything went white.

Everything went *"woo-hoo!"*

CHAPTER 20

Marty Expected the
Spanish Inquisition

Nellie and I and all the Krichards were excited that our mission had apparently been successful. That neither Nellie nor I had gone poof was also a reason to cheer. The success of our efforts to change the past, however, was more important than our individual lives. Had we put Earth on track for a brighter social and environmental future? The Krichards were busy doing an analysis via computer and expected to have some preliminary data soon.

In the meantime, my thoughts of the past turned to thoughts of the future. Even if Earth was now an absolute paradise, it would still be foreign to both Nellie and me. She wouldn't have any family or friends there, and though I suppose I could be married, I didn't have a sudden memory of anyone special in my life. The two of us also had our Krichard lovers to consider. That our relationships with them had been brief didn't diminish the fact that they were meaningful and intense. How could we just say goodbye and never see them again?

* * *

Several hours later, Captain Jagger called us into the conference room. As soon as we were all comfortable in our usual chairs, he

began, "Marty, Nellie, what you did in AD 31 was totally unconventional. In fact, as I monitored your progress from the ship, I
was convinced you'd fail. You didn't seem to take your job seriously enough, and embarrassing Jesus and then recruiting him to
work for you had disaster written all over it. Yet somehow, at least
based on our preliminary scans, you were successful." He paused
to give us a smile. "Keep in mind, however, that all we have so far
is the big picture. Based on our experiences on other planets, we
know it's the little things where problems tend to arise. Bruce has
been doing most of the analysis, so I'll let him take it from here."

Bruce nodded. "Thank you, Captain. First, you'll be happy
to know that Earth's environment is in significantly better shape
than it was in the original timeline. This is partly due to governments prioritizing conservation over corporate greed and partly
due to population reduction. In the original timeline, your planet
would have reached eight billion people in less than eight years.
Now, its population is just three billion."

Nellie looked at Bruce in shock. "Wait! Are you saying we
killed almost five billion people?"

"No. You can't kill people who never existed. All you did
was take the Earth back to where its population was in 1960.
Who knows? Those who believe in the concept of a soul might
even contend that those people will still be born, albeit at a
slower pace and perhaps in a different order. What I do know
is that growing from three billion to nearly eight billion in just
sixty years was unsustainable. More people means more pollution, more waste, and more pressure on resources. As you saw
in your timeline, Nellie, global warming had made life grim in
the United States, and it was much worse in other parts of the
world. By 2070, human greed and environmental recklessness
would have caused Earth's population to crash to less than three
billion people anyway. Now your planet has a second chance,
and because of your efforts, billions of people and incalculable
numbers of animals will be spared agonizing deaths."

"Are we still in the Bible?" I asked.

"Chrissie has been researching that," Bruce said, as he pointed. "So I'll defer to her."

"Yes, you're still there. But before you smile too brightly about it, you should know that the change from Jesus to Martyman and Mary to Nellie ripped the Bible off every best seller list. It's now an obscure book, not even available in English. Two original copies of your New Ten Commandments survived, however. They're now preserved in museums, and reproductions are available everywhere."

"On a related subject," Bruce said, "Nellie, you are no longer the first person to walk on Mars. Someone beat you to it by almost seventy years. Although human technology is still far behind Krichard technology, freedom from oppressive religions has allowed humans to advance much faster than they did in the original timeline. In fact, Earth's spaceships are on track to break the light-speed barrier within the next few years."

"Who is the president of the United States?" Nellie asked.

Bruce took a sip of his drink before answering. "Technically, no place called the United States ever existed. Instead, the continent that you knew as North America is home to just two countries. Great Bison, founded by native people, occupies the land west of the Mississippi, and Leiflandia, founded by people who crossed the Atlantic Ocean, occupies the land east of the Mississippi. Despite the divide, there is a lot of intermingling and little conflict. Basically, those who prefer to live closer to the earth and enjoy wide swaths of wilderness live in the West, and those who prefer a faster-paced technology-filled lifestyle live in the East."

Nellie and I looked at each other. Neither of us was quite sure what to think.

Chrissie placed her hand atop mine. "Remember when we were in the Chromosphere Cruiser looking at Jupiter, and you asked about Krichardia?"

"Yes. You said your world has fewer countries than Earth because breaking down artificial borders led to a greater understanding among ethnicities."

"Correct. And that's what happened here. Earth still has more countries than Krichardia—just fewer than it had before. That will seem strange only to you and Nellie. For all other humans, the number of countries and their names feel perfectly natural."

Nellie turned toward Bruce. "What about rights for women and people of differing sexual orientations?"

"From what I've seen so far, equal rights are so entrenched that they aren't even an issue. Although I'm sure there are pockets of misogyny and bigotry here and there, without major religions to provide ongoing support, such thinking has difficulty maintaining a foothold in mainstream cultures."

"Bruce, do you have any information on wars?" I asked.

"Earth still has wars, though they are much less frequent, and you'll be happy to know that neither of the two World Wars occurred. The reasons for this are complex. Major contributing factors include the lack of religious influences and the fact that some of the countries involved in those wars existed only in the original timeline. Also, everything you did in AD 31 had the potential to change the world. Who knows who might have met whom in the crowd as they waited in line to have their pictures taken? Just one child born to a couple who might not otherwise have met could have significantly affected the new timeline."

Nellie ran her fingers through her hair as she thought. "Did we prevent the Spanish Inquisition?"

"Most definitely," Bruce said.

"There goes one of the best Monty Python sketches ever," I said.

"Monty Python?" Bruce asked.

"They were a famous British comedy troupe."

Bruce picked up his handheld computer and scanned Earth's records. "Sorry. As far as I can tell, no such troupe has ever existed."

I stood. "Come on, Nellie. We have to go back and fix things. We can't live in a world devoid of Monty Python."

Nellie pushed back her chair.

Bruce stared at us with his eyelashes blinking multiple colors, unsure if we were really serious. "Marty, your memory of the old Earth timeline will fade just as your memory of Nellie did when she briefly disappeared. Be patient. Older memories last longer than newer ones."

I winked at Bruce, and we sat back down. "We were just kidding . . . unless, of course, no one in the new timeline has a sense of humor."

"I will keep that in mind as I continue my analysis." He nodded to Captain Jagger.

"Thank you, Bruce. That's all we have for now. We're going to stick around for a few days just to make sure we are leaving Earth in better shape than when we found it. In the meantime, Marty and Nellie, I think it's safe for both of you to visit the doctors to get your hair and skin color changed back to normal." He rose from his chair and started for the door.

"Tina, Chrissie, Nellie, can you stay for a moment?" I asked.

They nodded and remained in their seats.

I waited until everyone else left before saying, "Where do we go from here? Unless I have a wife and kids I can't yet remember, I really don't want to say goodbye to everything and everyone here and start life again from scratch."

"I feel the same way," Nellie said, "and I'm positive I don't have a wife and kids."

Chrissie looked at me with a mixture of pain and affection and whatever her blue glowing eyelashes meant. "Our regulations clearly state that we are not to take any humanoids home with us when we leave. Otherwise, we'd have the Earth equivalent of a person working at an animal shelter who keeps bringing home puppies. Our ships would fill up quickly."

I raised an eyebrow.

"Oh! I'm sorry. That was a bad example—even if you are just as cute and as much fun as a puppy."

I raised my other eyebrow.

"Okay, just forget everything I said about puppies." She buried her face in her hands for a moment before she looked back up at me. "We have animals virtually identical to dogs on Krichardia, and I love them dearly. Marty, I also love you dearly, but as an equal, not as a pet. We all knew we'd have to part ways sooner or later. Though I can't speak for Tina, I have been dreading the day our ship heads away from Earth."

"Actually, you can speak for me too. I don't know Nellie as well as you know Marty, but there is a spark between us unlike anything I've ever felt before." She turned to Nellie and gave her a quick kiss and long hug.

We sat in reflective silence for a moment.

"Let's go on a double-date and figure this out," I said.

"Someplace warm," Nellie added.

"Venus or Mercury?" Chrissie asked.

Nellie glanced at me for a preference. When I offered none, she shouted, "Venus!"

"Before we go, I'd like to get changed back to my natural appearance."

"Me too."

Tina smiled as she stood. "While you two visit the doctors, Chrissie and I will make all the arrangements and prepare the Chromosphere Cruiser."

"Let's meet in the cruiser bay in two hours," Chrissie said.

* * *

Three hours later, the four of us were eating dinner on Venus with the Chromosphere Cruiser in bubble mode. The flight there was quiet, with none of the woo-hoos or delighted screams of our past trips. Now as we looked outside, our view wasn't making us feel any more talkative. It was like being on a desolate, rocky plateau on a cold, foggy day—only the temperature outside was 870 degrees Fahrenheit. No one asked to don a spacesuit.

Nellie broke the silence. "What if Marty and I were to hide on the ship as stowaways?"

"The attempt would be futile," Tina said. "The captain will personally see you off in the hose room. Even if we successfully faked that, you'd eventually be discovered, and he'd have you on the next ship heading in the direction of your home planet."

"I still don't have any memories of my life on Earth, but I assume I have a house there that we could live in until we got established. It would be a new adventure for all of us."

"Tina and I would be like zoo animals there."

"I hear what you're saying, Chrissie, but with the proper clothing and makeup, maybe not. Plus, this new timeline sounds a lot more accepting than the previous one. You might love it there."

"Space is in our blood," Tina said. "As much as we love you two, sooner or later we'd grow resentful of being planet-bound."

"She's right," said Nellie. "It isn't fair of us to ask that of them."

We sat quietly again, nibbling on our food and sipping our wine.

This time, I broke the silence. "We could borrow the Chromosphere Cruiser and get lost."

Chrissie gave my hand an affectionate squeeze. "That's a nice thought, Marty. Cruisers seem fast in your solar system, but with their limited range and speed, we could never visit our home planet again. Besides, living in one for more than a few weeks would make us all feel claustrophobic."

"This isn't going to work out, is it?" I said.

Tina looked me in the eyes. "I don't see how it can. You and Nellie belong on Earth, and Chrissie and I belong in space."

"Perhaps we can talk the captain into swinging by Earth if we're ever near your solar system again," Chrissie said.

Nellie forced a smile. "This is way too depressing. If this will be our last time together for a long time, let's make the most of it and have some fun."

Chrissie's eyelashes flashed. "I agree! Let's put on some music. Marty, do you have any Earth rock and roll with you?"

"Sure. Before we left, I slipped a memory chip into my pocket with a bunch of albums on it."

I handed the chip to Chrissie, and she inserted it into the entertainment panel.

"Is there any Springsteen on here? I've grown fond of his music."

"Just go to the directory. You'll find most of his albums there."

"How about *Born in the USA?*" She waited for the music to start. "Hmm. The file folder appears to be empty. Let's try *The Rising.*"

Nothing.

Nellie and I shot panicked looks at each other.

"Oh, shit!" I said. "Try the Pretenders."

Nothing.

Chrissie stared at the entertainment panel screen. "I searched your chip, Marty, and none of the folders contain any music files."

"Hold on," Tina said. "After Marty pointed out my resemblance to Tina Turner, I downloaded some of her albums into my handheld. I'll feed one through the sound system."

Nothing.

"Could we have poofed Bruce Springsteen, the Pretenders, Tina Turner, and everyone else in rock from existence?" I asked.

Tina climbed into the cockpit and pushed the button to put the cruiser back into flight mode. "I can't tap into the internet from Venus. We need to be much closer to Earth."

Minutes later, we lifted off the surface, escaping the heavy Venus atmosphere, and headed toward home.

I couldn't sit still, so I started clearing the dirty dishes off the table. "I don't think I could survive without music."

Chrissie handed her glass to me. "Oh, I'm sure there's still music on your planet. It may not be rock or the artists you prefer, but virtually every society has some form of music."

"Can we listen to something from Krichardia?" Nellie asked.

"Of course." Chrissie walked over to the entertainment panel and started a song that reminded me of an out-of-tune cat in heat accompanied by a sitar. "This is a Krichardia favorite."

I put on my travel writer's hat, smiled, and respectfully

listened. When the song faded, I held out hope that I could relate better to the next one. . . . Well, it was a nice thought anyway.

Chrissie watched as I struggled to find a beat I could move to. "Here," she said, shaking her head, "let me help."

She grabbed my hands and led me in a dance around the studio cabin. Having her to follow made things easier, but I soon concluded that if there was one thing people from Earth were better at than people from Krichardia, it was at making music.

I took a break so Chrissie could give Nellie a dance lesson as well. Nellie did much better than I did. But then, she could probably find a way to dance to the sound of rainforest cicadas.

When the Krichard ship came into view, Tina cut the music. I had assumed we were going to check the internet from the cruiser, but we had definitely lost the mood, and the more advanced equipment on the main ship would be better suited for the job anyway. Soon the bay doors opened, and Tina set the cruiser down inside.

Once the doors closed and the room repressurized, Captain Jagger stepped onto the floor to meet us. "I'm glad you're back. I was a little worried I'd never see any of you again."

We all shot him innocent looks.

His eyelashes flashed purple. "Oh, please. I never would have made captain if I could be so easily fooled. Follow me to the conference room."

CHAPTER 21

Two Bathrooms!

As soon as the usual crew, minus Clarence, was seated, the captain began, "We've had a change of plans. Apparently, the moon doesn't hide us as well as it did in the original timeline. Although humans in the new timeline have no reason to look for us, we now believe they have the technological capacity to detect us behind the moon, Mars, and even Venus. I have consulted with my superiors to get their recommendations. They're quite intrigued that humans are now on the cusp of light-speed travel and would love to have an ally in this part of the galaxy. But rather than make direct first contact at this time, they prefer to observe for a while. As we speak, our ship is moving to a location where we can stay hidden."

I put up my hand. "Bruce Springsteen, Tina Turner, Mick Jagger . . . they're all gone! Earlier, you said, 'it's the little things where problems tend to arise.' That may be little for you, but it's big for me."

"The fact that you can still recall them so clearly tells me they aren't really gone. Tina, can you—"

"I'm already on it."

As we waited, some paced and others filled glasses or cups with their preferred beverages.

"Here it is," she said. "Bruce Springsteen lives in an area that geographically used to be New Jersey. Much of the E Street Band seems to be there as well, and they all work various factory jobs. Tina Turner seems to be missing, however."

"Try Anna Mae Bullock," I said.

Tina entered the name. "I found her! She is a retired university professor living in an area that geographically used to be Tennessee. I'm checking Mick Jagger now."

"Try Michael Philip Jagger."

"Yes, he's here too. Hmm. Music of some kind obviously exists on Earth since the bio I found says he failed miserably at every musical instrument he tried to play and that he finally gained regional fame as the host of a children's television show. I could go on, but I don't see anyone missing from the musicians and bands you've introduced us to."

"How can that be?" Nellie asked. "Are unfulfilled rock musicians somehow resistant to timeline changes?"

"That's an interesting theory," I said. "Can you just do general searches under jazz, blues, and rock music?"

Tina entered the information and looked at her screen. "There's nothing here."

"Classical, or opera?" I asked.

"Yes. Lots of that."

"Hmm. See if you can find anything on legalized slavery in Leiflandia."

Tina flashed me an inquisitive look before entering the information for the search. "All I see is a mention of the slavery ban that is included in Leiflandia's constitution."

I took a deep breath. "Well, I think I know what happened. Jazz and blues both originated with African Americans in the Deep South. Since slavery didn't exist in the same geographical region in this timeline, those genres of music either never took hold, or else they evolved into forms of music we are currently unfamiliar with. And, of course, without jazz or blues, rock and roll had nothing to develop from."

"As a girl from the South, I'm relieved that my slave-owning ancestors poofed from existence. I'd choose eliminating slavery over saving rock and roll any day."

"I wholeheartedly agree with you, Nellie. But since, apparently, many of the most important people in rock—and I assume jazz and blues—either exist now or existed in the recent past, perhaps there's still a way we can fool time and get a win-win out of this."

"How?" Chrissie asked.

"I imagine Bruce Springsteen still has 'Born to Run' somewhere inside him and that Muddy Waters had 'Mannish Boy' inside him until the day he died. Perhaps a visit to young versions of those two, as well as Elvis Presley, Louis Armstrong, and other influential musicians who didn't poof out of existence could start it all up again."

The captain waved the subject to a close. "We are way off track here. That said, Marty, if everyone agrees to my upcoming proposal, you might have a small—and I repeat, small—chance of saving your beloved rock and roll. First, however, Mr. Springsteen's namesake has something he wants to show you."

"Thank you, Captain." Bruce turned in his chair and looked directly at me. "During our preparations to return you to Earth, we checked to see if you have a family to go back to. It appears as if you are almost as much of a loner in this timeline as you were in the original one. Your parents both died fourteen years ago while trying to be the first married couple to cross Antarctica without assistance, and your sister passed away six years ago in a mountain-climbing accident."

"Hey, at least I came from a family of adventurers."

Bruce made an entry on his handheld computer, and a photo appeared on the wall monitor. "Though you aren't married, over the past several years, you've been involved in an on-again/off-again relationship with this woman."

Nellie and I shot each other wide-eyed looks. The woman's hairstyle was different, but it was most definitely Alison. "Well, it's a relief to know that I'm not married," I added before Nellie had a chance to comment. "Do I still live in what geographically used to be Montana?"

"No. It appears that what used to be Minnesota has a stronger hold on you. Knowing that you like things both ways, I'm not surprised. You own a house just east of the Mississippi River, in modern Leiflandia, with easy access to the wilderness of Great Bison." Bruce turned back to Captain Jagger. "That's all I have for now."

"Thank you, Bruce. Now that we have all of that out of the way, let's get to the primary purpose of this meeting and to what my superiors and I propose. Chrissie, Tina, Marty, Nellie, I think all of you are going to like our plan, but if even one of you objects, I'll send the humans back to Earth, and the rest of us will move on to our next mission. Bruce, please bring up a live shot of the Chromosphere Cruiser prototype."

The monitor switched to an image of Clarence standing next to a Chromosphere Cruiser that was larger and more badass-looking than the original—in dark pink, of course.

"Wow!" I said. "How come I haven't seen that before?"

"I mentioned it when I first made contact with you in Duluth," Chrissie said, "but so much was going on that it probably went straight into your implant and out your ears. We picked it up at the space station when we acquired the new time-travel attachment."

"And it's been sitting in the captain's cruiser bay ever since," Clarence added. "This is a prototype, so I've been spending all of my free time checking it out to make sure it's safe enough for a mission."

"So, is it safe?" Nellie asked.

Clarence smiled. "Not only is it safe, but it's also amazing! I'm going to switch to a handheld camera so I can give you a quick tour."

The picture on the monitor changed to a shakier image.

"First of all, this new cruiser is about 60 percent larger than the original. The increased size means more comfort on longer journeys. And it needs that, since the range has quadrupled from four to sixteen light-years. If necessary, this cruiser can travel from Earth to the space station where we got it without recharging. Most amazing of all, it's twenty times faster than the original."

"It sounds more like an interplanetary spaceship than a recreational runabout," I said.

"I agree. Although it still doesn't compare to the ship we're on now, it will actually outperform all but the top vessels of many advanced species. I'm now going to take you inside. . . . As you can see, the layout is similar, only more spacious and more luxurious. In the back, not only is there a large studio cabin, but there is also a smaller sleeping cabin behind it. *Oh! Oh!*" He hurried deeper into the cruiser. "Here's the best interior feature—*two* bathrooms!"

"Do the sides go down?" Nellie asked.

"Yes. It has the bubble mode feature just like the original." He turned and headed for the cockpit. "As security officer, I felt it necessary to add one customization. On the pilot's main screen, you will see an icon for weapons. Push that and a variety of defensive options will come up. You won't have enough firepower to defeat a large ship that is occupied by an advanced species, but it ought to be enough to get out of any trouble you find yourself in." He paused for a moment to think. "That's pretty much it. She's all charged up and ready to go."

"Thank you, Clarence." The monitor went black, and everyone turned to face the captain. "I asked Clarence to leave out one important feature because I want to talk to all of you about it personally. The new cruiser has a time-travel attachment."

My eyelashes couldn't light up, but I'm pretty sure my eyes did.

"This attachment isn't recommended for outer space use, however. You must land the cruiser where you physically want to go and make sure its systems are fully charged. Then you can enter your desired time, and the attachment will encompass the entire ship and take you there. The advantage, of course, is that you can all time travel together. The disadvantage is that afterward, propulsion will be offline for approximately twenty-four hours while the systems recharge. Needless to say, if you accept this mission, you are to keep time travel to a minimum. Also, if you screw up everything we've already accomplished, I will personally retrieve all of you and dump you on some desolate, barely habitable planet."

"So what is our mission?" Chrissie asked.

"We want you to go to Earth, try to fit in, and assess whether or not the planet has changed enough from its previous violent tendencies to make a good friend for Krichardia. You are authorized, if necessary, to make small changes to the timeline for the betterment of the planet. While you four are doing that, I will take the ship and the remainder of the crew on to our next mission. Depending on the distance we have to travel and the difficulty of what we have to do, expect us to return within six months to a year."

I broke into a wide smile. "Captain, it sounds like you've made Nellie and me part of your crew."

"Only as consultants, and only until I get back."

"And you say this mission is strictly optional?" Tina asked.

"Yes. If one of you says no, we forget it."

"I'm in!" I said.

"I'm in!" Chrissie said.

"I'm in!" Nellie said.

"I don't know," said Tina. "Six months to a year? That's a long time to be trapped with these three." She paused for effect, but her eyelashes were already giving her away.

"You are a terrible bluffer," I said. "Captain, we are all in!"

CHAPTER 22

The Handley Job and the Happy Ending

The four of us spent the next two days packing the new Chromosphere Cruiser with everything we could possibly need. Nellie and I had few personal possessions, but our Krichard companions brought clothes, toiletries, special foods, electronic gear, and even a portable auto-weaver attachment.

As for Tina and Chrissie's physical appearance, the doctors decided that temporary cosmetic changes wouldn't last long enough and that permanent changes would be too invasive. Instead, they designed comfortable, realistic human masks that the women could put on or take off in under a minute. They also synthesized a year's supply of makeup for any exposed areas that were too colorful. The extra benefit of this approach was that the women could be themselves whenever they were out of public view.

We also came up with a unique way to get to Earth without being detected. From the ship, we planned to take the Chromosphere Cruiser directly to Pluto, travel one thousand years back in time, fly to a secluded area near where my future Leiflandia home would be, and then jump back to present time.

Had we thought of everything? After the cruiser was fully loaded, one more item came to mind. I found Tina as she was shutting down her workstation and asked, "What are we going to do about money? I might have a job on Earth, but who knows if I make enough to support all of us."

"Let's see if Handley is still around." She tapped an entry on her computer and smiled. "Ah, there he is," she said, pointing to a picture of a balding man in a denim uniform. "He works as a biological refuse receptacle technician."

"He's a septic tank repairman."

"Can I assume he doesn't have billions in an offshore account?"

"I think that's a safe assumption."

"No worries. It takes a little longer, but I have a program that will search for the largest corporate bank accounts on Earth and skim just a little off the top. We will have all the money we need, and no one will notice that anything is missing. I'll set up an account for each of us at a bank near your home."

* * *

Finally, we were ready to depart. The entire crew met us in the hallway by the entrance to the cruiser bay, and we all exchanged hugs and said our farewells. I knew I would miss everyone, especially Captain Jagger, and though he didn't say so, I think he was going to miss me too. At the very least, our time together would leave him with some fond memories and an increased openness to unconventional methods.

We stepped into the bay and climbed into the new Chromosphere Cruiser. This time, Chrissie and I took the cockpit, and Tina and Nellie took the back.

I looked over my shoulder at Nellie. "Are you excited to start a new life?"

She smiled. "I think I did that the day we met. How about you? You're starting again too."

"Will I be starting a new life? Or will I be reconnecting with an old life that I'll remember as soon as I step into my house on Earth?"

Tina flashed an eyelash. "I guess only time will tell."

"Oh, bad pun!" I said as we all laughed.

No matter what the future had in store for me, I had just had the time of my life. I got to see, and outsmart, dinosaurs. I got to fall in love with, and even have sex with, a beautiful alien. I got to fall in love with, and not have sex with, a smokin' hot lesbian from the future. I got to visit AD 31, meet Jesus Christ, and even become the main character in the Bible.

That, for me, was enough for a lifetime.

Except, perhaps, "Can I drive?"

"No!" three voices shouted around me.

Chrissie pushed a series of buttons, grabbed the floor-mounted control stick, turned to everyone, and flashed an eyelash. "Hold on!"

We shot toward the door. It opened just in time.

"Woo-hoo!" we yelled.

Marty Essen grew up in Minnesota and resides in Montana. In addition to being an author, he is also a talent agent and a college speaker. He transformed his first book into a fun-filled, high-energy show, *Around the World in 90 Minutes*, which he has been performing on college campuses since 2007, making it one of the most popular slide shows of all-time.

If you enjoyed *Time Is Irreverent*, you will also enjoy Marty's two humorous nature/adventure travel books:

Cool Creatures, Hot Planet: Exploring the Seven Continents

Winner: Benjamin Franklin Award for Travel/Essay
Winner: National Indie Excellence Book Award for Travel/Essay
Winner: USA Best Books Award for Travel/Essay
Winner: Green Book Festival Award for Animals
Bronze: *ForeWord Magazine* Book of the Year Award for Travel/Essay
Bronze: IPPY Award for Travel/Essay
Minneapolis Star-Tribune Top-10 Green Book

Endangered Edens: Exploring the Arctic National Wildlife Refuge, Costa Rica, the Everglades, and Puerto Rico

Winner: Readers' Favorite Book Award for Environment
Winner: National Indie Excellence Book Award for Nature
Silver: Nautilus Award for Animals & Nature
Silver: Nautilus Award for Middle Grades Non-Fiction

For information on Marty's speaking engagements and signed copies of his books, please visit www.MartyEssen.com. For beautiful nature photography and biting political commentary, please visit www.Marty-Essen.com.

Readers are also welcome to write Marty at Marty@Marty-Essen.com, or to send him a Facebook friend request at www.facebook.com/marty.essen.

Please review this book. If you would like to read more Marty Mann and Nellie Dixon novels, the best way to make sure their adventures keep coming is to post a review on your favorite bookseller's website. Marty Mann thanks you in advance for any review you post, and Nellie Dixon promises to do a little dance in your honor if the review is smokin' hot.

CPSIA information can be obtained
at www.ICGtesting.com
Printed in the USA
LVHW090036090420
652753LV00005B/1305